Iran Strikes Back

L Ray Vinson

A CIP catalogue record for this title is available from the British Library.

www.bookpublisherslondon.com

First Published (2021)

Book Publishers London Ltd.

Kemp House

160 City Road London

EC1V 2NX

BOOK PUBLISHERS
LONDON

This book is dedicated to:

The professional Doctors, nurses and others at Emory University Hospital and particularly.

Dr. Akram Ibrahim , Columbus, Georgia USA And

Dr. Mani A. Daneshmand, Atlanta Georgia, USA

Without their considerable compassion and medical skills, this book would not have been completed. I would not be alive to have done so.

Thank you for your tireless professional effort.

L Ray Vinson

Contents

Prologue   vii

Chapter One   1

Chapter Two   9

Chapter Three   15

Chapter Four   24

Chapter Five   31

Chapter Six   37

Chapter Seven   47

Chapter Eight   55

Chapter Nine   62

Chapter Ten   69

Chapter Eleven   76

Chapter Twelve   84

Chapter Thirteen   91

Chapter Fourteen   96

Chapter Fifteen   102

Chapter Sixteen   109

Chapter Seventeen   115

Chapter Eighteen   126

Chapter Nineteen   133

Chapter Twenty	141
Chapter Twenty-One	145
Chapter Twenty-Two	152
Chapter Twenty-Three	159
Chapter Twenty-Four	167
Chapter Twenty-Five	174
Chapter Twenty-Six	180
Chapter Twenty-Seven	187
Epilogue	196

Prologue

On December 20, 1988, outside Katamak, Hirmand, close to the Iran-Afghanistan border, it was very cold—minus 4 degrees Fahrenheit— the ten members of the 65th Airborne Special Forces of Iran, known as the Powerful Ghosts, were moving away from the transport vehicle which was a gunship helicopter that was not piloted by a member of the group but by a regular army crew. They shivered as they exited the helicopter even though they had on heavy winter clothing designed for such weather. The wind was blowing which made the temperature even colder, the exit from the helicopter was like an electrical shock.

All ten members were well qualified including piloting helicopters, each spoke several languages including Russian, Urdu and English. These were the expected qualifications needed for this mission, understanding what was being said by all they may come in contact with, was extremely important. A misunderstanding could lead to disaster and a failure to accomplish what that had set out to accomplish.

It was nearly dark, around 7:30 pm, when they arrived at the border crossing. The group, all dressed in black, bearing no insignias, moved quickly and quietly. They had been transported from their home base outside Tehran. Waiting for them, were two transport trucks with Afghan regular forces drivers. The Afghans were being paid for their time and the trucks which included the fuel and an extra supply brought with them to insure they had enough for the trip, fuel was a precious commodity at this time in Afghanistan. The trucks had no markings, the markings which were on the vehicles had been crudely painted over to hide the Afghan army insignia The extra fuel consisted of 10, 20 Litre Jerry Cans which was enough to make a round trip to Rigestan, deep inside Afghanistan. Without using headlights, this trip, over rough terrain, would be difficult and dangerous. A faint moon hung high in the sky, which would be of some help to the drivers as they drove on what was not really a road but dirt worn down by use, it was mostly sand. The road had seen many a traveler who had traversed it for centuries.

This group of Powerful Ghosts consisted of one major, one command sergeant, two staff sergeants, two corporals and four private first class. The major and command sergeant both were veterans of the Iraq war and were seasoned combat experts. Even without insignias, it was obvious of the pecking order, since all had worked closely as a unit and trained to know their job and remember who was responsible for what, there movements clearly reflected who was in charge. They had with them a substantial arsenal of weapons: two 50 caliber machine guns, a handheld rocket launcher capable of taking down an airplane, five grenades each, each had a pistol, 5 automatic rifles, knifes, and enough ammunition to fight a sustained engagement. They also had heavy lead-encased blankets, cutting/ welding torches with two small canisters of gas. They were all experts in hand-to-hand combat, well trained in military tactics, sufficient enough that even the privates could take over command if needed. The ten of them believed they were equal to one hundred regular soldiers. No question, they were a tough bunch, their mannerisms and the way they moved together as a highly trained group showed as much.

The Afghan drivers helped them load the two trucks. It should take approximately 5 hours to drive to Rigestan without incident. The danger was the Russian military was moving out of Afghanistan and had moved the vast majority of their troops away. The Afghan troops were taking advantage and attacking anything that looked Russian: they would have to be careful or die before even reaching the first stop. The major sat in the front seat with the driver of the first truck, the command sergeant sat up front in the second truck. The remaining eight divided themselves equally and took over the back. All had weapons ready in case they were attacked. One man in each truck laid down on the floor peering out the back, constantly moving his head from side to side looking for danger. Once they were moving smoothly down the dirt road, they slept except for the two peering out the back and the major and command sergeant, who only relaxed and took a few quick naps as they drove down the seemingly endless dirt road.

They reached Rigestan without incident; the expected attack along the way had not occurred, and there were no roadside problems which happens often when traveling on such rough dusty roads. The two on guard in the back, the major and the command sergeant were relieved as it had been a stressful five hours. Upon arriving, the major immediately made contact, as had been arranged, just outside a joint military base, with a Russian helicopter pilot, who had agreed to take them all to Balbandin, Pakistan, stay on the ground until they completed their mission and fly them back to Rigestan. Iran had offered $100,000 US currency for this service, which was to be paid in no greater than twenty-dollar bills: $25,000 when they took off, the remaining $75,000 when they returned. The major handed the first $25,000 over to the pilot once the helicopter was loaded. The pilot also had with him a co-pilot who was grinning broadly. He did not count the money but only smiled.

Once the helicopter was loaded, it took off for Balbandin, the major and the command sergeant, for the first time, could relax. There was nothing to do but enjoy the ride. The two who had been guarding the rears of the trucks were asleep the moment they boarded, and it was completely loaded.

Balbandin was a small town in Pakistan. It had an airport with two regular scheduled flights departing and arriving every week. Tonight, there was no scheduled flights, the airport was closed for any flights. The flight took two- and one-half hours, and landed next to the terminal, which was completely empty, totally dark in and around the building, with no traffic, the moon which had given some light was now set and gone from the night sky. The terminal was a brick and concrete building with lots of windows, a main road went by the front entrance, which also had a parking area.

Upon landing, the ten of them exited the helicopter with planned precision. One of the privates set up a machine gun to protect the helicopter from anyone who might enter the area. He expertly camouflaged himself using a netting dyed to match the colors of the surrounding area, he covered himself completely: you would have to know he was there to detect that it was a person. He took with him the Russian pilot and co-pilot, gave them camouflage covers and instructed both to sit quietly under them. They were also told to not talk and not leave until the others returned. The other private moved toward the main road which was paved and established another defensive position. He also used the camouflage netting to hide himself from anyone driving or walking down the road.

The other eight gathered what weapons they deemed necessary: each had a pistol, a rifle, a knife, five grenades and one had a rocket launcher. It was roughly one kilometer to their first target. One private had a gas canister and a cutting torch strapped to his back, all believed they would encounter a steel door which would have to be cut open. The second destination was definitely a possibility; intelligence had detected the main and first site may not have the nuclear weapons they were after and only appeared to be a secured storage spot. The second site was well hidden with no guards; they would find out shortly which one held the weapons they were there to get. They walked at a brisk pace and looked for a building which they expected to be half-buried underground. You could only see a large mound of dirt with a steel door painted black for an entrance when they arrived. Outside were two guards, well-camouflaged, one to each side. The intelligence received was the guards were changed every four hours; the change was scheduled thirty minutes from now if the information they had was correct. The eight of them moved silently to within one hundred feet of the two, both guards were crunched behind sandbags with a machine gun ready to fire.

The two corporals slipped away from the others and moved like snakes closer to the two guards. Each slipped behind and to the side of a guard. The guards heard nothing; the two corporals inched closer. As if choreographed, each of the corporals was now only ten feet away from each of the guards. They sat silently for a few moments to make sure the other had reached the point of attack. They laid on the ground and squirmed closer to the guard until they were just two feet behind. At exactly the same moment, they took out their knives and slit the throats of each guard. Both of the now dead guards slumped down behind the sandbags as they died. The corporals pulled their bodies around and behind the sandbags so that the bags were both protecting and hiding them. They then took their place as guards.

The others had gone around back and located two trucks parked behind the mound. The trucks were both expected and needed. The major breathed a sigh of relief when he saw the trucks. Their mission would be difficult, maybe impossible, without them.

Twenty minutes later, the two scheduled replacement guards emerged from the steel door. Four of the Iranian special force's men were waiting. As they turned to close the steel door, two grabbed one each of the exiting guards and stabbed each in the heart with a knife. One of the Iranians held the door preventing it from closing. They dragged the two bodies away, motioned the others to join them and entered the building, while the two corporals stayed put huddled down in the sandbag bunkers. Inside, they knew there should at least be one other man. They moved quietly and slowly They saw the expected man on a bunk fast asleep. The major efficiently put one strong hand around his neck then thrust a knife through his heart, the man didn't know what was coming and felt only a slight sharp point before he died. The knife was razor sharp and penetrated like butter into his chest.

Inside the building, they found the keys to the trucks hanging on a rack made for just that purpose. One of the privates, who had now joined them, took the position of one of the corporals. The corporal and one other private took one of the trucks and drove toward the second location. Once inside, they paused for a few seconds as they heard the truck drive away, it was an important step as they needed to know the truck was on its way. After passing the dead man, they saw what was expected: a massive steel door, which, they hoped, stored three 50 kiloton nuclear bombs. The clock was now ticking. The ritual, as intelligence had discovered, was that every two hours the affirmation of 'all was OK' was sent back to their headquarters. They assumed this was done when the guards were changed and would need to be done again in two hours; the major had already set his watch for an alarm one hour fifty-eight minutes from now. The one remaining private was the person qualified to burn open the steel door. The private clicked his lighter to start the torch. He began cutting the plungers which were 25 millimeters round steel rods, the two plungers entered into the corresponding door through a thick steel plate, they were well designed and were preventing the door from opening. In thirty minutes, he cut through both plungers and pushed open the door. He had less than 5 millimeters which he could see to cut. Cutting such thick steel in close space requires a lot of skill, he had adjusted the torch to its finest flame.

It was not entirely a surprise, as inside the vault was found to be empty. There were no nuclear bombs, just small weapons and supplies. The major immediately ordered everyone to take the remaining truck to the other site. They had not heard from the two who had left earlier for the second site but only expected a call if something was wrong. The major called them on the short-wave radios each had with them.

"Unit four, this is unit one. Come back." "This is unit four."

"Nothing here. We are heading your way. What have you found?"

"We found an underground something. Still trying to figure out how to get in."

"We will bring the other truck and a forklift shortly." "10 4"

The men had located the loading planks for the forklift and pulled them into place against the rear cargo end of the truck. The sergeant then drove the forklift onto the rear of the truck, it was covered and barely made it into the cargo area.

By the time the remaining truck arrived at the second site, the two original men had located an entrance and were working on how to access what was a secure steel door covering which was blocking what was assumed to be the entrance. The "expert" on cutting tackled the second steel door; but this time, he had to cut the hinges as he could not see any plungers. He had to cut them from the side as he could not get to any other spot, there was just no room. The last hinge was cut after twenty minutes, they were made out of much thinner steel and cut faster than the plungers. The door slid slightly inwards as the hinges dropped away. The door was very heavy and required four of them to lift it out of the frame. Inside, encased in a lead shielding, were the nuclear bombs. The Pakistan army, the group realized, thought the alternate site to be so secretive that no one would find it and look for the bombs inside. Reasonably though, secretly hiding nuclear weapons allowed a Pakistan General to have access to weapons while the higher-ups believed they were safely secure in the alternate vault. Iran was fortunate to have intelligence which uncovered the possibility the bombs were in this location and not the main storage facility.

The bombs, not so large but heavy as each weighed approximately 1,400 kilograms as expected from the bomb details they had been provided. They unloaded the small forklift. The command sergeant drove the forklift into the facility, lifted one of the bombs, it strained at the load, for a moment he thought it could not handle as it strained to move, he then begin moving very slow as he headed toward the door. He masterfully loaded the bomb onto the truck and returned for another. He loaded two in one truck and one in another. He then drove the forklift back onto the truck, which had only one bomb. The group placed the steel door back into the frame using shear strength from four of the group, the private then 'tack' welded it closed. It looked as if it had never been disturbed.

The two trucks and the men drove toward the helicopter waiting at the airport terminal. The Russians were not allowed to witness the loading as they were still covered with camouflage mesh and posted near the machine gun, they were warned to stay under the covering until told they could move. The bombs were loaded onto the helicopter and covered with leaded blankets. This precaution to insure they were not detected by scanners for radiation.

The two staff sergeants along with the command sergeant loaded the forklift and returned the trucks and forklifts where they had found them. They carefully put everything, including the keys, back to where they had been found. The Pakistani government would not know how the bombs were removed or where they have been taken. The Pakistanis would assume the weapons were in the vault and had been stolen from there. Only the general who had hidden them in a different location would know, they had been removed from the guarded vault long ago! He likely smiled knowing they were hidden in a different location and were probably still there.

The three men double-timed back to the helicopter, where the Russians were now on board. Once the three sergeants returned, the two privates loaded the machine guns and got on board.

In less than three hours, they would be back in Rigestan with the three nuclear weapons. Soon, Iran would be a nuclear power.

The helicopter landed next to the two trucks that had brought the group to Registan. The trucks quickly moved to the helicopter. A forklift was brought over as the pilot had radioed ahead for it to be waiting. In 45 minutes, the bombs were loaded, two in one and one in the other, covered with lead blankets and in route back to Katamak, Hirmand. The Russian pilot and copilot were required to stay upfront while thew bombs were unloaded and then loaded. The major and command sergeant once again took the front seats with the Afghan drivers; the rest moved to the back with the bombs, this time two guards were on alert in the rear each laying down and peering out the back and to the sides. The Afghan drivers were not allowed to see what was being loaded, they were kept a distance away while the bombs were loaded. The major paid the remaining $75,000 to the Russian pilot, who again, only smiled.

The Major spotted something beside the road and stopped the convoy 200 meters away from whatever was there, the command Sergeant Major had spotted the same thing, both were trained to see even the slightest movement that was not natural. Two of the Iranians from each truck quickly slipped out and moved away and then toward whatever was out there. The Major had radioed them the moment he saw something. The trucks set there when suddenly 3 men in camouflage clothing carrying rifles stood up and started toward the truck, two others had set up a machine gun in the road, another was moving toward the rear of the two trucks. One of the Iranians laid down behind a sand dune and when the man headed toward the rear came by, he jumped him and slip his throat, he made no noise.

One of the 3 heading toward the truck shouted out in Afghan, "Do not move we are confiscating these vehicles, if you want to live just walk away."

Suddenly all 3 dropped to the ground as they were shot by the Iranians, they had fired using a silencer on the weapon, it made almost no sound. Then the 2 manning the machine guns also dropped to the ground. The Iranians quickly removed the bodies to beyond the sand dunes and returned to the trucks. The Major believing, they were safe ordered the convoy to continue.

Four hours later, they crossed back into Iran, which, as of this moment, was a nuclear power. Three trucks with drivers and a forklift were waiting at the same spot they had originally departed from along with a helicopter. One bomb was loaded onto each truck. They were careful to cover the bombs to ensure radioactivity could not be detected from the air. They were also careful to not allow anyone to see what was being loaded. Once securely loaded, the two staff sergeants and one of the corporals separated and boarded the three trucks. The trucks departed, each heading in a different direction to different locations. Only the driver knew where they were headed and only then after opening a sealed package in the glove compartment. The remainder of the special forces unit with their equipment boarded the helicopter and was flown back to Tehran for a much-needed rest.

Only the President and the Supreme Leader would be aware of the bombs, there locations and that they even existed

Chapter One

A top-secret meeting of military leaders and the Iranian President was held in a location away from any normal government facility, it seemed every word spoken for the last several months in primary government offices was either being overheard by American intelligence or was being leaked. It made no difference, this meeting had to be held in a totally secure site with no chance of either a leak or be overheard. Hassan's staff thoroughly checked the location for any possible listening devices and ran new security checks on all who would be present. It took 45 minutes to complete the security needed when all finally were seated, each person was thoroughly checked. They could take no chances.

President Hassan Rouhani sat at the head of a large oval table that had eight chairs with writing paper and pens in front of each, they would allow nothing to be brought in, cell phones were taken, all pens, pocket knives and anything else that could be converted to a transmitter were placed in a basket two hundred meters outside the meeting area, At each entrance, stood four guards, armed with machine pistols, two helicopter gunships were circling a full kilometer away, one north of the site and the other south. High in the air were three fighter jets whose purpose was to protect the gunships. On the ground was a contingent of revolutionary guards, Iran's most feared military, the guard patrolled the area with dogs to make sure no snipers were present, and no one was close enough to intercept a conversation using long-range listening devices. This meeting had to be held in secret and once held remain so. The purpose was to begin planning of a military retaliation against the United States and Israel for what they had done and were doing to the Iranian people. Discovery of the plan would invite a preemptive retaliation by the United States, it would prove disastrous for the Iranian people if the plan was discovered.

Hassan opened the meeting, he was deliberately dressed in a black western style suit, he wanted the look of someone bad; maybe and undertaker or gangster, he was angry and held his fist up in the air clenched tightly as he began to speak.

"There is no family in all of Iran that has not being impacted by the economic damages being done to our country. I am tired of Iran being beaten down by the United States and Israel, it has gone on too long."

All at the leaders at the tables made mocking sounds in agreement.

"We must now take action! The American President imposed these sanctions on the Iranian economy, breached agreements reached after years of negotiating with most of the world, including the United States."

Two of the men sitting at the table banged lightly with their fists in agreement with him.

"The United States because of its currency, banking and trade controls have forced other countries to also enforce these new illegal sanctions. Most of these countries do not wish to do so and actively have tried to go around the currency and trade issues. The new American president made it a priority to breach the treaty during his campaign for the Presidency, even though Iran was complying with all the terms. They are bullies and must be dealt with."

All of the powerful men at the table clapped but quietly.

Hassan was now banging the table with his fist as his anger rose to a higher pitch.

"President Trump promised he would do this to us, and he has. What he now wants is complete capitulation to the demands of Israel, as to how they can treat the Palestinian people and other Muslims, which is to control them, something Iran will never allow. Israel considers the Jewish people above those of Palestine and other Muslims, and the lowly believers must act and do as any inferior race should. They must adhere strictly to a policy of containment and restrictive actions and movement, almost as if they were slaves, maybe worse than slaves. Iran wants all Muslims to be treated as equals and insist they be allowed to seek their own destiny. The United States continues to supply massive, sophisticated weapons to Israel to be used against us and the Palestinians, but we are forbidden from providing any assistance. Donald Trump has the nerve to demand we negotiate new terms with him."

Hassan threw his arms in the air and spat as those words came out of his mouth.

"No!" we will not allow this, 'No' was said in almost unison by the men at the table.

Seated to Hassan's right was General Kenan Shiraz, the head of the army and a popular figure in Iran. He also banged on the table in agreement with Hassan. Others at the table were, to the left of Hassan, General Pejman, the head of the revolutionary guard. Next to General Shiraz was Air Marshall Namdar, an experienced pilot and head of all air forces and missile systems. Directly across from the Air Marshall sat Admiral Mokri, a legendary naval officer. At the other end of the table across from Hassan was defense secretary Javon Darzi. All looked dazed that such a gathering was being held. Normally the President would meet with individuals not with a group. The Supreme leader did so but not the President. It was a historic meeting.

"Mister Trump does not realize who we are and what we can do. Most of you are not aware, Iran has 3 50 kiloton nuclear bombs well hidden in three secure locations. We acquired them in 1988, they were taken from Pakistan as the Russian army moved out of Afghanistan. We can do much damage to the United States and Israel with them, and we will and must!"

"Using our nuclear abilities against them is the answer," said General Shirazi who had only recently been informed of the existence of Iran having a nuclear bomb.

He was only aware one existed not three. "It is a question of when and how, not if!"

He smiled broadly when he learned there were three.

"I completely agree, but none of us have the authority to make that decision. Only the Supreme Leader can do that," said the President who said so with an obvious distaste in his word emphasis and movement indicating it should be him who can make that decision, after all he was the elected official by the people.

"Then we must present our arguments to him," said General Shirazi Iranian pride is important.

"I will try and make arrangements for such a meeting, I agree we must convince him to let us teach them a lesson," said the president.

Admiral Mokri rose from his seat and spoke as if he was talking to children, quietly choosing his words carefully.

"Getting a bomb into the United States will be highly risky and difficult. My guess is each will weigh maybe even as much as 3,000 kilograms and be 2 kilometers square. A large heavy package to be handling. That size will require special equipment, very difficult to hide and easily detectable. We have worked on different scenarios to smuggle things into the United States for many years with little success. We once tried a submarine making contact with a pleasure fishing boat 30 kilometers offshore. Three times we tried and three times the boat was searched by the US coast guard when it returned to shore. The crew was held and investigated although they were given nothing but an empty box. Think of the devastating impact had they discovered a nuclear bomb and traced it to us! We better be damn sure we will succeed before we try anything!"

Air Marshall Namdar said, "you are correct we better be sure. I too have tested several types of situations, at one time I wanted to bring a missile across in pieces then put it back together. We were able to get many of the pieces across the border, this from Mexico but many were stopped and held until someone could explain what they were. We finally gave up, the American's have Xray machines mostly designed to find illegal drugs, but they also will stop possible weapons, the shapes are detectable. The ports also have installed radiation detectors which would easily find a nuclear bomb. Admiral Mokri is right we better be damn careful!"

General Shirazi banged his hand on the table, "gentlemen, it can be done! I have been smuggling items into the United States for some time now, never anything as large or as complex as a nuclear bomb but let me assure you I will test something that size and weight to see if I can!"

"How!" ask Admiral Mokri.

"It is better if I don't disclose. President Rouhani has been fully briefed on how." Said General Shirazi.

"I am aware of the successes of General Shirazi, but we need to also examine other possibilities. Can we get a bomb into Mexico or Canada? If we can, does that not help our chances of bringing one across the border. I would like each of you to develop a plan to first get one into Mexico and Canada then across the border." Said President Rouhani. "let's adjourn for two weeks then reconvene."

Ten days later, he was able to arrange a meeting with Supreme Leader, Ali Khamenei. The meeting was to be held in another secure, secret and remote part of Tehran, hidden from the prying eyes of spies who seemed to report every move the government planned, especially related to anything they planned against Israel or the United States. It was as if someone was always in the room with them, recording every word. Iran had long suspected the United States had installed devices that allowed them from afar to listen to every word said in the Supreme Leader's offices, conference or meeting rooms or areas in the office complex. Iran had tried to detect and remove such devices many times but found only a few. It was even possible, Iran had concluded, the listening was being done from a satellite far overhead. They were now installing a system that could reflect any listening beams, but it was months away from completion. For this reason, this meeting was being held away from any place that could be monitored. Hassan Rouhani had insisted on a secure location and high security. President Rouhani's staff had handled the security and, as with his meeting with the military, super security measures were in place. No one could get close to the building and there was no chance of them being monitored.

When the meeting finally started, Iran's Supreme Leader, Ali Khamenei, sat at a large conference table with a group of Iranian leaders, chairing the promised meeting. Ali Khamenei had first resisted then conceded to hold it, his sixth sense told him it would only lead to bad things for Iran. He knew the subject and was reluctant to being forced into a decision, although he knew he must.

Hassan Rouhani had given the Supreme leader a private briefing on what he wanted to do. The military had done so as well; the military was not invited only Ali Khamenei's senior civilian advisors. He was now well aware of the desires of the military.

"I agree, we must retaliate," the Supreme Leader began, "even though it means America will strike us, with a far superior military power, and do much damage to our country. To do otherwise will mean our people will forever be deemed weak and cowardly. It is only a matter of when, and to what extent, we must do this."

"Your excellency," said Javon Darzi, the minister of defense.

"You are aware; we have the three nuclear bombs we obtained secretly from Pakistan many years ago. They have never acknowledged the loss, and the Americans are unaware that we have them and only a very few of us are aware We can destroy an American city or more and threaten to do more damage if they do not end the sanctions. The military is working on how this can be done; I am confident they will have a doable method."

"How many Americans will die if we do this?" asked Kasper Hirazi, the health minister.

"Millions at least,", answered Javon. "We could however, plant it in a shipping area. It would seriously harm their economy without as many casualties but there would still be many thousands to die."

Hassan Rouhani banged his fist on the table, "Why do we care how many Americans will die! Look what they have done to us! They put a dictator in power over our people who killed thousands and thousands of us just to hold onto his power and he stole our money to live a life of luxury. All this to control our oil, not someone else's, but ours. When we rebelled, the United States supported him and not our people, and when we took hostages, they stole our money and put economic sanctions on us. It took us 30 years to get them to return our money and only when we agreed to stop development of nuclear weapons and give up the same power to defend ourselves as equals to other countries, particularly Israel, who vows to destroy us. We trusted them to abide by the agreement in turn, we were to destroy or give away most of our nuclear storage and the capability to enrich uranium. We now have no nuclear stockpile. We do not owe them any kind of mercy, killing more will be better! We gave them all we agreed, but they didn't abide by what they consented to do".

Hassan had now turned red with rage. "And now, they want more! They send billions of dollars to Israel to buy weapons to threaten us and control the Palestinians and then accuse us of being terrorists when we do the same for our allies and they insist, we must do nothing to protect ourselves. If we agree to stop any defensive moves, only then will they keep their word. I say kill as many as we can. They deserve to die and cannot be trusted with any agreement!"

"They will be forced to retaliate and will kill millions of our people," said Ali Khamenei "it is not a good end result."

"We must find another way," emphasized Kasper Hirazi.

"There is another way," said Aftab Karimi, the deputy defense minister. "And that is what?" asked Javon Darzi.

"The American or the Israeli people are not our enemies. It is only two men who have caused all these recent problems: Donald Trump and Benjamin Netanyahu. That's who we should target!" responded Aftab Karimi.

"Kill them and you will have their people against us, and they will still be forced to retaliate," noted Ali Khamenei.

"I do not propose we kill them. I propose we destroy their businesses, take their money, cut off their credit cards, their ability to make loans, do to them as individuals what they are trying to do to us! Also, do the same to their family members as they are doing to ours!"

The Supreme Leader stood and waved his hands over the group as if he was blessing them,

"I like the idea, if it is possible. We harm no one physically, but harm the ones harming us, in the same way they are harming us. I say let's try it. We have little to lose. Do you have a plan?"

"Only a concept but it will not take long to develop one. I can give you a rough outline in two hours", said Aftab Karimi.

Ali Khamenei then stated they would take a two-hour break. All left except for the defense minister and his deputy.

Two hours later Aftab Karimi presented a rough plan on how the property owned by Donald Trump and Benjamin Netanyahu could be damaged. Ali Khamenei nodded his head that he would like to try and see if this could be done, it was so much better than starting a war they could not win.

The minister of defense proposed his deputy, Aftab Karimi, be put in charge of such an effort and be given sufficient budget to get the job done.

Ali Khamenei stood up and said, "I agree, we must try. How much will you need to get this done?"

"I will need substantial American dollars for what we will do in America. We will also need more for specialty electronic equipment and many educated Iranian professionals and, of course, facilities, and skilled Iranian computer experts. The mission will require a substantial amount."

"We will provide whatever funding is needed. I expect details of the needs and an itinerary of the steps you believe this effort will involve within the next few weeks."

The minister of defense ended the meeting on that note. Aftab was requested to stay.

"Give us an immediate needs list," said Javon Darzi.

"Let's see I already know, I will need a list of the most qualified computer experts in Iran, the fastest and most reliable internet connection available, and, of course, a location to work. I can give you much more detail tomorrow."

"What you ask now, will be done by morning."

Hassan Rouhani stood and waved his arms to get everyone's attention. "This is all wonderful, and I hope it works, but, with the Supreme Leader's permission, I would like to continue the planning of blowing these evil people to hell – just in case it is needed!" Hassan knew at that moment, if he had the chance he would blow up as much of America as possible!

Ali Khamenei said, "I agree but this will be a last-ditch effort if all else fails, and only when you receive my specific permission."

"Agreed," responded Hassan Rouhani.

Chapter Two

Aftab Karimi was well liked by the people he worked with and for, he was a moderate and fought for sensible responses, he did so above board and did not believe in anything underhanded. He confronted those he disagreed with to their face with calm and logic. He was a father with three teenage children, had a home and country he loved. He did not worry about what he had told someone as he strived to always tell the truth. His belief was, as long as he always told the truth, he did not have to remember what he had told anyone, as it would always be the same. He was well educated and had what was equivalent to a master's degree in business. The Iranian leadership expected him to rise to a position of great power in the future. He was trusted by the higher Iranian leadership which was very important.

Aftab spent late into the evening working on what he had deemed his 'needs list'. He even designed a rough layout of a building that would fit his now, known requirements. His mind was moving fast, he could see the likely path to damage the Trumps and Netanyahu, but he must be able to clearly present that message to those who he would bring on board. Make the property Trump and Netanyahu owned be reduced greatly in value was the path, how they would be able to do that was a whole different story. He knew for certain he did not want to destroy the property as they, both Trump and Netanyahu would just file insurance claims and get the damage reimbursed. It had to be by creating damage that only a small part would be reimbursed. He could conceptually at least, see that damage to a hotel, for instance, that would make people not want to stay in the future, the loss of business was the type of damage insurance companies would not reimburse.

Aftab went to his home and informed his wife and children he was being assigned to a top-secret project and would be unable to make contact for at least the next few weeks, maybe longer. It had happened before, so his wife was not concerned. He did send a message to both the President and the Minister of defense, he requested access to personnel records to look for people who he can select as; chief of security, a deputy ,a person to supervise the computer experts and a supervisory procurement person.

After much thought, Aftab had come to the conclusion that he must start with a strong security person as a leak would destroy the chances of success. He also needed a strong deputy to push forward things as he got them moving. He was not qualified to know if the computer people he would bring on were or were not capable and doing what they needed done, he also must have a qualified person to put in charge as there was going to be many needs and he must have a person who could get purchased what they needed and fast and then supervise what they would be doing.

When Aftab woke the next morning, he had received a response from both the President and the Defense Minister, he was given unlimited access to the records and a personnel supervisor, to help him find what he was looking for. He dressed and went directly to the location of the records. Aftab wore more western style clothing, a sports coat with dress type pants and a button-down shirt. He felt much more comfortable wearing pants than the long robes many wore which, he believed, was only to impress the religious fanatics. He located the supervisor, Lila Rasul, a stern looking lady who wore a hijab not a burka. Aftab was pleased he was assigned a sensible looking person. "Miss Rasul, I need first a person who has great knowledge of security and the ability to handle other people."

Lila spent thirty minutes on a computer then gave him a list of ten people who would meet the qualifications he was looking for; she ordered the records pulled.

Aftab gave her, his next 'need', which was a computer supervisor who had lots of experience and credentials. She left, got on the computer while Aftab began reading the files on the ten-security people.

As Aftab went through the folders of security types, Lila had given him, he paused at the name Nash Heydari. *This man*, he thought is *perfect. He is a former intelligence officer, a moderate, which is important, well educated, is presently teaching international law at the University of Teheran.*

Aftab called the University and ask, could they possibly arrange for Nash Heydari to meet with him. Ten minutes later he received a call from Mr. Heydari.

"Mr. Heydari, my name is Aftab Karimi, I am the deputy minister of defense, I have a problem I would like to discuss with you. Could I possibly buy you lunch to talk about it?"

"Well of course, please call me Nash, everyone else does, I am honored you asked. Where and when should we meet?"

"If you are at the University there is a place not too far from either of us, the Malek Café, it is excellent."

"I have heard, what time?"

How about we both leave now?"

"Meet you there soon, I assume you know what I look like?" "I do, see you soon."

Aftab returned back to Lila who was assisting him "I must leave for a short while; I also need an experienced administrative manager to act as my deputy and another position is a procurement specialist especially in government procurement. You did a good job, looks like your first list will work out fine."

He then left and headed toward the restaurant, when both arrived, they shook hands. Aftab's first impression was positive. Aftab was wearing his normal dress of a western style sport coat and a button-down shirt with dress pants, Nash had on the same but a standard no button down no collar shirt. There was an instant chemistry between them.

"Nash, very glad to see you. Please call me Aftab. I need your expertise; I hope you can help."

"I will certainly try."

"I need a head of security for possibly several months. We must not have any leaks or anyone spying on our operation, you have the credentials. It will mean you will be away from your family for many months. Can you help?"

"Certainly, when do I start?"

"Right now. You can assist me in selecting three other positions that I must fill. We can drive to your place for you to pack if you like. We will notify the University that you will be taking a leave of absence."

"Ok, I do not live very far, should only take a few minutes. Wait until we are away from this area then let's both turn our cellphones off, then we can talk with a certainty we will not be overheard. We cannot be too careful."

"I will turn mine off now. I have much to explain to you."

Aftab was relieved, he had his chief of security who would also be helpful in selecting the other positions he needed now."

Once they were in a completely secure environment they could talk and only when Nash approved, Aftab was smart and told Nash, he was now in charge of security so when he approved them talking, they would do so, both had now turned off their cell phones.

"We can talk now, no possibility of us being overheard.", said Nash. Nash felt comfortable working with Aftab.

Aftab gave him a very brief and limited outline of what he was to do.

"We have decided America and Israel must be punished for what they are doing to Iran. I have the support of the moderates to not harm anyone physically but doing economic damage to the leaders of both the United States and Israel. It will be a tough job, I will be the person in charge, we can do it that way and not start a war where lots of our people get killed. You will be essential to our success, if word gets out the plan will be doomed. That is why you are my first to bring on board."

'That was smart, normally security is what is thought of after a failure. How many people are you thinking you will need?"

"My guess is forty." "Wow!"

Nash and Aftab headed straight to the office where the personnel files were located. Aftab handed him the files for a computer expert, he began reading each file carefully. Aftab started working on the files for a procurement expert. After slightly more than 30 minutes, Nash handed Aftab a file.

"I know this man; he also teaches at the University. He is smart, reasonable and supervises his staff with kindness and compassion. He gets a lot out of them by respecting what they do and who they are. His name is Rasheen Abbasi, I do not believe there is anyone in Iran with more knowledge of computers."

Aftab quickly flipped through the pages of the files. "Do you think he will want to leave his family for what could be months willingly? I want no one who is not part of this team voluntarily."

"I believe if it will help the Iranian people and also prevent a war. He will leap at the chance."

"Let's go talk with him, I am not having any luck with the list I have right now looking for a person to become our head of procurement."

Aftab again, contacted the University and requested Rasheen Abbasi contact him. Aftab and Nash continued to go through personnel files. Nash also had rejected all of the procurement individuals found in the files. The lady had no luck finding anyone with the qualifications Aftab had listed for his deputy. Forty-five minutes later they received a call from Rasheen Abbasi.

"Mr. Abbasi this is Deputy Defense minister Aftab Karimi, I am here with Nash Heydari and we would both like to discuss a position we need to fill. Are you available right now?"

"Yes, where should we meet?"

"I think it best if we pick you up and have this discussion somewhere private. Can we come get you now?"

"Yes, Nash knows where my office is located, I will be waiting outside."
"Good, we are on our way."

Aftab and Nash picked up Professor Abbasi twenty minutes later.

Rasheen got into the car and immediately Nash told him to turn off his cellphone, he also with hand motions putting his finger to his lips told him to be quiet for a few minutes. Aftab was driving and drove to the outskirts of the city then pulled over.

"Sorry for such cloak and dagger but what we need to discuss with you is a highly confidential project to benefit our country. I have seen your credentials and know you can do the job. It will entail you being completely away from your family for weeks at least, possibly months. If you can agree to do that then we can discuss what you will be doing next."

"If it will benefit my country then I will be glad to help!"

"Ok, then you are in and now a part of this team." Said Aftab. "What this is about is, we have decided to retaliate against the United States and Israel for putting our people in such dire predicaments. We discussed a military option but decided what we can and should do is attack them economically as they are doing to us. It is two men who have caused all the suffering, Donald Trump and Benjamin Netanyahu, not the American or Israelite people, we do not wish to harm them. We plan on hacking into their financial and bank accounts, take their assets and damage properties they own. We need your expertise to do this."

"What will I have to do this with?"

"I plan on having the most powerful internet connection in Iran, the most up to date and dominant computers and as many assistants as you may need. I anticipate around forty people to be working on this."

"How about facilities?"

"We should be getting a building in the next day or two. We will completely remodel it to fit our needs."

"Then we will get it done!", stated Rasheen.

Chapter Three

Over the next several days, Aftab gathered more of the staff, telling them no more than what he absolutely must, to get the job started. Secrecy was essential; a leak would destroy the chances of the plan to work. Nash took over the security and created procedures necessary to protect the information and entire process, as more people came on board. Rasheen provided a list to Aftab of computer experts who he believed could do the job. Rasheen paced as he talked and wrenched his hands together, a habit he had developed while teaching, it allowed him to think. All who knew him well was aware following his pacing would be something brilliant coming out of his mouth.

Aftab was given office space consisting of a building with two floors, with each floor easily housing 40 people. Using the list given to him by Rasheen, he began a search of personnel records for the brightest Iranian computer experts. He wanted 15 geniuses with knowledge of whatever computer hardware that was needed. He wanted those people as soon as possible; they would be the key to establishing how the offices needed by each were to be configured. He also wanted housing: cooks, janitors, and more security for all the staff. He had decided that once they started, they would not be allowed to leave. They would not have to make their own beds, cook meals, wash clothes, or do any other thing that was not related to the task in hand: Which was to steal and or damage the assets of the Trump family and Benjamin Netanyahu! Rasheen had taken over the selection and narrowed the list down to ten.

Late the next day, Aftab had been given temporary quarters which would house 25 people and had some working space. Nash spent considerable time making sure the building was secure. Aftab was delivered 10 computer experts from his list of 15. They were blindfolded and. brought into a room. He spoke to them as if they were his children.

"You are here because you are the best we have. Your country needs you. You have already agreed to participate, or you would not be here. We want no one who is not here willingly. We must have absolute secrecy regarding what you will attempt to do, which is why you were brought here under such unusual undercover conditions. You will be rewarded handsomely if we succeed. I want you to be comfortable. Whatever your needs are to get this job done, it will be provided. I also want you to contact your families and assure them you are OK and have been drafted to work for your country. You will be with us for weeks and, possibly, months. All reasonable funds your family needs while you are here will be provided, I will give you contact information to give to them, and this contact will arrange for their needs. Do you have any questions?"

Several of the men raised their hands, Aftab pointed to the man on his far right.

"We have no clothing, or other personal items. What are we to do?"

"Someone will get your sizes, the type you like to wear and a list of other items you may need. Don't forget to list any medications. They will provide you with clothing and all other things needed. I do not want you to know where you are located. You cannot leave this place until we have completed our goal. We will make you as comfortable as possible. I hate to do this, but it is absolutely necessary, I hope you understand."

He turned to one of the men in the center and pointed to him. "Will I be able to speak again to my family?"

"Right now, the answer is no, but as we get organized, we will try to accommodate some contact. What I can promise you is, your family will be well taken care of."

He then turned to a third man. "Is what we will be doing legal?"

"Yes, what you will be doing will make you and your country proud. This effort is necessary to defend our country."

Aftab then allowed each of them to contact their families which was overseen by Nash who was pleased with how all was handled, after providing them with the contact information their families could use to seek help. Nash also reemphasized that he would send someone to check on them regularly.

After everyone had made their calls and settled things with their families, Aftab sat down with them using a large conference table. He had pads and pens for all. He quickly got down to business. "We are going to hack into many banks and financial institutions around the world. Your object will be to take funds from people who have been damaging Iran"

Nash had scanned the room again for listening devices before they got started. "This also will mean we will have to discover the account numbers being used by the people we will target, what financial institutions they use and how many accounts they have. There are a number of people in the United States and Israel who are our enemies and are harming Iran and your own families. Our job is to harm them as they have harmed us! I need to know the type of computers and any other equipment you will need to do this. It would helpful if all of you would get together and create a shopping list of what you will need. Can you do that?"

Almost in unison, they answered "Yes!" However, you could see in the eyes and demeanor of several who had skepticism as to what information they really would have and if this was even possible.

"Let me be clear. We are going to hack into the President of the United States and his family's personal bank, investment accounts, and income sources. I also want to know every piece of real estate they own, anywhere in the world! Include on your list, any assistance from other people to include other experts whose skills you may need to get this done."

The group worked late into the night, only stopping for food that was brought to them.

The list was long and comprehensive. It took them through the entire next day. Early in the evening of the second day. they presented a finished a list to Aftab. He was pleased with the work they had done. Rasheen had worked with the group since they first arrived. Aftab had not yet officially announced Rasheen was in charge of the computer operation. Aftab's reasoning was he wanted them to be part of the larger group first before they separated into a group of just computer hackers. Rasheen had agreed with the way Aftab wanted to handle the start of this effort.

The list began with the computer hardware they would need, followed by very specific software, power requirements and air conditioning. Emphasis was put on the amount of heat these computers would generate, as they would malfunction if they were not kept cool. The second group of items were the internet requirements; the internet source had to be hard-wired into the building and stable. The internet going down could mean a large loss of time and possibly lost data. Proper furniture and lighting were also emphasized as the work is tedious, and comfort equals fewer mistakes. None wanted to use Wi-Fi, not even for printers.

As for additional personnel, 10 computer experts would be enough, but they would need 6 'grunts' with computer knowledge to assist as needed. The work should be in two 12-hour shifts, equally divided.

Aftab provided portions of the list of items needed to four different people. He did not want any one person to be able to piece together what they may be up to. He had still not found a person who would be in charge of procurement, he used four military buyers at different locations to find and purchase the items on the list.

He was given contact information with the Iranian guards of the construction and engineering division, a Colonel Rasma. Whose name he had been given by President Rouhani, he made arrangements and went to the Colonels office for a meeting.

"Colonel Rasma, I am Aftab Karimi, I need several items from your people. I do hope you can assist me."

"I assume that I can't question anything you ask of us?" answered Colonel Rasma with a slight grin.

"You must have received that type of order from someone but not from me. What we plan on doing is, extremely important."

"We have. As I understand, it is more than just very important and sensitive it is critical to our nation."

"It is important and sensitive only to the extent that we need and wish to be left alone. I have several staff members who have been given a task that must be done if we are to be successful, and I desire you to assign someone to work with each of them, as each task is complex and will require careful coordination. My list of the major items we need is:

"We want a 100% reliable and the fastest internet connection available. This will include a system and a redundant system that is hard wired with no other users. We cannot afford for the connection to ever go down. And we need it installed yesterday. I will show you on a map where it is to be located."

"I have a major who is an expert on cable installation and another who is the most knowledgeable person on the internet in Iran. I will arrange for them to meet with you the moment we finish here. Both are located in this building"

Colonel Rasma wrote the names of two men on a piece of paper and handed it to an aide. "Find these two men and have them come here as soon as possible."

"I will need some secure fencing: two rows with security electronics, dogs and guards patrolling the building we will be using. A temporary storage building to be constructed in the area between the rows. This building will hold temporarily any, and all deliveries. Another similar building will be inside the main compound. This building will be a holding area, before anything is moved inside and act as another checkpoint for inspection, which we will do."

"We have capable people; I will have them available to meet with whoever you assign for this task. Just tell me who, when and where."

"I will do so in the next hour. The building we have been given needs a lot of new partitions, a kitchen, showers, bathrooms, substantial air conditioning and electrical connections. All of this needs to be done quickly. I think the most efficient way is to give us a crew of men capable of doing this work along with a purchaser to buy whatever we need."

"If it can be made to work, I will have someone come tomorrow, meet with whoever you have. He will bring with him a carpenter, a plumber, several laborers and an electrician along with tools and supplies to get to work. No reason to waste even a single day. I am aware of the urgency"

"Fantastic."

Aftab made several calls to his people to arrange for them to meet with the Colonel's crew the next morning. He also ordered drawing paper, tape measures, and pencils. They would need to work late to develop the partition, shower and bathroom layouts needed. Aftab contacted Nash. Nash, who now had four people under him, wanted two of those he had assigned to security fencing to come to the Colonel's office to meet with his people now.

"Colonel, the men who will handle the fencing design will be here within the hour."

"Good. I will have the people they need to meet with come here as quickly as possible."

Aftab was overjoyed at the attitude and assistance of Colonel Rasma. He intended to tell his superiors of the treatment he had received. Aftab later learned Ali Khamenei had personally called the Colonel to request absolute cooperation. Ali Khamenei was no fool and well aware of the power of the Iranian Guards and knew that without their full cooperation this project would fail.

The two 'experts' on cable and internet had been waiting in a side conference room for the Colonel to see them. The Colonel and Aftab walked into the conference room. Both Majors rose to shake hands.

Colonel Rasma said, "Majors, this is Aftab Karimi, a personal representative of our Supreme Leader. We are to provide him with whatever he requests and will do so as quickly as possible. Aftab, this is Major Hussein. He is our most knowledgeable person on the abilities of our internet, and this is Major Abdole, who is extremely qualified in installing cable especially underground for long distances."

Aftab shook both their hands. "I am so glad both of you are available to assist with this project. Let me quickly tell you what we need. We must have an internet connection that will be 100% stable. As a precaution, I am asking you to run two separate lines."

Aftab laid out a map showing the end location. "This is where we need the internet. We will, due to security concerns, not use wireless devices of any kind. I need the building wired to connect ten stations with the possibility of adding more if needed."

Major Hussein spoke first. "Our most reliable connection is available approximately two kilometers from this point," putting a finger on a spot on the map.

"My recommendation is, we do this with underground cable. The ground in this area is firm but not hard or have much rock issues. The Colonel briefly told me what you will need, I have two crews on standby ready to start today. We will run two separate cables as you request. The equipment I have will dig and bury the cable at the same time, roughly one meter deep. We will run them side by side."

"You guys are amazing. I could not have asked for anything better."

"I will have a team ready to make the connection as soon as the cabling is complete."

"We will build a distribution junction box at the building so you can run as many connections as you need and can also add more as required," said Major Abdole.

Aftab was smiling. He shook the Colonel's hand and patted each Major on the back, "Colonel, you have some fantastic people!"

Shortly afterward, two experts in security, particularly fencing, showed up. Three of Aftab's people who were aware of what was needed were already there. One was Nash Heydari.

After introductions, they started immediately. Names were not important, but the contact information was. They each wrote down their respective emails and what were their responsibilities.

"The object," Nash Heydari. began, "is to prevent anyone unauthorized from entering the facility. We want a double system with two main gates. The first gate is to inspect and pass the person on to the second gate. There, they will be inspected and questioned again. We want two guards and a third hidden from sight who will kill anyone who tries to enter either of the gates without approval. The change of guards will take place one guard at a time, so that we always have five guards who have been there for a while."

"Sounds like we really need two gates and a preliminary checkpoint," stated a Lieutenant who had been sent by Colonel Rasma.

"I would agree," confirmed another of the Colonel's men. "Why?" Nash Heydari asked.

"You do not want anyone fumbling for identification or documents at either of the actual entrances. Anyone fumbling for information sets it up for bad things to happen. You want the first checkpoint to verify that authority exists for them to present their credentials to get in and, if they have the proper credentials, we will, instruct each to keep them in their hands until they get to the next step. You will need a man to verify the authority to go forward before anyone tries to enter and another hidden with a machine gun, just in case someone tries to breach."

Nash Heydari rose and pointed to the map, "We will need at least 40 meters from the first fence to the next. Our great concern is deliveries. To resolve this, we will want a temporary storage building constructed and all deliveries will be offloaded, inspected and reloaded with our own people before being brought into the compound. Our greatest weakness is someone might smuggle listening devices or other electronic surveillance inside. We intend to inspect, scan and dissect, if necessary, every item before it enters the compound." He laid out on the table a design for the temporary storage building. It was a simple building, 6 meters by 12 meters 5 meters high. The building had a dirt floor with no doors but openings for a drive in and out at each end. The design was for a delivery truck to drive in, unload, then drive around the fencing and then move back out. Another temporary structure of approximately the same size was to be just inside the second fence. Workers would unload, inspect, then pick up the goods with a forklift and move to the second structure where a second group would inspect and deliver to the area of the facility where they will be required. There, a third inspection would take place before and then once again after the merchandise was unpacked.

The security people for the Colonel were impressed.

"That is a well thought out system," said the second Colonel's man. "It will be difficult if even possible to sneak something in as a delivery."

"My recommendation," the Colonel's man, a lieutenant, said, "is that each fence will be four meters high and razor-wired. Also, to include a series of bollards just inside the first fence and just outside the second. This will prevent a speeding vehicle or truck from running over the fences and getting in.".

"Now when can this get done?" ask Nash Heydari.

"It will possibly take a week to get this much wire to the site, but my crew can begin setting the post and bollards tomorrow.

Chapter Four

Aftab and six of his staff worked late into the night in the unfinished building, using it to meet, as inefficient as it was, gave them a better sense of what was needed for the layout requirements. They all walked around the inside of the large rooms, marking in chalk on the floors what they believed would be essential for the space needs.

Rasheen said "The computer hackers need private space as total concentration is necessary".

Aftab conceded, and they drew out 10 private offices, each with individual air conditioner, three electrical outlets, and two internet connections. Someone then recorded this on the drawings paper to scale.

The seven then moved to the second floor.

Aftab said, "We need private places for our people to rest and sleep undisturbed. I think the entire floor should be only a living area."

Nash took a measuring device and handed Rasheen the end of a chalk marker pulling one end toward him. He measured a reasonable amount of space, roughly two meters for a bunk bed length and had Rasheen move toward the end wall. Nash then snapped the line leaving a mark all the way down one side of the room.

"I believe double the width of a bed will give each person enough room especially if we have footlockers that will slide under the beds."

Aftab agreed and Nash with Rasheen's assistance marked off another two meters for each bed. This layout would allow for twenty bunk beds which would sleep forty people. Aftab took the chalk line and also gave one end to Rasheen, the two marked off an area for a couple of couches and a space for a television with an extra computer screen and console for playing games.

"This is great" said Rasheen "our hacker guys love computer games!"

All moved to the end walls and laid out two large showers, six toilets and four urinals. Around the corner at a different room on the second floor. The drawing guys were busy putting all this on blueprint paper.

Aftab told one of the new engineers,

"layout on paper a dining area that will seat 50 people, a kitchen with ovens, stoves, sinks, grilles, refrigeration, with space sufficient to cook 150 meals a day."

The engineer, Kenan Mizael, the youngest of the group, shook his head up and down.

Aftab then turned back to Nash. "Nash, we have no females now but let's allow for separate spaces just in case, can you take care of that? I had rather be prepared."

Nash responded "Of course."

Later, Nash drew out a wall with a door and a separate but smaller shower, three sinks and two toilets.

In addition, Aftab on the first floor created an office space for himself.

The next morning after looking through many folders provided by Lila Rasul, Aftab finally found an employed a purchaser, a travel coordinator and a deputy. He was not ecstatic with what he had ended up with, but it was the best he could find and much better than nothing.

At 8 AM the following day, a crew of workers arrived, looked over the drawings Aftab's group had prepared and, with hardly any discussion, began the work. They first took marking paint and laid out the lines for toilets, sinks, and showers. The soil was very sandy, and simple drainage lines would be sufficient for sinks and showers, but a complete septic tank with drainage lines would be necessary for the toilets. The crew, obviously, was well qualified and worked with astonishing speed. As the crew laid out the lines, another crew cut trenches into the slab concrete and the elevated slabs. Another dug deep drainage ditches. Aftab stood and watched with absolute astonishment.

Within 8 hours, 20 more men arrived with specific instructions as to the task they were to do and began work. One group of 4, ran electrical conduits to each location marked for electrical outlets, internet connections, air conditioning, all air conditioners were to be window units. Another group of 3 men roughed in for the electrical distribution system, 4 others dug trenches to connect and supply water to the building as the previous connection was only a small pipe that would not suffice for the present needs. Three others ran hot water lines to the showers and kitchens. The remaining crew laid out and calculated the quantity of materials required for the partition walls, outside buildings, drywall, roofing, electrical wire, lighting fixtures and even paint. Colonel Rasma had already ordered two tractor trailers to be loaded with the most common items that would be required. He scheduled delivery to the site for the next morning.

Aftab watched along with his staff in pure admiration. Never in his wildest imagination would he have believed that this project could move with such speed and efficiency. His experience working with the Iranian bureaucracy was that so much red tape existed it takes months, if not years, to get approval to modify even a small room owned by the government. By the morning of the second day, the drainage pipe had been installed along with the air vents through the roof. Gravel was being placed into the drainage lines and the septic system. The tank for the septic was sitting on the ground; it had been delivered sometime during the night. Nash established a system where every hour his security people scanned everything being installed for listening devices. They discovered two devices in the first few hours. Colonel Rasma was notified, and the culprit was dealt with severely. He took each device and scanned them for fingerprints and DNA. In both devices, a fingerprint was detected. Aftab ordered the device to be replaced with ones that would transmit the sound from a local television station.

Colonel Rasma tortured the culprit until he gave them all the devices he had been given and a list of any other people who may be involved. As expected, it was the Americans who had paid handsomely for the installation. The American agents had a standing order for any new or modification of a government building to be 'bugged' with such devices. The covert counterpart for the Revolutionary Guard took over. their techniques were anything but kind. Most were broken when they were finished with them. They were either dead or wished they were dead. The Guard had no problems in bringing in their close families to be tortured if the person resisted.

The result was the arrest of 50 American agents. All were tortured until the repeating listening devices they knew about were located. As expected, the devices had been planted in nearly all sensitive buildings, including the homes of most government officials. The system worked like a repeater; the conversations were received by a device that sent a signal to another repeater. This continued until it reached a computer, which converted the data to an encrypted information format and was transmitted to the American CIA via satellite. This enlightenment of how the American spy system worked made them understand how the American government was so aware of Iranian plans and why so many had failed.

The Revolutionary Guard's counterpart to the American CIA recorded the location of the devices as they were found. It also now had the intelligence about the frequencies the devices used to transmit. The intelligence arm of the Guard began transmitting fake conversations using the frequencies in the assumed voices each location would have overheard. Over the next several weeks, the Guard monitored the now-known locations of each repeater and the computer system encrypting the data. The monitoring uncovered ten people, they were arrested and forced to provide more information on the contacts and functioning of the group. They intended to continue to transmit a false narrative to the unaware Americans.

The speed of the project was nothing more than incredible. In just a week, the project had reached a point where the actual mission work could begin shortly. The trenches and cable for the internet were complete, tested and functioning. Septic systems for both the toilets and other drainage were finished. Window air conditioners were installed in holes in the outside walls created for them. Partition walls stood everywhere; electrical wire could be seen snaking through them. The kitchen, showers and bathrooms could now be identified as what they were to be. Doors, toilets, kitchen equipment and hardware were stored anywhere there was space to put them; the trusses for the two storage buildings were stacked outside. The fence poles and bollards were installed; the fencing was to be delivered in the next few days.

Eight more listening devices had been found in materials being delivered. The Guard quickly found the culprits. The devices had been installed into the door casing by the door manufacture. The supplier was only aware that the doors were to be installed in a government building, but not the location. The discovery meant many more facilities were bugged. The company records identified where the deliveries had been made in the past. The practice had been in place for 5 months but still entailed more than a hundred doors. These devices transmitted at a different frequency than the others and caused much detail work to locate the repeaters and the computer system to encrypt and transmit the data. The Iranian government was furious but kept their cool so that the knowledge about the detection of the devices was kept secret. The Guard created detection equipment capable of locating these devices and began canvassing every government building and home of high-ranking officials. Many more were found and neutralized. The Americans would have overheard nearly every conversation any government official had with anyone.

The fake data now being transmitted was having an impact on the American policies toward Iran. The conversations provided knowledge that Israel was afraid of the current American government and was bringing and hiding defensive nuclear weapons into the United States just in case they were ever needed.

Hassan Rouhani, the President of Iran, broke down in giggles when he reviewed some of the misinformation being picked up by the American spy devices. Hassan referred to one fake planning conversation being transmitted as creative genius. Portions of the transcript read as.

"Mister Ambassador" (speaking to the Mexican consulate) we have a mutual problem with the current United States government and believe there exist safety measures we should take.

"And what might they be? We cannot afford issues with the United States!"

"Iran believes you cannot afford not to. You saw from their latest moves on immigration that, even though they had just signed a trade agreement with you, they broke it and demanded more concessions. Where will it end, what new concessions will they demand tomorrow?"

"Yes, that is true, we are concerned."

"This is the same as they are doing to Iran, we reached agreements and now they want more, or they will resume sanctions. We said 'No' and they did resume sanctions. They can't be trusted."

"What do you propose we do jointly?"

"Iran has short range missiles we can deploy along your border with the United States. These missiles launch from temporary movable vehicles which can easily be camouflaged They would only be used as a last resort...."

The fake plan as continued provided information formulated jointly between Mexico and Iran; it was confirmed. Mexico would allow Iran to install a number of yet undecided missiles along the border which could be aimed at American airports and cities. The missiles were low flying with a range of 700 miles. Mexico explained that they have been sickened by the current United States Regime's treatment of their people and those who have migrated from the south. Also, a very brief mention of a Canadian alliance, with no particular details given, was mentioned. President Rouhani could only imagine the efforts that would be made by the Americans to thwart this plan. Mexico nor Canada has any knowledge of any of this! The United States had sent special envoys to Mexico and Canada to try and determine how serious this threat was.

****

On a Wednesday night, the walls for the two storage buildings were raised. The walls consisted of large timbers for posts attached to top plate beams with plywood siding. The trusses would be installed during daylight; the lighting fixtures would be attached to the trusses. Probably by the next day, plywood decking will be installed, followed by shingle roofing.

By Saturday evening, the storage buildings were scheduled to be completed, the fencing material had arrived. Drywall was now being installed over the partition walls; paint was stored inside as was the electrical outlets and fixtures. Aftab expected the desks, bunk beds and other furnishings to be delivered by Monday, he was very pleased. Refrigeration remained a slight problem, but that was expected to be resolved soon.

By the end of the next week, fencing was complete; the partition walls were painted, all electrical devices were installed, the toilets, showers were connected but not yet functioning, the water heaters were yet to be delivered. Aftab decided to go ahead with the installation of the furniture. The computers would arrive in four days, which would mean they could get to work.

****

The fake information had been so convincing that the American government was searching all trucks and trains coming from Mexico or Canada thoroughly; and Canada retaliated by searching, in turn, all the vehicles coming from the United States into their country. Vehicles were backed up on both sides of the border for miles; the cost had to be staggering. The United States could not explain why they were doing this, just that "it was a precaution."

President Rouhani doubled the effort on leaking fake information over the next several weeks. He created a narrative among Britain, France, Germany, China, Spain, Japan, Russia and South Korea about the current danger of the United States. The narrative included replacing the US currency as an international trading currency with something more reliable such as the European or Chinese currency. This was primarily because the United States was using its power to force other countries to follow its demands. Although they had negotiated a joint agreement earlier, but now, the US did whatever it pleased with no agreement of other nations.

The United States was frantic and sent ambassadors everywhere to resolve the issues. Of course, none of these countries were even remotely aware of anything. Donald Trump was livid, blaming members of his cabinet for incompetence, none of which he believed was his own fault. Because he was required by law to do so, the Secretary of the Treasury notified Congress about the currency problem and was immediately fired the moment Trump was made aware he had notified Congress.

President Rouhani was delighted that his fake news efforts were paying such dividends.

At the end of the third week of construction, all the buildings were complete, the computers were operational, the supplies had been delivered, and all had been checked and rechecked for detection devices. The complete staff would be in place by tomorrow. The Revolutionary Guard had been placed in charge of security through the first and second checkpoint Nash's people took over before anyone was allowed into the compound. The staff consisted of 10 computer experts, 6 grunts to work with and for the computer experts, 3 agricultural experts, 3 metal experts, 3 engineers, 5 clerical support staff, 2 cooks, 2 janitors and household staff, 2 security experts and 1 deputy to Aftab. The total staff was 38, all were ready and anxious to get to work.

Chapter Five

Aftab brought his ten computer experts together, they were exhausted after working on the list of required items for nearly twenty straight hours, they now began to verify all had been considered properly. He had already appointed Rasheen Abbasi, a tall professor in his thirties, who taught computer science at one of the universities, as the leader, he was certainly the most qualified. Aftab announced to the other nine that Rasheen was the supervisor and would be in charge of the computer operations. He and Rasheen had known this for a long time but decided to wait to tell the others. Before Aftab said even a single word, he had security scan everyone, including himself and the entire room, for any listening devices. He was positive that everything was clean, but it was better to be safe. Because they now knew quite a lot about the many types of listening devices that could be planted, the scanner was much more efficient in finding them. It was a not- so-pleasant a surprise when the beeper went off and a device was discovered inside a just-delivered table leg. Aftab ordered several of the men to lift the table and take it outside. Then he contacted the Revolutionary Guard using his secure cell phone, he wanted the person now responsible for following up on the devices as they were found. The person from the guard rushed as it was important to follow up quickly, he removed the device and went straight to the table's manufacturer. The rest of the room was found safe, so Aftab knew he could continue safely. They would have to once again review all procedures as the table should not have gotten past the first check point.

"Our starting point for this effort," he began, "is to locate any real estate, buildings or other structures owned, partially owned, managed or controlled by Donald Trump, the current President of the United States, his companies, his sons Donald Jr. and Eric, his daughter Ivanka, his son-in-law Jared Kushner, Ivanka's husband and Benjamin Netanyahu, the current prime minister of Israel. Trump and Netanyahu have conspired together to harm us, our children, our wives, and our parents. We plan to retaliate for what they have done. We intend to damage, in some way, every piece of property owned by them and bring down their value. Later, we will attack their other investments."

Rasheen Abbasi raised a hand. "Yes," said Aftab.

"How long do we have to do this?"

"As long as it takes, however the sooner the better. Although, if we do not get to damage all, or if we don't get to all, then, it is their good luck."

"We will begin by assigning each of you a primary target. I want you to start by doing just a simple search on the internet and see what it brings up. We know, for instance, that Donald Trump or his company owns nineteen golf courses and the Trump Tower in New York City. There are many other properties. When you discover one, one of our clerks will create a file on that property and put into it all information we gather, and then, we will build from there. You must identify exactly where this property is located— what country, what city, what state, what county, all the necessary identifications as if you were interested in buying. The next step is to find the recorded property boundaries, then the location of any utility lines, easements, and so forth."

Rasheen Abbasi stood up and began pointing fingers, "Let me give each one of you assignments; by assignment I mean find all the properties, bank accounts, credit cards, and so forth. Rasheen paced as he spoke, grasping both hands and squeezing them. They had all by now become accustomed to how Rasheen brought his intellect forward and just smiled. "Rashan Darzi, you will search for Trump corporate properties managed or owned by the company. Shahzad Hashemi, you will do the same for Donald Trump personally. Nima, you will take Donald Trump Junior. Arash, you are assigned Ivanka Trump, Bijan, you have Eric Trump, Kenan you will handle Jared Kushner. Mainchin, Arastoo, and Aarush, you will handle Benjamin Netanyahu. I suspect his information will be harder to pin down. I want each of you to have the clerks write down on this large marking board each of the properties and to whom it belongs as you locate one. We have engineers who will do more detailed work and build on the file as soon as you give them an address."

All nine of the computer experts headed toward their assigned computers, excited and anxious to find out as much as possible on these people. The five clerks began building file folders for each of the names given, making many folders for each, which were then to be separated by property.

The latest found device created a raid on the furniture manufacturer's plant. A cache of the devices and two culprits who were responsible were found. Though nothing new was discovered about who and how they had been recruited. The two just simply disappeared and were not heard from again. A massive manhunt was started but they apparently had well established escape plans to be used, if they were ever discovered, they could not be found.

The security for the remodeled building was now in place. The Revolutionary Guard had taken over that aspect from all points before allowing entry into the compound. It was an impressive setup: the outer entry had two guards to check identification and other papers, they were supported by a well-hidden man covered in camouflage netting matching the area grounds, manning a machine gun. Each of the guards carried an MPT-9, which is an Iranian version of a handheld machine gun, each also had grenades attached to their belts. The second gate had two guards, also armed with MPT-9s and grenades. Their backup was a well-hidden guard to the left and on the right of the opening. Once someone got past the first and second gates, there was a large space before the third gate that led to the actual compound.

Aftab felt comfortable that the computer folks had begun and would be busy and needed no further supervision from him for the next day or two, they were in good hands with Rasheen. He had now on board three agricultural experts, he had them brought to an area where they had installed desks and a conference table: this would be their home for some time. When they were all present, he once again had the entire room and every person scanned for any listening devices. This time, all was clean, and he could proceed without interruption.

"Gentlemen, this is a great task that you are given. Let me familiarize you with the starting point. Our objective is to make two individuals and their families pay for what they have done to our people: Donald Trump, the current President of the United States and Benjamin Netanyahu the current Prime Minister of Israel. We have, right this minute, skilled computer experts finding out every property owned by these men and their families. Your job is to come up with ways through which we can make those properties less valuable. For instance, we know Donald Trump owns at least nineteen golf courses. My ideas are that you will kill the grass on all those courses and kill it in such a way that it will be very difficult to grow back."

Jamshed stood and waved his hands. "We are well aware of what those bastards have done to our country and wish them much harm. Yes, we know how to make grass die and make it difficult to regrow. The problem will be the delivery. Obviously, they will not stand back and let us spray something on the grass or other items."

Aftab was immediately impressed with Jamshed Rostami who was not much for physical appearance, he was short and a little overweight with longer hair than Aftab preferred, but there was something bright and open about this man, he alluded knowledge. Jamshed was dressed comfortably with Serwal type white pants and a loose top. He smiled a lot which Aftab also liked.

"Jamshed, that is exactly the problem, but other than golf courses, how else can we damage the value of these properties?" asked Aftab.

"Nearly all properties," Jamshed said, "especially those owned by investors, have elaborate filthy expensive landscaping many times at extremely large cost. A single tree may cost thousands of Rials. We can kill each tree, all bushes and plants although not easily!"

"OK. You have access to computers, dedicated for your use; the clerks have been instructed to give you full access to the folders they are creating. If you desire copies, they will make them for you. I suspect you will want to bring up satellite images of each of these properties. Divide them up among you. I want you to have, at the end of each day, an open discussion on how you plan to deal with each of these. In fact, my desire is for you is to present to me a comprehensive plan on what needs to be done and how you think it can be done. Once I have it, the second part is for us to decide how we are actually going to do this. Get started. The clerks already have listed several properties and created many folders. I will be back tomorrow."

Aftab started to walk out then stopped and came back, "Jamshed, I would; like to make you the supervisor of this group would you mind overseeing the progress?"

"I would be honored" answered Jamshed.

Aftab left the agricultural group and requested the three metal experts and three engineers be brought to their designated area. When they arrived, he repeated the security procedure: everyone was, again, completely clean. He began, repeating nearly verbatim what he had told the other groups.

"Gentlemen, as I have already told our computer and agricultural experts, this is a great task you are to be given, let me give you the starting point, our objective is to make two individuals and their families pay for what they have done to our people: Donald Trump, the current President of the United States and Benjamin Netanyahu the current Prime minister of Israel. We have right this minute, skilled computer experts finding any property or buildings owned by these men or their families. Your job is to come up with ways through which we can make those properties less valuable. You will be able to look at satellite images of all these properties and even, get the original building plans on most. You will also see how the agricultural experts plan on damaging the properties. Trump and his family own, we believe, they own more than one hundred properties. Netanyahu owns quite a few as well. Your job is to give us ways to damage those properties in a way that it will not be obvious that they have been attacked. I only have one concept running through my mind, which is to destroy the metal in their plumbing fixtures and stop up the sewage to each of the buildings."

All six of the experts laughed.

"Stopping the sewage systems should not be so difficult, but damaging the fixtures will be," Gulzar Charmchi, a metal expert, said. "But it can be done."

"Glad to hear that," said Aftab.

"What kind of information will we be given to work with and how will we proceed?" asked Aram Alinejad, an engineering expert. Aram was exceptionally smart; he had a PhD in engineering and was officially Doctor Alinejad but preferred just Aram. He dressed in more of a western style which came from his attending a University in Spain for his PhD. Aram preferred to shoot straight he did not like beating around the bush and wanted straight to the point answers to his questions.

"I have, right now, a group of computer experts identifying all the target properties. They have clerks building folders on their findings. We hope to tap into the permits for each so that you will have sketches of each structure. Also, we have a group of agricultural people working on the exterior. They will be producing satellite images of each property. You have already been given full access to each folder; I want you to add any new information so that everyone is always on the same page. The clerks will give you copies of whatever you need from the folders to work with. We do not want the damage to the structure which you may decide to do be obvious."

Aftab started to walk away but turned toward Aram, "I hope that answered your question, it is important I give you the information you need."

"It did," answered Aram.

Later the next day, Aftab brought the entire team together, which, as of now, consisted of 10 computer experts, 6 computer grunts, 3 agricultural experts, 3 metal experts, 3 engineers, 5 clerks, 5 security experts, 2 cooks, 2 janitors, 1 executive assistant. A total staff of, including him of 41. Aftab, as was the case for every meeting, began with a security scan of the area and all personnel. All were clean, of course, but this was to emphasize the importance of constant awareness of security. Nash smiled as the scan was performed, he could rest assured, this project would not be compromised.

He seated them in no particular order in the main conference room. Aftab made eye contact with each as they entered and either patted them on the back or squeezed their hand.

"It is time to bring all of us together as we will be here for quite some time and we all, have the same goal. Please feel free to contact anyone at any time you feel the need. I would like for each of you to consider one item for which there isn't a person responsible yet. I have decided that I may want to introduce bedbugs to all the properties that have overnight guests, such as the hotels. If we are able to pull this off it would be a major blow, to the Trump organization. I am not sure which discipline should have this responsibility or if I should recruit someone who is an expert on insects. I would like your opinion. Will each of you please stand for a moment, introduce yourself, and state your expertise?"

Aftab held his hand up and pointed, "Let's start from the left."

Each person then stood and addressed the group, saying why he was selected, Aftab encouraged questions after each had spoken. It took well over two hours to complete but he accomplished his objective: that they understood and respected each other as a team and learned that they should work together.

Chapter Six

Regardless of the success of the disinformation campaign and the discovery of how the Americans have so far been able to listen to the conversations of so many Iranian officials, Hassan Rouhani, decided it would be wise to prepare for a nuclear attack on the United States. The fact the Americans had planted so many devices was reason enough to bomb the hell out of them, they needed to be severely punished. He wanted the work being done by Aftab's group to do the damage they planned but the chances of success were low and also, he selfishly hoped it would fail, He wanted all Americans to suffer and suffer greatly!

The secrecy of the three nuclear weapons Iran had in their possession meant that he must work with people who would not know what they were really doing and would follow instructions without questions such as 'why'? He needed two small backhoes, two trailers capable of hauling the backhoes, two trucks that could also haul a bomb, and, of course, drivers, laborers, and two nuclear experts capable of examining the bombs. Hassan decided he would deal with only two of them now. He must be absolutely sure they would work if needed. He realized they had been in storage for over thirty years and would need to be examined for corrosion or any other thing that could have gone wrong over the years.

Hassan had four different meetings in separate rooms within the same location, his first was with a nuclear expert who had tremendous knowledge of nuclear weapons, especially those of the age when these were acquired, a Dr Javed Sorouri. He had everyone he would talk to or meet with all searched and scanned for any form of communication or tracking devices before the effort to locate, find and examine two of the bombs began. The third would remain hidden. Hassan must be positive the bombs have been tested and were ready for use. Bringing the equipment to the site and uncovering each would be tricky. None of the people involved must know where they were and be unable to return to the sites later. Only Hassan was currently aware of the location of the two bombs he had selected although the information was available to others, it was sealed and may never be opened by anyone else, he would retrieve the two bombs soon. The information as to how the bombs were obtained and the locations was also stored in archives available to his successor, whenever that time came. Hassan read part of the detail report prepared by a major from Iran's special; forces unit known as the 'Powerful Ghosts". The entire report was dated December 20,1988, Hassan's interest was the trip from Rigestan, Afghanistan to the Iranian border. The bombs had been brought to Rigestan using a Russian military helicopter, Iran had paid a Russian pilot to temporarily 'borrow' the helicopter. They then trucked the bombs to Iran,

Three trucks with drivers and a forklift were waiting at the same spot they had originally departed from along with a helicopter. One bomb was loaded onto each truck. They were careful to cover the bombs to ensure radioactivity could not be detected from the air. They were also careful to not allow anyone to see what was being loaded. Once securely loaded, two staff sergeants and one corporal separated and boarded the three trucks. The trucks departed, each heading in a different direction to separate locations. Only the driver knew where they were headed and only then after opening a sealed package in the glove compartment, the remainder of the special forces unit with their equipment boarded the helicopter and was flown back to Tehran

Each truck continued its separate path. From the report of the drivers. the first arrived at its destination, near daylight, at a desolate spot in the desert. There was a concrete bunker built deep into the ground. Instructions pertaining to what they were to do were in a separate package, which was also sealed. A backhoe was there, to be used to unload the bomb and place it on a pedestal built inside the bunker. The sergeant, using the backhoe bucket, picked it up and moved the bomb to its new home. He kept it covered completely with the blankets, the driver did not need to know what was underneath. He closed and locked the heavy wood and steel door. The backhoe driver, as instructed, began taking a large mound of dirt piled up next to the bunker and covered the entire structure. He used the blade to smooth off the site, leaving it to look undisturbed like everything else around it. They then loaded the backhoe onto the truck and drove away. This same scenario was repeated on each of the other sites at different locations, this from the drivers reports.

Only the President and the Supreme Leader should be aware of the bombs, there locations and that they even exist They now had the ability to use them against America or Israel, if they must. No one connected to our unit will ever disclose what we took from Pakistan.

Hassan after absorbing the information on the bombs and their locations found in three separate reports, was ready to meet with his nuclear experts and General Marsal. He had with him, the exact locations of each bomb.

"Dr. Sorouri, I am so happy you have agreed to meet with me"

"I am grateful to be chosen, how can I be of service, call me Javed please."

"I must warn you, that when I divulge the details of the mission you will not be allowed to go back to your home until the work is complete. It will take at least several days. I do hope they warned you."

"They did."

"Good, now allow me to share some highly classified information."

Javed Sorouri leaned back in his chair and listened to every word being said.

"Javed and please call me Hassan, in 1988, more than thirty years ago, Iran acquired a nuclear device from Pakistan. We built a small structure out in the desert to house it, made it so moisture could not enter and then covered it with lead blankets. We need you to go to the site, which you will not know the location. Inspect the weapon and make any repairs needed to insure it will function if ever needed. I am thinking it will take you several hours, but you would know better than anyone as to how long it will take."

"Will only be a wild guess as to how long, until I look it over. I can inspect and do any minor repairs. I will need certain specialty tools and supplies."

"Can you give me a list?"

"Yes, I can do that now, if you like."

Dr. Sorouri began to write on a pad, listing the items he would need. The list included specialty screw drivers, cleaning acid, a generator, small air conditioner, a fan, battery operated screw drivers with extra batteries, petroleum paste, 30 meters of 18 gauge covered copper wire in four different colors, red, blue, yellow and green, copper wire connectors with different types of screws and sized, three different types of battery operated firing mechanism and continuity testing meters.

He then began to explain the purpose of each so Hassan could expand the list as maybe required. "There are several different types of screws used by Pakistan to attach the wires to the device. Since I don't know right now what type, we will need to bring all that they could be. I need the generator, air conditioning and fan because it will be very hot inside, a mistake could destroy the device, so it is safer to keep the place cool while I am working. There is likely corrosion, I will need to remove and clean each, I also will need to replace any that have gone bad.

"And the wire?"

"Each wire must have a solid contact; I suspect many will have to be replaced. The colors of the wires will be red, blue, yellow and green.

"And the firing mechanism tell me what you mean?"

"Thirty years ago, the bomb was to be set off by one of two ways, it could been set to explode when dropped from an airplane, impacted by use of a missile or set off using a radio signal. My guess is this one is radio controlled. We need to modernize and update the firing mechanism. I am assuming you will want to detonate remotely."

"That is correct, do you know if our military has such devices?"

"Yes, they do,"

"I believe it would be wise for you to give more precise information to our supply officer. I will have him brought here right now."

And hour later the supply officer arrived and wrote down each item needed. Javed Sorouri gave him contact information if he needed to discuss further. The next morning most of the items were delivered. The firing mechanism would be delivered the next day. Javed Sorouri was pleased.

After Dr. Sorouri received, checked and then rechecked the items, he was ready to go to the site.

Hassan had one other nuclear scientist which he needed to have the identical conversation. This scientist Dr. Omid Darvish was much younger than Javed Sorouri but gave an almost identical description and list of what would be needed. As with Dr. Sorouri he had him coordinate with a purchaser who delivered the items by the end of the next day. Hassan had made a decision to wait to look and handle the third bomb for later. His plans for now only involved the two.

The third person he met with was brigadier General Marsal. He outlined what he wanted him to do in so far as arranging for drivers, operators, helicopters and other items that would be needed to securely get people to the sites in a way where they could not return and transport the scientist to the site where they, also could not return.

General Marsal ordered the backhoes, trailers and trucks delivered to the different locations he was given by Hassan. He had the drivers, one for each, head out to a point far from where the bombs were buried. Over a period of two days, the drivers were changed four times, each time driving for several hours before stopping, a helicopter delivered the new driver, the pilot was given coordinates only after lifting off. The coordinates were then destroyed. The old driver was dropped off at a location where a new driver was picked up to be taken to yet another location to be dropped off. This scenario was repeated for each four times. There was essentially no possibility the pilot could repeat the process as to where he had been or was going. Finally, the trucks stopped, unloaded the backhoe and drove away. Several hours later, for each site, a helicopter arrived and dropped off two men, one a backhoe operator and the other a supervisor. A helicopter had earlier dropped a transmitter that emitted a signal. The supervisor located the signal turned it off and directed the backhoe driver to begin digging. This occurred at each of the two sites.

Each of the nuclear bombs were hidden in an underground bunker. The only entrance was through a heavy steel door, the entire facility was completely covered with dirt and made to look no different than the surrounding area. One could stand on top and not know it was there.

Both of the backhoe drivers were hesitant to begin with, as there appeared to be nothing there but just sand and dirt. Fortunately, the operators had been well briefed, and each found the steel doors to the underground structure in less than an hour. Once uncovered, the driver and the supervisor walked several hundred yards away to a different signal being emitted, which a separate helicopter had also dropped. The supervisors turned off the signal and waited. A separate helicopter was hovering nearby. When the signal was turned off, the helicopter came to the spot, picked up the two men and flew away. A different helicopter landed, carrying Javed Sorouri at the first and Omid Darvish at the second. both nuclear scientists. On the ground to the side of the steel door was the items from their list, which included a box of miscellaneous supplies, scientific gear, a generator, a small air conditioner and a backhoe operator These items were at each site. Each man went to work: the backhoe operators drove the backhoe to the door, hooked up two chains to the door handle and, using the backhoe blade, pulled open the heavy steel door. The operators had been instructed to not go inside but instead drive a hundred feet away and wait for instructions. However, Javed Sorouri instructed his operator to wait just outside. Dr. Sorouri went inside and, for the first time, saw the nuclear bomb. He covered it up completely then instructed the driver waiting outside to bring the air conditioner in and get it operating. Both the scientists were surprised that the bombs actually existed but now knew why such secrecy was necessary and where they were located. They certainly could not get back to the site. Once inside, each scientist removed a camera from his backpack and began taking pictures. Hassan's instructions were to stop after each task and take photos. Dr. Sorouri at the first site saw some corrosion and, for the first hour, spent cleaning, painting and otherwise repairing corrosion damage to the bomb casing. After repairing, it was opened. Inside, was a maze of wires attached to a trigger device. The scientist took many pictures since they might be needed in the future and to comply with the instructions received. The bomb was armed, to be detonated by remote control or once armed, by dropping from a high altitude. The scientist removed the remote-control device and all the batteries and installed the more modern trigger with new and more advanced batteries. This took two hours. The scientist then applied an anti- corrosion waxy lubricant on all the connections: this included unscrewing and then reattaching each of the more than one hundred connections. It was necessary to replace more than half of the wires and connections. This was a slow process as each wire had to be measured, cut from the rolls of wire, the ends peeled to expose the wire, a new connection installed, then reattached to the bomb. It was a scary and stressful effort. Twice Dr. Sorouri had to stop and rest. He walked outside to stretch his legs.

"Are you done" ask the driver.

"No, not yet maybe another two hours. Even with the air conditioning, he was soaking wet. He drank two more bottles of water before going back inside.

After another hour and a half of reattaching wires. Dr. Sorouri retested the continuity of each connection to be positive he had properly reattached each correctly. Once satisfied the bomb would explode if triggered, Dr. Sorouri reattached the bomb casing, took great care in covering up the bomb with new leaded blankets wrapping both tape and rope, it was important, he was told, that anyone else coming into the structure would not be aware of what was under the covering. He then left the structure to, once again, locate the backhoe and driver. He found the driver asleep against the front tire and woke him by calling his name. The driver followed instructions, he drove to the door, removed the air conditioner and generator, closed the door, again using the blade and chains after inspecting and applied new door seals. The operator covered up the entire structure dressing the area. So, it appeared to never have been disturbed. The operator, now with Dr. Sorouri as a passenger, drove several kilometers away from the site, parked the backhoe, and covered it with a camouflaged tarp. He then placed a tracking transmitter on the seat and turned it on. Around 45 minutes later, a helicopter landed and picked up both men. There was no possibility that they could find the location again.

Meanwhile, the second crew had accomplished pretty much the same. However, once the casing was removed, Dr. Omid Darvish realized that the connections to the wires were all corroded. This meant each of the more than one hundred connections had to be changed to new ones. This effort took considerable time as each wire had to be cut, stripped to exposé new wire, and a different connection installed. The connections were compression types: very small, and a perfect connection had to be made on each wire or risk failure. Pressure was put on each wire, sufficient to pull apart if it was done less than perfectly. Dr. Darvish had a small test kit and decided he must test the continuity of each new connection before going to the next, it was slow and painful, but a bad connection meant the bomb would not explode Several failures occurred, which required the entire process for that wire, be redone. Once all was installed, he retested each of the connections again, he was much more careful than Dr. Sorouri, Dr. Darvish also applied the same anti-corrosion waxy oil to each connection. This entire effort took around 9 hours. Dr. Darvish was exhausted by the time he was done. The finish was similar to the other site, with the pickup scenario also being the same. The details worked out were impressive, all to ensure no one could return and find the bombs. The pilots posed the highest risk of being able to return to the spot, but they had no idea why, but were not fools, and knew something highly sensitive was at the site. To lessen it, they were given sealed envelopes with directions to various locations using instructions such as: fly northeast 30 minutes at a given speed until finally given the order, land and wait for a signal to be broadcast and fly to that spot to pick up people or drop off. After each instruction, the pilot was ordered to tear up the instructions and throw them out the window. The return was the same: flying in different directions until the beacon was transmitted that took them home.

The next morning, a tractor-trailer arrived at each site and loaded the backhoe which included the air conditioner and generators. The operator drove for several hours before abandoning both and being picked up by a helicopter. This situation continued until the backhoe and trailers were delivered back to their home sites. Only the two scientists had any idea of what they had uncovered, and they had no idea where they were located.

The truck drivers and the forklift drivers were allowed to go home. The two scientists, however, were brought directly to Hassan Rouhani to be debriefed, they were brought at different times, each knew nothing of the other. Each of them explained to the President the condition of the bomb they had examined. They also provided the cameras they had used to take the photos. The President reiterated the importance that this knowledge should never be shared. The Americans were doing serious damage to Iran and should the nuclear bombs ever be needed to protect the country, then we now know they are ready and waiting. The scientists, of course, agreed as they were well versed on the damage being done by the American sanctions. The President later reviewed the photos—absolute proof that Iran had, in its possession, nuclear weapons.

Hassan had created a task force to study and create a theoretical way of getting a nuclear bomb into the United States. The study concluded it could be done by inserting into a container of bananas being delivered to the United Sates from Central America. Based on this conclusion Hassan then created a different group to get a bomb from Iran to Central America.

All participants believed this was nothing but play acting in that Iran had no nuclear abilities.

Satisfied the possibilities were real and could be done, Hassan assigned the task of shipping a highly sensitive 2,700-kilogram radioactive item to South America without being detected. His earlier task force had concluded the highest chance of success was to bring the bomb into Central America among a shipment of bananas through the Long Beach docks in California. This was the busiest dock in the world. Bananas were unique, in that, they were placed in steel shipping containers at the location where they were grown and transported. United States inspectors inspected and sealed each container before it was loaded on a ship heading to a US port. Once they arrived, they were brought through a different entry point without a second inspection. This was important as bananas had a short life and could not withstand long periods of offloading.

The group assigned the task went to work immediately, computing a way this could be accomplished. The shipment could be done, they concluded, by modifying a supply ship that commonly crossed the Atlantic Ocean to reach South and Central America. The modifications would be to drop the radioactive device into a water-sealed structure, protected by an additional layer of lead, then into the water just before it reached a Central American port. The structure would have extremely strong magnets and be positioned underneath the ship before the magnets would be activated. The radioactivity would not be detected underneath the water, especially with the lead covering, and no Central American country would be looking out for it. Once the ship docked, an underwater vessel would go beneath the ship and attach itself to the structure before the magnet was deactivated. It would then bring the structure containing the radioactive device to a location away from any inspectors who might detect its presence.

Hassan was satisfied that the plan to transport the weapons to the United States was doable. Now, he needed only to decide where he would place the bomb, as he had decided to only transport one. New York City was tempting, but the city had the best security anywhere and the likelihood of being caught increased substantially. Chicago and Los Angeles were the softest places, with less security, and would do substantial damage to the economy beyond just killing people. The Los Angeles area has the largest and busiest shipping port in the world, and Chicago is the center for rail freight. It would take many years for them to recover from the damage a bomb would do no matter which city it was exploded.

Hassan contacted the Supreme Leader to discuss the current status of the plan. A meeting was scheduled for the next day.

"My Leader sir," Hassan said, "we have developed a doable plan to get one of the nuclear bombs into the United States. My view is the success rate is high. I am greatly concerned about the success of the current efforts being undertaken to damage the president and his family. Their chances of success are not high in my opinion. As such, I would like your permission to take the weapon and have it ready to detonate if and when we deem it is the right thing to do."

"You are requesting that we proceed to a point with the plan, but only to a point?"

"Yes. We have many options once the device is in place." "Such as?"

"I now have many photos of the two bombs. My thoughts are, if the other effort fails, we give the United States and Israel copies of the photos and an ultimatum to stop what they are doing to us. Israel will not know we are bluffing. We also plan on planting a non-nuclear device in a different city to prove that we have planted explosive devices and will explode one if necessary. A device will be planted in Israel also."

"Are there any identifying marks that can be traced back to us should the devices be discovered or the less-than-lethal explosives?"

"No, I will be 100% sure there is not. Can I then assume that I can proceed with getting the nuclear and another device to the United States?"

"Yes but let me repeat. Make sure that at any step it cannot be traced back to us!"

"It will be done."

Chapter Seven

President Trump screamed at the Chairman of the Joint Chiefs at a special called meeting of his cabinet. It was an early morning called meeting, early morning for President Trump was 10 AM. They all sat around a table specifically designed for such meetings.

"What the fuck have you been smoking? You don't see any risk in the fact that Iran plans on installing missiles along the Mexican border to kill thousands of our citizens! Holy shit!"

"Mr. President," General Washburn said. "None of our intelligence agencies have established that as a fact. We recorded some folks talking and that is all we have. We do not know their names, their positions, or anything else. Our efforts to confirm have yielded nothing. We have concluded that Iran has discovered our listening devices and are filling us with crap and nothing else.".

"And you think the same about the plans we uncovered to harm our currency? That the person we are secretly recording, this Muhammed and whatever his other fucking name is, must say it before we can accept it as a fact? That is fucking stupid, and you should know that."

"Yes, sir. We do believe this is fabricated for us to hear and not true."

"My God, have I nothing but fools around me. Does anybody else share his nutty views?"

The heads of the CIA and the Secretary of Defense raised their hands. The others sat silently knowing that it was no real risk, unwilling to face the wrath of the President.

"So, we have a majority who believes as I do that this is a real and significant threat. General, I order you to immediately prepare a plan to attack both Iran and Mexico. If this threat escalates, you will enact those plans. Also, you are to deploy a large force near our southern borders and monitor any effort to install a missile system. I want complete plans on how you will accomplish this within 48 hours. Do we understand each other?"

"Yes, sir. But I must inform you, I have a duty to inform Congress."

"General, if you do that, consider it your resignation. I do not believe it necessary, and I am sure you are aware that the moment Congress is aware, the whole damn world will be aware."

"Mr. President, it is the law, and I must." "Then consider yourself fired."

The President turned toward the Secretary of Defense. "Jim, you issue the order to the Deputy Chairman."

"Mr. President, it is the law. I will also have to inform Congress. I will not break the law!"

"Are you fucking men? Do you not have balls?"

"As I said, I will not break the law, and neither will the Deputy Chief of Staff."

The President was now red with fury He kicked over the table to the right and then in front of him, "Chicken shit motherfuckers! General, I retract my order to fire you, do what you must!"

"Mr. President, with all due respect, you fired me, and I will stay fired. I will not participate in this nonsense. Everyone here also knows that this is no threat to us. They are just afraid of your retaliation."

"Just carry out my orders, General!"

"Mr. President, you will have to order someone else. I cannot, and will not, do what you have ordered." The General rose and walked out the door.

"Jim, it is now up to you to get our military to obey my orders."

"Mr. President, I will try, but it is a foolish order. Why don't you just allow us to send drones along the border and, if we detect something, we can then go from there? We will know what to do should we discover something."

"This is horseshit, but for now you do that, and I will get back to you. Sending drones! Do you still need to notify Congress? And it is not if you, it is when you find them!"

"Yes, sir. I am afraid so."

"This is the stupidest way to run anything. I need to be able to make a decision and a decision that is to be obeyed without question!"

The President, still cursing, walked out of the room.

Jim turned to the remaining cabinet members. "You should be ashamed because you would not speak up. This nation has lost our most capable and experienced military officer. Your job is to tell him the truth."

"We completely agree with you, but you know as well as we that once we do, he will get even with us, and maybe even force us to leave. We cannot protect the American people if we are not on the job."

"Sad, isn't it?"

General Washburn went straight from the White House to the Pentagon and put in his retirement papers, effective immediately. The Deputy Chairman of the Joint Chiefs, General Carter, took over the job the moment the papers were signed. President Trump sent a nomination to the senate the next morning, for the deputy to take over the job permanently even though he had never even met the man.

The Secretary of Defense forwarded to Congress a formal notification that the President considered Iran and Mexico a threat and had ordered drone surveillance of the border. Congress was upset that they had not been informed earlier. They then learned that there was also a threat against the currency of the United States and the President had fired the secretary of the treasury as a result.

The military shifted three drone squadrons to begin patrolling the US–Mexico border. Mexico filed a formal protest as they had not permitted use of their air space.

****

Aftab had a morning progress meeting with Rasheen Abbasi, who gave an update, "We have made substantial progress on several of the properties owned by Trump and have created a priority listing of targets. This is based on the research of what proprieties were most newsworthy. The first two are the Mar-a-Lago Golf Club and the Trump Tower in New York City. These properties are constantly in the news and must be of supreme importance to Trump. Others have been assigned a priority, but not enough information has been developed yet to be able to discuss."

Aftab listened intently then was given a typed information summary for the two properties. He decided to bring in one of the agricultural, metal experts and an engineer. Aftab quickly briefed the three; "Rasheen's team has identified two properties as priority targets, we need to develop an attack on them."

Rasheen introduced Mashan Darzi, who had actually done the research.

When the three experts were seated, Mashan began. He started with Mar- a-Lago. "This property is an elaborate private club, with gold plating everywhere, parties, weddings are common, and it has many rooms. It has a championship golf course with 27 holes. Thus far, we have concluded it has 20 acres of total property, a 100 x 50-foot pool plus one smaller, a significant beach on the Atlantic Ocean, 6 tennis courts, 12 individual rooms, 6 suites, 9 cottages and 7 Cabana type beach cottages all for guest. Each of the rooms are expensively decorated with many amenities such as private spas. We believe, in addition to the 27 holes of golf on the main hotel area, there is a much smaller course on the property. It looks like as many as 6 restaurants. They have many reported health violations uncovered during inspections at the restaurants. President Trump has a private residence there. It is served by public utilities including water and sewage.

"We have tapped into the accounting system and have available copies of all invoices and payrolls for the past three years. We can also determine who the current guests are. We may be able to go back in time to get a daily account of the guests. The accommodations are extremely expensive. Only the very wealthy can afford to stay."

Pointing to the three experts, Aftab asked, "What do you think we can, and should do to this property?"

Jamshed Rostami noted, "In view of the many health inspection violations, I believe our starting point should be to make the guests of the restaurants sick. Do we know who supplies them with fresh fruits and vegetables?"

"Yes, I do. Give me a couple of minutes," said Mashan.

Mashan did a quick search on a laptop computer connected to the main computers.

"Two suppliers. One, 'Universal Grocers', looks like they make weekly deliveries of a range of food stuff, including fresh fruits and vegetables. I can give you pictures of the uniforms they wear and the markings on their trucks. The other appears to be much smaller companies, 'Cruz Vegetables'. My guess is they deliver locally grown stuff. I can give you their truck markings also. They do not appear to wear uniforms."

"Fantastic!" said Jamshed. "We should be able to spray this substance I have in mind on them before delivery. It cannot be washed off and will make anyone who digests it very sick but will not kill or do any permanent harm."

Aftab had a big smile on his face. "I like that! How difficult is it to get this substance and how quickly can it be done?"

"Very common ingredients. It is a mixture of several items which are different type mold fungus and mycotoxins that produces a toxic effect. A 4-kilogram container could spray an entire shipment and still have much left over. The substance will be invisible to the naked eye and cannot be easily removed, it also has no odor."

"This should mean Trump will be sued by a lot of people, and since we will know who stayed there and also from the charges who ate in the restaurant, we can certainly notify some of the shyster lawyers to seek them out. I say, let's get this aspect moving. It can be done independently if anything else. Now, what else have you seen?"

"We believe that the grass on both courses is watered and fertilized using water from the largest lake. Assuming we are right, it will take someone to verify on-site. There is a pump to bring the water to a feeder system, allowing fertilizer to be injected into the water. This way, you can add whatever element is needed at the moment, on the grass, with little labor cost. We can introduce a ground cover poison into the system and kill all the grass that is being watered by the system, which is likely all of it," said Jamshed.

"Is this all done by Trump employees?"

"Yes, I could not find any company that maintains or cuts the grass on the golf courses. What I did find was a supplier who furnishes canisters of all types of fertilizer. The canisters screw into a feeder system which, when the grass is being watered, puts a set amount on the grass. They then just change the canisters."

"Wow, if we could substitute our ground poison into the canisters, they would do this for us!", said Aftab.

Everybody laughed.

"It is possible with a little luck," said Aftab.

Jamshed said, "For our next area, I believe we should address the living quarters of the guests. We talked the other day about introducing bedbugs into the guest quarters. That would be devastating to the Trump organization. It will be very difficult, but I do have some ideas gained from many discussions with the other folks. We kicked around lots of possibilities, one was to raise and send the bugs from here, none of us believed that would work. Another was to raise in Mexico and bring across the border, that we concluded it just added to the risk, best to do is raise them in the United States."

Aftab asked, "So how can we, what are your thoughts?"

"First, we will need to create a new company in the United States. This company should be called 'Bedbug Research'. We are going to need to breed and raise several million of the little critters right before their eyes in the United States. We will be safer doing so in the open."

"That makes sense. So, how do we raise them?"

"I don't know the answer to that. I do know that we have people in Iran who do know and that is who we need to find and bring them on board."

"I will see what I can do. It is obvious that we need such a person. When we get such an organization and the bedbugs, what do we do then?"

"Could be easy, with the right luck. From the invoices, I have pulled, they hire a company that treats all the guest quarters for all types of bugs and rodents. The company comes regularly, looks like once a quarter. It typically takes them three days to go through all the rooms and buildings. Looks to me like they come back when the units are vacant. A lady named 'Valerie' is their contact person. Having a contact person rather than a set schedule, tells me that they do not know which units will be vacant until the day they show up and then they assign them to treat specific units per day. What we will need to do is, have someone dressed as one of the employees show up instead. We can call the company and reschedule the work. We plant the bedbugs in each unit we are to treat. It should work."

"It does sound like it will. We can further contact whoever stayed in the unit, assuming they contacted bedbugs and have them speak with the newspapers; this should make the Trump organization very happy!"

"There are a few more items we need to discuss on Mar-a- Lago: one is, we spoke of causing leaks in the entire building. I spoke with our metal experts last night. I think they should explain how this could be done."

"Yes, we came up with some ideas," said Gulzar Carmchi, a metals expert who was known throughout Iran for his expertise. "First, we have to locate the water supply and the hot water source. There is a muriatic acid we can put in the water, not the other way around! Even though it will be diluted, the acid will, within a week or two, cause all the metal parts to corrode and render them incapable to hold back the water pressure normal for such type structures. Every fixture in the entire complex will leak and spew water. The place will be flooded. The hot water is important because it sends less water but a higher concentrate of acid, and, most water heater systems have a high amount of metal, so we also will do serious damage to the hot water system."

"Trump is really not going to be happy!"

"OK, a few more items," said Jamshed. "We can and should damage the landscaping over the entire complex. This involves hundreds of large trees, mostly palm trees, maybe a thousand bushes and ten thousand landscaping plants that are replaced often. It's probably not worth damaging the landscape plants because they can be replaced in a few hours, but the trees and bushes will be harder to replace if we kill them. We also can, and should, sully the soil around the trees."

"So how do you propose we do this?"

"I have located a company in the invoices, 'Gonzales Landscaping', that appears to be the landscaping contractor. They bill for planting trees, bushes, and, on a regular basis, adding fertilizer. The fertilizer is special for each type of plant. I have the uniforms they wear and the markings on the trucks. It should not be so difficult to show up as one of them and poison the trees and bushes", responded Jamshed.

"It can be done," continued Jamshed who was now standing and gotten excited. "We have a number of substances that will kill a tree and the soil around it; does not take that much. We also have substances we can spray on bushes that will do the same."

"Okay, the last item for Mar-a- Lago. We talked about stopping the sewage system. I don't know any reasonable way to do that, but we turned it over to the engineers last night. Hopefully, they have a plan."

"We do," said Aram Alinejad, one of the engineering experts who Aftab had grown to have a lot of confidence, "Several options, depending on the way they are hooked up. Most sewage systems operate using manholes to lower or raise the sewage as it travels to the place where it is to be treated. We can choose as many spots as necessary and fill the pipes with cement. We can do the same with any manholes. This will cause all the sewage to rise back up into the hotel rooms, the kitchens and all restaurants. It will be a mess!"

"We looked at the tennis courts and swimming pools, but it looked to us like the risks will be greater than the rewards", said Jamshed

"Aftab is correct, when we get all this done, Mr. Trump will be most unhappy", Said Aram who liked to speak directly to the point.

"One other possibility", said Aram, "The military, ours included, have available what is called 'Stink Bombs'. We believe we can modify the ingredients so we can spray this substance on the carpet and walls. Assuming we are correct, the smell will not become overpowering for several days after being sprayed. When we back up the sewage, they will send cleaning crews to clean up the mess and likely replace the carpet. We send people at the same time to spray this substance on the new carpet and walls.

"Oh, that would be nasty!", said Aftab, "I love it"

"All of us are still working on the Trump Tower. It will take a few days to come up with an action plan", said Gulzar.

Chapter Eight

Hassan Rouhani stood before a mirror in his bathroom, smiling, speaking to his reflection. "I bet a nuclear bomb accidentally detonated will do as much damage to those bastards as one that is intentional. Once, I get this one in place, an accident may just happen!"

The now-approved plan to transport a nuclear bomb to the United States was entering into a reality phase. Engineers had completed a design for a special box to be used to ship the bomb which would make it undetectable to harbor security. It would pass easily through the radioactive detection system used by most harbors and port complexes. The box was made of aluminum to make it lightweight, then covered with a thin coating of lead on the inside and outside, it did have a steel plate welded to the very top, this, to allow for a magnet to attach. Another box was designed to put the entire aluminum and lead box into to make it completely waterproof. This box was extremely rugged, capable of being towed underneath a ship for long distances. A cable long enough to swing under most cargo ships could also be attached. The covering had an extremely strong electric magnet powered by batteries encased inside. Pushing a button remotely could turn off the magnet; the box's steel plate welded to the aluminum, would attach to the magnet and keep it upright. The purpose of the magnet was to attach itself underneath the ship when approaching a port. The bomb being underwater would also make radiation difficult, if even possible, to detect.

Well before and without total authority, Hassan had arranged for a shipping group to study how to best get a box measuring 4 meters by 2 meters weighing 1,450 kilograms secretly into the United States preferably out of Guatemala. Naveed Fikri whose family had been in the shipping business for generations was recruited to do the research. Hassan believed the man was a genius and welcomed his suggestions., he had requested it be provided in person.

"Mr. President, I have studied the request you gave me and have a likely solution."

"I am anxious to hear, my objective is to know we can, not to actually do."

"I understand. The weakness I have found in the American system is bananas. The United States imports 5 million three hundred thousand tons of bananas each year. Bananas have a short shipping and consumption life, they spoil easily. They are stored and shipped at precisely 13.2 C. There is a unique container called a 'Banavac' which creates the correct amount of air and so forth to allow them to arrive undamaged. The package which is a strong perforated cardboard box has vent holes all around. Typically, the box will have two layers of 10 stalks of bananas. They will be packaged in a refrigerated storage facility. The packers place the bananas in the boxes, seal them. The custom inspectors look them over after the box is sealed, as it has holes all around. Once inspected, 20 of the boxes are loaded in a refrigerated steel shipping container. The custom officials weigh the entire container, as they know approximately what this number of bananas should weigh. Once he is satisfied, he will place a special tamper proof lock on the container which will not be removed until it reaches the United States."

"So, you can put something in the box surrounded by stalks of bananas, and it will not be seen?"

"That is correct. However, the problem is the weight. We must then compensate for the increase; 1,450 kilograms is very heavy."

"How do you propose to do that?"

"We must remove a total of 9,600 bananas from a full container, this from each box what I have calculated as 550 bananas from each stalk. In total that should then equal what the weigh would be if the entire shipment was just bananas. This will be difficult as the removal must be random.

"Will this require any special boxes?"

"Yes, I think it will be much safer if the box could also be made of corrugated cardboard. It has a less chance of being spotted or detected."

Hassan thanked him as this was a wonderful well thought out plan. He was confident if they ever needed it, it would work.

Hassan had arranged for his secretary to record all that was said, he then had her transcribe.

Later that same day, he had the Revolutionary guard special forces unit provide a plan for getting such a box across Guatemala. The plan required an advance unit of 4 men, be in place prior to the box containing the nuclear bomb landing in Guatemala, a gunship helicopter and two special forces guards to accompany the bomb in a truck. The helicopter would be on standby in case the truck had any issues. They would serve as a rescue unit.

Hassan had ordered the construction of the box along with its covering and magnetic function to be done quickly. He was concerned the Supreme Leader would change his mind and placed a high priority on getting it made. Several weeks later, he was told it would be delivered later in the week. This knowledge set in motion a separate plan. One of the bombs was targeted to be dug up, he decided to use the one inspected by Dr. Sorouri as he was the most experienced. and delivered to a location near the docks. He had arranged for a lot of distractions to insure no one would know it was a nuclear bomb, all before a backhoe dug up the door, entered, loaded it on a truck as it was completely covered with lead blankets no one would know what it was, he ordered the backhoe operator to securely tie more ropes around the blankets then add two canvas tarps and also secure them to the item which was covered. He had them construct a lifting sling which was slid under and around the tarps. The contraption made a cradle for the bomb but allowed it to stay completely covered. He also had a security supervisor to ensure the 'contraption' was never uncovered. It was then, using the sling, picked up with the backhoe placed it on the back of a cargo truck. The bomb was covered up again, once inside the back of the truck. All the coverings created a neat hiding place, it was strapped down inside the back of the truck using webbing to be sure there was no movement. The operator never saw what it was he was loading or transporting. The truck had also gone through a series of drivers to get there. So, the chance of ever returning to the site was nil. Once the truck left, the backhoe recovered the opening and, once again, made the property appear undisturbed.

The truck, after two days of misdirection, arrived at a storage warehouse. The cargo, completely covered in the lead blankets and other coverings, was lifted, using the sling and placed inside the special box built for the secret one-time shipping.

A cargo ship was leaving in the next few days: its first stop was Guatemala's port of Barrios. The port was perfect; there was virtually no security and no one who would detect a nuclear device. Hassan had arranged for a five-ton truck with all-terrain capabilities waiting. He also had ordered the Revolutionary guard to implement their plan, the construction of the special cardboard box, he had three made, just in case. In addition, he had recruited an Iranian who lived in Guatemala to hire a crew to load the 'special' boxes, remove the needed number of bananas and repack the box.

The ship *The Magi Star* loaded the special made shipping box for the bomb, the next day and set sail the day after. The ship was loaded with plastics, ceramics, and saffron. It would offload, pick up bananas and then deliver them back to Iran. It was a ten-day sail. The ship slowed to a near stop five kilometers from the Guatemala port; the 'box' was lowered with a crane attached to long cables, the ship turned so the box would flow with the movement of the ship and the currents to underneath the hull. The magnet was turned on and, with a loud thud, it attached itself underneath the ship. The ship then sailed slowly into the Port of Barrios. Divers dropped down into the water and reattached the cables. The captain decided that he could offload in a way much easier than the complex plan he had been given. He made contact with his superiors who permitted him to make the change. The original plan was to have another vessel pull up beside them, which would take the cables and pull the 'box' on board. There, it would travel away from the main dock and transport the 'box' to shore. When the captain realized there was no security, he ordered the five-ton truck to drive to the dock, and, using the ship's crane he had the long cables reattached and simply picked it up and loaded it directly onto the truck waiting at the dock.

As he loaded the 'box', two of the elite Iranian Revolutionary Guard marines, a part of the Powerful Ghost, legends in Iran, sneaked off the ship. They were heavily armed and could speak fluent Spanish. The driver had already loaded 6 additional 5-gallon containers of gasoline and enough food and water for several days. One guard climbed into the front seat, and the other into the rear of the covered bed of the cargo truck. The former had in his hand a GPS device that would assist them in getting across the almost unmapped roads. He also had a folder with detailed maps, depicting every inch of the route. He had studied them so well he could follow them without actually consulting the folder. A Guatemalan driver was sitting behind the wheel. The two were dressed as peasants, no military insignias were present.

The trip began on a modern road, CA9, which, within 30 kilometers, had turned into not much more than just a dirt path. The distance they needed to travel was roughly 420 kilometers. At times, the maximum speed they could expect was 20 kilometers per hours. It would be a long and tough trip. Just as the sun began to set, the senior marine among them decided to stop. His orders were to take no risk by rushing. Arrival was what was the most important, not the speed.

It was 2 PM before they got started on the truck; they had traveled only 4 hours. None of them were aware of what the cargo was, just it needed to reach a port on the Pacific Ocean in Guatemala. In another part of Guatemala, the Iranian military stood posed to assist, if necessary, with a helicopter gunship. They had taken another ship two weeks before with the helicopter on board. They set up a camp roughly halfway from the arriving port to the final destination. They would be ready to assist if the marines had trouble. A tracking device on the box allowed them to know exactly where they were at any given moment. Both of the Iranian military on the truck was ordered to contact the standby group at any sign of trouble.

On the second day of the trip, they were still traveling on CA9, which now was just a cleared trail in dense jungle. They rounded a curve and saw a roadblock with a paramilitary man holding an RK47. The Iranian in the rear did not hesitate and jumped off the back of the truck, carrying enough weapons to defeat a small army. The Iranian on the front seat clasped his weapon and readied himself to fire. He was aware that his teammate had gotten out of the truck because that is what they had been trained to do. They would not hesitate to take these men out. The marine who exited the truck made contact with the standby unit first.

"We have been stopped by what I believe are bandits. They are creating a roadblock. I suspect I will have to kill them all. I can see three of them, I don't think there are any more."

"OK, if you do not call us back in ten minutes we will be on our way." The truck had a GPS device, so the army unit knew exactly where they were. The unit boarded the helicopter and started it up, just in case.

"OK."

The man guarding the roadblock was joined by two others; one motioned for the driver to get out of the truck. He hollered at him, "What are you carrying?"

"I do not know. Just a heavy box and some supplies."

"Well, it is ours now. So is the truck. If you and your passenger want to live, leave the truck and walk away. If not, we will kill you. Either way, the truck will be ours."

The moment he finished his little speech, two of the men guarding the roadblock fell to the ground, bullet holes in their heads. The one who was speaking turned and said, "What the hell!" a second before he too dropped to the ground.

When it was clear that they were safe, another contact was made to the standby unit.

"We had to kill all three, but all is well." "Good, call, if you need us."

They hurried and dragged the bodies just off the road deep into the jungle, taking with them the rifles and pistols the three men had on them. The driver took their jewelry and money. All this took less than 15 minutes. They then dragged away the limbs used for the roadblock and were soon back on their way. They made contact again, with the standby military reporting that the situation was under control.

Three hours later, they stopped again for the night. This time, they established perimeter security in case the bandits had friends, or a different group tried to take their cargo and truck.

They had traveled 190 kilometers in nearly ten hours of driving. It was very slow. Late in the afternoon of the third day, they began to see signs of Guatemala City, and the road gradually became better. Since they were on a well-paved surface, they continued till dark and were now on the western side of the city. As the road narrowed into a path again, they stopped for the night. The GPS indicated that they had another 120 kilometers before reaching Monterrico. There, a different group would take the cargo and transport it to the Port of Quetzal, when all the arrangements had been made for the next shipment. They did not know where it would go from there.

Monterrico is roughly 20 kilometers from the port of Quetzal where ships often travel to the Long Beach port in California.

The two marines dropped off the 'box' to a storage location the next afternoon. They had been given fake identification as Turkish citizens, money, and were expected to make their way back on their own. When the box was safely taken from them, they contacted the standby unit to tell them their job was over. Both men looked at each other. The first and most senior marine said, "I think I may stay in this area for a while. How about you?"

"I have decided I would like to see Mexico and head north."

"Good idea. I am thinking of Columbia. They have lots of drugs and could use someone like us to protect the shipments."

"OK, see you around."

That said, the two marines dispersed, now just ordinary people. Ordinary people who could kill anyone in an instant.

Chapter Nine

Early the next morning, Aftab met again with the group handling Mar-a- Lago.

"I think it would be wise for me to go to the United States and organize a recruitment campaign to get the people and supplies we'll need. It may be premature since we are still behind on making arrangements for the other properties. But let's start by making a list of what we can accomplish now."

Rasheen stood up and began, he paced as he talked. "There are certain things we need for Mar-a-Lago and we'll need the same for all properties. Someone to watch each property for a certain period of time and report details about security, how best to get into area. We can develop a checklist unique for each property, listing everything we will need. We should note where we will get certain supplies, such as the poison to kill the grass, or the muriatic acid to kill the trees. And also, the quantities that we will need. Most importantly, we need people to carry out the tasks we have laid out. This, in my view, will be the most difficult."

"The bedbug nursery needs to start now. It will take a while to grow the numbers we will need," said Jamshed.

"Also, the exact location of the water supply and, if possible, the hot water system. If we can tap the outgoing line from the hot water, it will increase the amount of acid dramatically," said Gulzar Charmchi.

"We must monitor each of the suppliers we have identified for all the properties, it is essential we know how they come and go and who they contact while there.," said Aram, "I do hope we have developed the ability to do that." Aram stared at the entire group with a most serious face as he spoke, they all knew from the look on his face, he was absolutely right and knew it.

"It is very obvious that I need to be present in the US at least for a while. There's a substantial number of things to accomplish, and it must be done in absolute secrecy. There are a few properties in the area near the United Nations building that I can use as an office. It would be helpful if one of you could get me a listing of any properties just in case I need. I will have a restriction on travel, but I need to be close to the UN building so it will not be a problem. Hopefully, they can get me private working space at the UN building that, would be much better as the Americans will be watching. 160-kilometer radius, that is my understanding of the travel restrictions I will have placed on me by the United States, it may get me deported if I exceed that limit without permission. That limit will be a problem for me to view the Florida properties."

"We will have it for you in a few hours," Rashee replied. "Also, we have some news on Netanyahu. He owns an apartment in Manhattan and five other properties: two in Spain, two in France, and one in Israel. We are getting more details each hour."

"Good. He is an important target. Get me the address of the property in Manhattan. It can't be far from the UN building."

Next afternoon, Aftab left for the United States. The group continued to work on Trump's and Benjamin Netanyahu's family properties. And by the next afternoon, they had identified properties belonging to Donald Trump. Jr. and Eric.

Donald Jr.'s property was sketchy, as most of them had been given away to his former wife or lost during his recent divorce. They noted down the addresses but guessed that the property could not be bothered as it was no longer his. Eric's property, other than his home, consisted of joint ownerships with Trump, including several golf courses. They would be grouped with the Trump properties, but they would not damage the homes of the children, even they, did not deserve such. The group, which was working on the bank accounts, credit cards and aspects other than properties, was progressing well. Several had been found along with the numbers, expiration date, security codes and zip code of the addresses.

Aftab's arrival in the United States was surprisingly uneventful. The immigration people at Kennedy Airport were aware he was coming, treated him with respect when he arrived. He later learned the US state department had classified him as a moderate and thus a desirable Iranian official.

When Aftab arrived at the UN building, he immediately met with the Iranian delegation. With him was a list of thirteen properties to look over, and all were within a few miles of the UN headquarters, the UN delegation had no specific knowledge of why he was there. His group had now identified 58 properties that Trump owned or had an interest in. 19 of those properties had golf courses, 13 had a hotel, and 33 were either built for residents or were a combination. He wasted no time; he was given a bulky tourist camera and a small but indiscrete one after a formal request, whose pictures could be transmitted to Iran securely. He sat for an hour studying a map and marking which route to take to see each property without the driver realizing what he was doing. Even though the driver was an Iranian employed by the delegation, Aftab believed it was wiser to let him think that he was just sightseeing. He wrote on a page of a yellow paper tablet large numbers from 1 through 13. He would take a photograph of the number corresponding to the property he was photographing. He had sent the addresses to Iran corresponding to the numbers. This way, those back in Iran would know which photograph was of which building.

Aftab had also marked the map with the numbers 1 through 13 and written the address of each building on a separate page. He intended to refer to that page to verify which building he was looking at. He also carried with him a laptop that had photos from the internet of all the Trump properties he wanted to see. He and his driver left at 10:15 AM. He directed him exactly how and where he wanted to go. Aftab wisely included common tourist spots such as the Empire State Building, the Statue of Liberty and Broadway. He told the driver to go slow as he wanted to sightsee and to not go anywhere in particular. As they cruised, he took some photos with his small secretive camera and also with a larger tourist camera. He took a photo of the page with the number, then the photos of the corresponding building, he was careful not to let the driver know he was taking photos with the secure camera, he often put it side by side with the larger tourist camera to hide it He often asked the driver to go back around the block. Photographing took most of the day, and by the end of it, he was well- versed with all 13 properties.

The properties that were living quarters, he decided, should be handled differently than the hotels and commercial spaces. They would tap into the water lines and sewage lines but not try to add bedbugs or kill the landscape because doing more damage would likely not hurt Trump but only those who lived there. He could see no reason to harm the people who had leased or purchased condominiums any more than was necessary. The water and sewage were a different story because Trump would be held responsible. Only one of the properties he had photographed was a hotel. He planned to make the people who ate there sick, kill the landscaping, destroy the faucets and other plumbing fixtures and introduce bedbugs.

Once Aftab had gotten the photos and transmitted them back to Iran, he requested permission by the United States to allow him to go to Orlando, Florida to visit Disney, other parks and some of the other attractions. He believed that it certainly would not hurt to ask. The Iranian government forwarded the request and, within one day, it was approved for a four-day visit. The Iranians believed this, was because Aftab was a known moderate and had been classified as such by the United States state department in his official position as the deputy defense minister as he had always been publicly against many of the radical ideas being pushed by other Iranian leaders. He was never considered a risk by the US state department.

It took a few days to plan the trip. He needed a double in Orlando as he expected the American government to keep close tabs on his whereabouts as they did all Iranian officials in the United States. The only ones allowed were members of the UN delegation and each was considered a risk to the US. He went to a local Walmart and purchased what he needed for the trip, including a baseball hat, several pullover long sleeve dark-colored shirts, blue jeans, white socks, dark sunglasses and sneakers. He was careful to buy common shirts and shoes that Walmart had plenty in stock. His double would need an identical wardrobe. Both Aftab and his double were given throwaway cellphones. They left for Orlando on different flights and from different airports, Aftab from Newark and his double from La Guardia. Aftab was amazed at the number of airports in the New York area. He had arrived at Kennedy and came to know about two other major airports within a short distance. It seemed like a horrible waste, but they all appeared to be really busy with many flights arriving and departing each day.

On the morning, his fight was scheduled, Aftab sent a coded message to his assistant. "We need to hack the New York City Building Information System (BIS). We will need a permit to dig anywhere in the city. This system gives police and other authorized personnel permits and thus approval to dig. We must be able to create and insert a permit as we will need to dig in a lot of places. My guess is Chicago and other major cities have a similar system, so look for those also."

He had a direct flight to Orlando and by early evening he was checked into his hotel. He would use taxis to get around to the different parks. A car had been rented for him, but it was parked several blocks away from his hotel. He planned on leaving early the next morning and drive to Miami. His double would wear the same outfit Aftab would have on for breakfast. Aftab then would change and disguise himself before walking the few blocks to the car.

The next morning, he had a leisurely breakfast and returned to his room. He was wearing blue jeans, a red pullover long-sleeved tee-shirt, sneakers and a New York Giants-baseball hat. Fifteen minutes later, his double, dressed exactly as him, walked out the door, taking the hotel shuttle to Disney World. Aftab waited another fifteen minutes. Then, wearing a blue golf shirt, a green hat from the master's, dress shoes and expensive slacks, he walked out the side door, and the three blocks down to the waiting car. He drove quickly to the Florida turnpike and then all the way to Miami only stopping for gas and a snack at one of the rest stops.

His double made it into the park without incident, but within minutes someone bumped into him, apologizing profusely. He knew it was an old trick to plant something on him and ignored it for several hours. He then went to a restroom, found the tiny object attached to his shirt, pulled it off, reattached it to his hat, and continued as if he did not know. He planned on losing it sometime during the day. He did not yet know how he would do that.

Four hours later, Aftab reached the Miami area. His GPS was set on the Doral Golf club address, which he reached easily, it was only a few miles off the interstate/turnpike. He boldly went straight to the front desk and inquired about a golfing reservation for a small group. The price for 3 rooms and golf was unusually high but he acted like it was well within what he expected. The agent was cordial and invited him on a tour of the facilities, which he gladly accepted. He had earlier snapped a photo of the number he had assigned to the Doral facility. Lots of photos were secretly taken as he toured. He requested to see the golf course. They escorted him to the pro shop, where a young man in a golf cart drove him around. Aftab acted excited and requested to be taken to the 'famous' water hazard.

The young man laughed. "Don't be afraid when you see how difficult these holes are."

"I can't wait. I have some friends who think they play like pros." "These holes will bring them to their knees."

When Aftab saw the lake and the pumping station on the edge, he nearly blurted out "Yeah!"

He could see how easy it would be to plant the chemicals to kill the vegetation on the course and he took lots of photos. He tried to count and estimate the number of trees and large bushes they would also need to kill.

It was a lot; the course was beautiful. He frankly hated to do the damage they would do—but Trump deserved it.

He left after two hours. He was given a small welcome packet and a number to call and confirm the dates. He breathed a sigh of relief and smiled a 'mission accomplished' look. He could visualize this entire site with nothing but dead grass, trees and bushes. He could also envision Trump's employee's being afraid to make the call to relay what they were seeing when all began to die.

He left and headed to Mar-a-Lago. One hour later, he pulled into the entrance and began his routine. They were not as accommodating as Doral but did seem to see big profit possibilities as he upped the number of rooms and people he was considering bringing. He had again taken a photo of the number he assigned to Mar-a-Lago before he got out of his car when he arrived. His escort was OK but somewhat rude. He obviously did not want to be assigned to such trivial duties. He did take him on a tour, which included most places around the hotel Aftab wanted to see and he could snap dozens of secret photos. When the tour was completed, Aftab requested to visit the golf course, which was what his party was primarily interested in. The guide took him to the pro shop, and, after a few minutes, left. The young man from the golf shop was somewhat more accommodating and excited to show off the course. He drove him around the famous course in a golf cart. Aftab, like before, wanted to see how difficult the water hazards were.

"Your folks will find themselves being presented with an impossible task to overcome these hazards," the young guide said, his hands making the motion of golf balls splashing in the water.

Aftab laughed. "I will enjoy punishing my friends!" He observed the pumping stations on two of the lake areas. They were neatly disguised by landscaping but could easily be used to poison the landscaping and grass. He also noted the number of trees and other landscaping. They were magnificent; would be nearly impossible to replace.

Aftab, having had a successful day, began his drive back to Orlando. He had received a text from his double about the tracking device and gave him the order to lose it on the shuttle back to the hotel. The Americans would think it just fell off and would plant another tomorrow. He transmitted the photos to Iran before reaching Orlando. He was giddy with his success. He wished he was back in Iran to put some of the things he had discovered into action.

Chapter Ten

The Iranians responsible for the fake conversations to deceive the United States being recorded by the United States CIA were back in full swing with more misguided information. They kept the chatter constant but carefully planned the information they wished to be overheard. From the President's bragging tweets, they were aware that the US was sending drones along the Mexican border. They also had agents who confirmed that the drones were making regular flights. The conversations being overheard by the US concentrated on two things: one was how to overcome the drones and, two, further information on the currency. The conversation with the Mexicans was beautiful. The Mexicans spoke in Spanish, which was then repeated in Arabic by an interpreter. "It is a waste of time for the Americans to send the drones." "We have installed camouflaged netting over the areas under construction and from the air they cannot be seen. They are spending millions to uncover nothing." This was followed by laughter. Another was "China is coming along well with its plan to replace the US dollar. Russia and the European countries are excited about the progress. We expect that, in the next few months, all transactions will be converted to the Yuan. It will be good to see the US having to use the Yuan in its international trades!"

Trump was given a summary of the conversations by his intelligence briefer and went ballistic. He called a special meeting of his cabinet to include the National Security team. "Are you going to be fucking wimps again or are you gonna do something about this?" he screamed at the people present.

"Mr. President, this is fake! Our drones can see through any netting. We have resolved that possibility years ago," said General Carter, the current Chairman of the Joint Chiefs.

"Horse shit, more fucking excuses! We need to take action. I will order you for the last time. I want our military on the border."

The entire cabinet froze and was visibly afraid of the consequences this might have.

"And Mr. Secretary of State, do your fucking job! Get people to China and stop this before it has really bad consequences on us. Do you not understand the danger?"

"Mr. President, you are being manipulated by the Iranians. None of this is true," advised the Secretary of State.

"I want a show of hands as to who believes that crap!" said the President.

Everyone except the Secretary of Education and Commerce raised their hands at first. Slowly, they also raised theirs.

The president threw his writing tablet and walked out of the room. "Fucking gullible idiots!"

****

The box containing the nuclear bomb was now safely hidden away in Monterrico, Guatemala the Iranian agents were making arrangements to house the box in a shipping container filled with bananas. It was heavy but not large. The Iranians had constructed a false bottom on a shipping container, inserted the box inside and put it in line to be filled with bananas. Bribes were paid to be sure that the bananas completely covered the box before the US inspectors looked over the contents. The Iranians built the cover so that the expected weight of the container would be within the expected range once a certain number of bananas were removed. The United States inspector whose entire life was to inspect and be sure all were safe before loading onto a ship headed to the US, looked inside and then looked at the weight of the container, closed the door and secured it with the special lock. There would be no further need for inspection until the recipient had the container in their possession.

The next morning, the container was moved to the dock and lifted aboard a ship stacked high with containers. After the last one was loaded, the ship departed for Long Beach, California, the busiest docks in the world. In five days, the container would be unloaded and picked up by the company Iran had hired.

Once docked in Long Beach, the container was unloaded with no concerns from any inspector— within six hours, Iran had a nuclear bomb on American soil.

The plan was to bury the box in an already prepared location. The logistics to get this done was harrowing. The box was delivered to a location several miles away from its final spot. A driver then loaded the box onto a different truck. The driver was taken on a long journey to nowhere. After several hours the drivers were changed twice until finally the box arrived at its final location. The final driver did not know the address where he had arrived, a passenger was giving him turns and movements for some time before he arrived. The last driver believed the box had been delivered from out of state. A backhoe and operator were waiting, they had no idea where they were, just somewhere in the Los Angeles area. Once the truck with the box arrived, using the backhoe, the box was lowered into the hole. The backhoe operator had no knowledge of where he was or what was in the box. He believed these were criminals who were hiding loot. Within an hour of the box being lowered, a nuclear technician was taken on a wild goose chase where several changes of vehicles and drivers were used, none of which knew the final location. After several hours of such diversions, a driver brought him to a spot and dropped him off. Within minutes, he was picked up, blindfolded and taken to the location of the bomb. He immediately went to work arming the bomb and inserting a coded detonator that would be used to set the arming device in motion whenever it was needed. He made a call on a disposable cell phone when he was complete. Minutes later, he was picked up and again blind folded; a crew came who were delivered in an enclosed truck who had been riding in the back for two hours, so they did not know the address and covered up the location where the bomb had been buried, it looked completely undisturbed when finished. They drove the backhoe onto the truck using loading planks They believed they had gone a great distance but had no idea where, the truck was enclosed with no ability to look out. The bomb was in a trench only three feet deep and would destroy many blocks to complete total destruction and many miles with radiation poison to include all the docks when exploded. The crew worked and were pleased when they finished as it looked undisturbed. They were unaware of what they were covering up, as it was made to look like a sewer line which was a fake pipe directly above the covered bomb, but they suspected it held likely illegal drugs. When the crew was picked up, they were once again placed in a covered truck and, after going in circles for two hours, were dropped off where they had started. It made no sense to them why a crew much closer was not used unless it was very valuable drugs.

The dangerous information end of this operation was the person who dropped off then picked up the technician and crew. None of the others could find or tell anyone where the final location was.

Iran had the last driver escorted across the border to Mexico. There, the agents arranged for him to be transported back to Iran. The technician only knew there was a bomb but had no idea where it was located.

Hassan Rouhani was excited. He felt like a powerful king who could kill at will. He ordered the next step in his plan to be accomplished. The agents he had in the United States had gathered explosives that could do considerable damage but kill few people, and that too only if they were just unlucky enough to be in the wrong place at the wrong time. He had selected a spot in Chicago and New York that would do considerable damage to the building but, with a little luck, would not kill anyone. The bombs were made of military-grade C-4 with remote detonators. The first target was an office building in Chicago. His agents had monitored the building carefully; there was never anyone working late at night. The building had steel columns with precast and stone as an outside covering. The explosive devices would be well hidden in the basement and attached to two of the columns holding the building up. They were camouflaged as AT&T telephone boxes with wires running up and through the ceiling. The other building targeted was in New York City. It housed retail shops that were only open during the day. The building, also a steel structure, had a marble façade. It was a six-story building; the third floor, once full of offices, had been vacant for many years. The shops were on the first and second floors. The fourth through sixth housed a combination warehouse for the shops and several attorney's offices, which had little foot traffic, their clientele included mostly debt collectors, the transactions done mostly by mail or email. The bombs were attached to the columns penetrating the third floor. All the columns had been encased with paneling for decorative appeal; the agents simply removed a sheet from two different columns, planted the bombs, and then replaced the covering. Unless some major remodeling was being done, the bombs would likely never be detected.

After placing the nuclear and C-4 bombs, Hassan Rouhani struggled with himself not to make demands of the Americans now. He wanted to send a threatening letter, photos of the two bombs, and demand that if the sanctions were not lifted, the nuclear bomb would be detonated within ten days and, as added proof of their capabilities, Iran had non-nuclear device that would be detonated in 48 hours and if the Americans did not respond to the demands, he would then set off the nuclear devices. He relished at the thought of Trump squirming at the mess he had caused. Hassan, as he was required, contacted the Ayatollah and informed him that the nuclear device, as well as the two other conventional explosives, were in place. The Ayatollah, immediately with a loud voice, beating on the table as he talked, ordered Hassan not to do anything but wait. He would let him know when and if, a demand would be made. Hassan responded he would, but in his mind, he knew he might just disobey the order and start the process anyway. Trump deserved to face the problem of how to save millions of Americans.

The Ayatollah had received a report of the infighting between the Unites States Cabinet and Trump. He laughed as he realized how gullible Trump was. He also realized that this is why Iran had the current problems with the United States. Trump was being fed untrue information by various people and entities, information he believed without proof. He refused to listen to his advisors who knew that Iran posed no threat to the United States. Iran's only sin was in the eyes of Israel, who believed the help Iran gave to the Palestinians was an act of terrorism. Why didn't Israel and Trump understand and accept that Palestine has a right to self-govern and return the lands taken from them? That is all Iran wanted.

Hassan was also very pleased with the latest information. With Ayatollah's urging, he ordered the disinformation effort to be not only continued but increased.

The group responsible for the disinformation worked feverously to come up with various plans to play on Trump's weakness. They had concluded the best scenario was to pretend to involve Canada, Mexico and China in a mutual defense effort. They constantly carried on conversations depicting ordinary government business transactions. The conversations included the concerns for eavesdropping by foreign governments and what protections were in place. The Ayatollah's office complex had been fitted with electronic devices that emulated signals that prevented any transmission outside the complex.

The Ayatollah's messages were recorded and taken to another location to be transmitted; this was the only way a message could be transmitted outside the complex. The same was also used for all key government officials. The United States' spy agencies took special notice of this disclosure and were working hard to locate and record the transmission of the messages.

The disinformation group discussed the problem it had with information being disclosed from a super-secret location. They were convinced it had not come from any devices in their offices. There was a daily scan of any listening devices or other types of electronic surveillance. So, it was just not possible for their conversations to be heard and recorded. The consensus was that the Mexican government and possibly others were being recorded by the Americans. They must contact their counterparts in Mexico to warn them. The counterparts, who did not exist, were happy to continue with the ruse. Trump had also done much damage to the Mexican economy. Further discussions decided that the best way to do this was through their United Nations envoy. They would purchase throwaway cell phones and communicate with throwaway phone numbers they had been given by the Mexican authorities. The disclosure must be stopped before their plans were harmed. No one should ever mention that this was all a ruse. Trump was convinced the communications through throw away cellphones was not good as they would not be able to overhear. He ordered the CIA to monitor all cellphone emulating from the Mexican delegation.

Carlos Rodriguez, the fictious, head of the Mexican delegation laid out what information they needed to transmit to their UN envoy. The recorded conversations with Iran noted they needed more security as some of their plans were being discovered by the United States. Mexico had gotten some real word on what was happening and wanted Donald Trump to be led down a path of nonsense and uncertainty this could be done by continuing to allow fake data to be overheard and or discovered. Thus, they never denied any of it. They liked the false information of the missiles and drones but could not allow the United States to ever be aware they had participated in the ruse. Any overheard conversations confirming any threat must always be from the Iranian, not from any Mexican officials.

The outline for the latest escalation of the ruse was complete and also brilliant! They now began discussions with fake Cuban authorities. The Cubans would be ever so delighted to damage the United States; they too had faced damage from Trump's madness. The former US President had started a program to look for solutions to the long history of sanctions to the Cuban people. The program was working and would, in time, bring back normal relations. But Trump, with no rational reason, closed down virtually all contact and any interchange with the American people. It was sad.

The plan overheard by the CIA was that Iran would bring its short-range missiles to Cuba. The short-range was 1,500 miles, which meant they could reach many United States cities from a Cuban base.

Trump walked into the cabinet meeting with a stack of recorded conversations. "Have any of you fucking idiots seen this?"

"Mr. President," said the CIA director, "This is fake and meant for us to hear. We are double checking our sources but are convinced they know they are being recorded and creating things for us to overhear."

"Well, it is a damn good thing you are not the president. I guess you will only be convinced when the first missile hits us!"

"It takes a lot of effort on the ground to make this happen. No such effort is being undertaken," said the Secretary of Defense.

"Did you not hear them say they had moved the location several miles into Mexico so our drones could not see what they were doing? This is fucking ridiculous! I want action and action now!"

"Our drones can see for more than twenty miles and our satellites have unlimited range. There is no construction ongoing capable of launching a missile!"

"You are willing to risk millions of lives for such horseshit. Well, I am not!" Turning toward the Chairman of the Joint Chiefs, he said, "You will prepare plans for the immediate partial invasion of Mexico and possibly Cuba. Do you understand, General?"

General Carter hung his head with an obvious expression of disdain. "Yes sir, I do, you do understand I must inform congress!"

"It is stupid fucking rule but do what you must, but you wait until we meet again, as I might change my mind.!"

Chapter Eleven

Aftab, back in Iran, was meeting with his senior personnel early in the morning, as he had much to discuss: "Our next step must be one of action, which means, to actually do damage to the madman's property. I think we should do this so on several fronts. First, we make some people sick by tainting the food. Second, we cause leaks in several of the places that have many residences and, third, we cause sewage backup in at least two of the more upper-class hotels. Of course, we also will damage or destroy the landscaping. What do you guys think?"

"What properties do you have in mind for each?" asked Rasheen.

"I believe 200, 220 and 240 Riverside and Trump Park Avenue," said Aftab. "We can install 55 gallons drums of acid at each in a single night. The acid should make the plumbing fixtures leak within a week. For Trump International Hotel and Tower in New York, Las Vegas and Chicago, we already know who supplies the fresh food. For these, we make customers sick and, finally, in Trump International Washington and 610 Park Avenue, we stop up the sewage."

"I follow. We have lots of data already on all of these properties. We can acquire permits to do whatever we want for all the New York properties. So, the list is good. We just need to get the logistics on how to do it down pat," said Rasheen as he walked around the room in small circles

"For the sewage stop ups," offered Aram, "I have discovered a substance we can pump into a manhole. It will last about five hours and then just disappear. The workers who come to deal with the stoppage will see nothing but a stoppage at the flow pipe into the manhole."

"Incredible," said Aftab, "How does it work?"

"It is like a gelatin but much firmer and stronger. We will mix and create the substance as it goes into the manhole, and it will instantly form into a hard gel until we completely fill the manhole. At that point, sewage will back up, causing the entire system to stop. The backup will begin almost the minute it hits the gel. Depending on the amount used, the system will begin to overflow into the toilets, bathtubs, showers, and sinks within hours. It will make a real mess!"

"Sounds great. How difficult is this substance to make or obtain?" asked Aftab.

"It is a mixture of several components, mainly gelatin and dry ice all of which we should be able to buy at common places, maybe even a Walmart," said Aram. "We will be prepared to add a sort of anti-freeze if needed, what will happen is we will have a frozen mixture that will resemble a firm ice cream."

"Maybe we should hit more than two properties. Let's do some reconnaissance and locate the manholes and find out how difficult it will be to fill them. How long do you think it will take at each manhole?" asked Aftab.

"If we attach a pump to a water truck and a dry sprayer for the mixture, maybe 10 minutes. Or if we can get our hands on a concrete mixer that can generate hot water, we can dump the load in under 5 minutes." Said Aram

"Let's hit as many as we can to include those outside the United States," said Aftab. "We will have a separate group that will handle all of the New York area properties, other than those I visited."

"There are 6 properties in North America, not including those in the New York area. One of them is in Canada" said Gulzar who stood and began a prepared presentation of all the properties and the planned attack that their planning had come up with.

Gulzar then passed out a printed list of properties and then stated each as he checked them off with his pencil.

"Albemarle Estate a Trump Winery and hotel, Charlottesville, Virginia, Trump International Hotel and Tower, Chicago, Illinois, Trump International Hotel and Tower Las Vegas, Las Vegas, Nevada, Trump National Golf Club,

Los Angeles, California, Trump International Hotel and Tower Waikiki, Honolulu, Hawaii, Trump International Hotel and Tower, Vancouver, British, Columbia. It will require at least 3 teams to look over and provide all the information we will need since one of the United States properties is in Hawaii. We need to know the exact location of the manhole. All permits needed to open. Other requirements are a rental place to rent a water truck or mixer, safety markers to protect the opening from traffic, pumps for the water and the dry mixture. All of this needs to be done just before daylight at each location. Also, we need to locate where to buy the ingredients and arrange water supply to fill the truck."

"How about the properties outside the United States?" asked Aram.

"I show 17 properties: this will be a major task. The properties we found are here." Gulzar pointed to another chart and read off the names.

Le Chateau Des Palmiers	St Martin	Carb
Trump Towers	Pune	India
Trump Tower	Mumbai	India
Trump Tower	Kolkata	India
Trump Tower	Delhi	India
Trump Residences	Bali	Indonesia
Trump Residences	Lido	Indonesia
Trump International	Lido City	Indonesia
Trump International	Bali	Indonesia
Trump International	Doonberg	Ireland
Trump Tower Central City	Makati	Philippines
Trump International	Aberdeen	Scotland
Trump International	Turnberry	Scotland
Trump World	Seoul	South Korea
Trump Towers	Istanbul	Turkey
Trump International	Dubai	UAE
Trump Tower	Punta Del Este	Uruguay

"Our conclusion is, we will need 9 teams to get this done properly, plus the New York group, with the same information needed for all." He pointed to more charts and listed off the names. "Team 1 will handle LeChateau Des Palmiers at St. Martin, Caribbean and Trump Tower at Punta Del Este in Uruguay. Said Gulzar.

"St Martin and Uruguay are not close, nearly 6,000 kilometers apart, but St Martin is small. It should not take long to figure out how this can be done. We may even need to import the ingredients. I believe we will need to fly to Buenos Aires, then on to Uruguay and again need to import what we need." Added Rasheen who was sitting and uncomfortable, he did squeeze his hands as he spoke.

"It is likely that we may delete these two properties and leave them alone as they are much easier fish to catch! Said Aftab.

Gulzar pointed to another chart his team had prepared and read the summary. "The other properties and teams would be:

Team 2 will handle, the four Trump properties in India."

"The distances between some of these properties are great. We may likely require two teams to handle." Stated Rasheen, he had now stood up and was pacing again. The others in the room just smiled at the now familiar habit

"Teams 3 and 4 will handle, the four properties in Indonesia and one in the Philippines." Continued Gulzar.

"It is nearly 3,000 kilometers between the Philippines and Indonesia, I think these teams will run into similar problems and should coordinate their efforts." Added Rasheen as he now was walking around the table.

"Team 5 will handle, the one property in Ireland and the two in Scotland." Continued Gulzar.

"There should not be supply problems for any of these, and the locals hate Trump and maybe even would help if they can be trusted!" Noted Aram.

"Team 6 will handle the one property in South Korea." Said Gulzar. And "Team 7 will handle the one property in Turkey and one in Dubai."

Aftab and his team stopped for a short lunch break, they had been going for five straight hours and Aftab could see they were all becoming exhausted including him. After lunch he ask Gulzar to continue.

"Team 8 will handle all the properties of Benjamin Netanyahu we can locate. Team 9 will handle all properties of the Trump children and son-in-law. The distance between the two are not close but the problems should be relatively the same. It likely will take several days each to gather the information needed to do the job."

Aftab clapped his hands in appreciation for the outline he had just heard. "I think Gulzar and Aram should handle all the planning for the acid. Jamshed can handle the poison of the foods. Rasheen can be in charge of planning and the creation and selection of the 9 teams. In addition, Shahzad and Nima will continue the hacking efforts on Trump's finances. We all need to get to work. Are there any questions about what each of you is to do?"

"Many of us are going to need to travel. How soon can we plan to leave?" asked Rasheen, he had stopped pacing and was sitting down.

"As soon as you can be ready and have an itinerary, run it through me. Let me remind all of you, you will be on foreign soil and foreign soil that is our enemy. You must be extremely careful as being caught not only means failure but it means you will spend the rest of your life in prison and may even be executed as spies, caution is the way we must proceed." said Aftab.

"The same with funds?" asked Rasheen "We will need budgets and so forth soon.".

"Yes."

Aftab assigned workstations to each group, who, without comment, moved to their assigned spaces. They were an efficient group and grabbed a clerical person without being told who brought writing and filing supplies to the area for their use.

Aftab looked on, in pure delight, watching the machine he had created working like clockwork.

Gulzar, assigned to install the acid, had assigned 3 people plus a clerk. He started as soon as everyone was seated. "At least 2 of us need to go to

New York City as part of our United Nations staff. We have 4 properties and, if all goes well, maybe more. We must ensure that we can input building permits for those properties. Who has solved that problem?"

Shahzad had hacked into the New York system. It was a difficult and excruciating effort. Shahzad had enlisted the help of two of the other hackers who had coordinated the bombardment of their computers to continue with billions of hits to the New York system until the correct sequence of codes were found that allowed access. Two separate passwords were required, one to allow sign in, to the primary New York system and the other after the first access to sign into the part authorizing entry into the permit portion. The access was designed so issuing a permit would be limited to only a few authorized people.

"Shahzad told all of us that he could now hack into the New York system an issue permits at will," said Gulzar.

"Will you go get him please?" said Aftab.

Gulzar left. Four minutes later, he returned with Shahzad.

"Shahzad, glad you could join us. We have four properties in New York City and want to make sure that we have the building permits that will allow us to work at night. We should finish what we intend to do around 6 A.M." Said Gulzar.

"Give me the addresses. I do not think it will be a problem."

"200, 220 and 240 Riverside and Trump Park Avenue, which is at 502 Park Avenue, all in the city," answered Gulzar.

"Can I get back to you in 30 minutes?" "Yes, of course." Said Gulzar.

"If you know the exact date, I can enter them now. We must have an exact date for a digging permit in New York City."

"I'll give it to you tomorrow." answered Gulzar, "I will have to be sure and will coordinate with Aftab."

"Ok, we need a storage place. Who can handle that?" ask Aftab.

Rasheen raised his hand. "I looked at this earlier. We can rent a temporary storage place. The cost is small, and they are all over the city. Americans tend to buy more stuff than they have room for and rent these places. Dumb as shit, I think."

"Good. Find us one as close as you can to the Riverside properties," said Gulzar

"Will do."

"Next, we will need to rent a truck capable of pulling a trailer with a small backhoe, plus the drums of acid and tools." said Gulzar

"I will find us a rental place for a warehouse type and for a truck. Several companies have them," said Rasheen, he was back up pacing again.

"As to the design of the system, our engineer says we need 'hot patches' for both steel and plastic since we do not know what type of water pipe we will encounter. We need both here so we can practice the installation. Rasheen, can you get us some?" said Gulzar

"Yes sir, should not be a problem, I have a supplier who can deliver as needed." answered Rasheen.

"Our engineer also says that we will need a tool to install two 2.5-millimeter holes, one to attach to the 'hot patch' and the other to install an air vent to the surface. I think a flexible pipe would be better. It will have to run to the surface so it can be accessed from above, it can be installed into some type of grid. Level with the ground. We must make it completely flat, so it is not easily visible. We will need to also have a 5-millimeter hole that will house a safety pipe to refill the drum with more acid. We think they will replace the metal valves within a week or so of the flooding. With the added pipe, we can do it again if we wish," noted Gulzar.

"Oh yes, I like that," said Rasheen who was back sitting down.

Later, the team responsible for the manhole stoppage met to determine what they would need and who would be in charge.

"We will need a large quantity of gelatin," said Aram. "You mean like the kind you cook with?" asked Rasheen.

"Yes, the same. To do what we need to be done, we will need to mix it with hot water. My rough estimate is 7,600 liters per manhole, and the water must be hot."

"Wow, so we need a water truck that can heat water," said Rasheen "don't know where we can find one, can't be many around, probable a concrete company may have that ability, but it would be something they created, I would think."

"We may need two separate units one just for mixing and one just for heating water. After heating, we will possibly need to add some liters of Ethylene Glycol. Then as it begins to thicken, add 3 liters of dry ice, the dry ice before the glycol. It will be best if we always have a couple of canisters of carbon dioxide at hand, just in case we need extra cooling. This mixture will become like clear hard plastic in just a few minutes. It will stay that way for maybe 5 hours then slowly turn back into liquid," explained Aram

"Don't you think we need some practice?" asked Gulzar.

"Yes, of course. Rasheen, can you arrange for the ingredients?" "Yes, no problem."

Both groups practiced until they were confident that they could do it blindfolded. Most of the time, the solid gelatin turned back into a liquid within 6 hours. The water was heated using gas burners and pots. The mixing was done using a portable concrete mixture. They needed to improve on this. Aram now questioned if the Ethylene Glycol which was brought into the mix to be sure it was not just solid ice which could be a problem really added anything. Aram believed the problem was better controlled by monitoring the amount of dry ice.

Chapter Twelve

It was Monday morning; the President's cabinet had just started their normal meeting. All the members were especially tense as the President had a look that he had been waiting to order something that none of them were going to like.

"Have you carried out completing my plans to invade Mexico and Cuba, General?" asked Donald Trump.

"No, sir. It takes longer than a couple of days, and we also have to inform Congress about the planning," said General Carter.

Trump threw his tablet on the floor. "As I said before, that is bullshit. This order is executive privilege, just for me. Just because I am curious, nothing else! So, no need to bring those slimy bastards into this discussion!"

"Sir, my orders are absolute. I must notify Congress when such plans have been made or are in the works."

"Then just fucking forget it for now. I don't want them slimy bastards in my business."

****

Aftab had taken the advice of Gulzar and ordered them to practice what they would be doing in New York. He created two groups, one for the gelatin mixture and the other for the acid. The two practice groups stayed in Iran, each received a duplicate drum, emulating the containers for the acid and the ingredients for the gelatin mixtures separately. The practice was being done a few kilometers away from the main secure facility, they did not want the equipment operating inside nor the necessary holes or torn up areas to be at the facility. They moved people to two different sites to begin the practice. They started early in the morning with a backhoe that dug down to a depth expected for the main water supply using an expected 20-centimeter size pipe. One pipe was plastic, another was steel, and yet another was cast iron. The test began with digging a trench one-meter-wide and 1.2 meters deep. A 20-centimeter plastic pipe, 2 meters long, was laid in the bottom of the trench, simulating a main water supply line. A 'Hot tapping sleeve' was placed around the pipe. The Tapping sleeve was designed to penetrate the pipe ending with a valve which, when turned on, would allow fluid to flow in or out of the line. The tap was made, and then a full drum (of water) was lowered from above and to the side of the pipe. Soon, they discovered that they needed to create a seat for the drum at least 12 centimeters above and to the right or left of the pipe. A similar sleeve tap, but a much larger one, was placed around the drum, connecting a 10-centimeter flexible pipe, which had installed a low stop valve already that would only allow backward flow from the drum to the waterline. Two punctures were made into the drum, for an air vent and as a refill entrance. Both the air supply and the refill pipes were raised to ground level: one was attached to a drain that would allow air to come freely into the drum, the other was sealed with a screw-on drain cap where it could be easily removed, and more acid could be added if necessary. A separate engineering group had already tested and verified that, as long as air could get into the drum and equalize the pressure, the acid would flow into the waterline. The acid would be drawn out as water was flowing in the pipe it was connected to, it created a suction action.

The group did the exact same operation using steel and cast iron. The entire operation was down to 45 minutes. Added time would be required if there was concrete or asphalt above the pipe. The crew required a backhoe, a truck capable of hauling the backhoe trailer and enough room to haul the drums and the tools required. Aftab decided that this group was ready to go to New York. He ordered flight arrangements and the necessary United Nations visas. They were excited. Now Trump would get a taste of what the rest of the world felt when economic war was declared. Iran, Cuba Venezuela, Syria and a few others were suffering now Trump would know what economic war tasted like.

The second group had many difficulties. A manhole was constructed 3 meters deep and one-and-half meters wide. The type of water heater used was not sufficient; it did not get the water hot enough to make the gel sufficiently firm to hold back sewage. After several attempts, each with varying degrees of frustration as the gel did not harden or hardened so quick it would not flow out of the mixer. Aftab had commented what they really needed was an old lady supervisor who made gelatin salad often. a kettle used by roofers was brought to the site. The kettle was designed to bring tar to over 400 degrees Fahrenheit and heated a sufficient quantity to mix with the gel. A portable cement mixer was used to mix the boiling water with the gel. The group decreased the amount of Ethylene Glycol as it reduced the effect of the dry ice. They also increased the amount of dry ice. The formula was now 2 liters of Ethylene Glycol. As it began to thicken, 5 liters of dry ice was added based on a 7,600-liter manhole. This mixture should provide as much resistance as 40 PSI or 3 kilograms, sufficient enough to hold back free-flowing sewage. The sewage should back up and create a clog that will itself-would hold back further sewage. The final mixture stayed firm for 5 hours, then turned into a liquid. They realized that they also needed a cooler with enough foam to keep the dry ice cold and, just in case, several canisters of carbon dioxide, the type used for fire extinguishers. The canisters would supply an added shot of frigid cold if necessary. Cold, frigid cold, was an absolute necessity since forming the gelatin into what would be a nearly frozen block of ice in just a few moments was essential to it working properly.

The group was satisfied that it could heat the water, mix the ingredients and pour it in a manhole in less than 1 hour.

The group then celebrated and prepared to go to New York.

One week later, the message was received that the items requested had been obtained and would be waiting in two separate warehouses in Manhattan. Aftab selected UG, Inc., which stood for Under Ground, as the name of the company that would install the drums. Magnetic signs were ordered to place on the vehicles. Manhole Installation and Inspection Services was the other name selected; signs were made for them as well. The acid was ordered under the name of Pool Services, Inc., it was delivered directly to the warehouse. Other items such as the tapping sleeves, magnetic signs, valves, pipe, cement mixer, finishing tools, water barrel, shovels, mattock and carbon dioxide fire extinguishers were also delivered.

Aftab decided to move the group handling the golf courses timeline forward. There was no reason why the assault on the golf courses should not proceed at the same time as the other property attacks. He found an area in Iran with large palm trees to determine the best way to destroy the trees. Palm trees were unique and would require drilling into them to make them die. Destroying the trees on the golf courses would be difficult and time-consuming. They had to get the operation down to a few minutes per tree—that would be very difficult. Aftab insisted that they damage no trees in Iran. He knew that the poison they would shoot into the trees would work—it had been well tested. So, he ordered his crew to use only plain water for practice. It was the drilling that would take time.

The golf course crew arrived, armed with several devices: battery-operated hand drills and watering cans with tube-like pouring spouts. Around the base of trees, with a 13mm auger-type bit, they began by drilling 5 holes. One of them stood behind the drill operator and filled each hole with water. It took 1 minute and 40 seconds. Another person also drilled 5 holes into the tree, followed by a person who poured water in each hole. This took 5 minutes 20 seconds— too long. They had a more powerful battery-operated drill that used a 20-volt battery, and it reduced by 1 full minute the time, the drill was more powerful and drilled faster. The carbon steel auger wood bit, they found, was the fastest, bringing down the time to 2 minutes 33 seconds, though it still needed reducing. Many of the golf courses had several hundred trees, so the multiplier would not work.

They wanted all 19 golf courses done on the same day and on a moonless night Once the grass and trees started dying on one course, the tightening of security at all golf courses would make it nearly impossible to do the others. Aftab's person in charge of obtaining the right people assured him that he would recruit one crew for each course, and they would be ready. The problem now was to train them and get the right equipment and supplies in their hands. He wondered if it was too difficult a mission. The courses were spread out all over the United States, then Europe, India, Saudi Arabia, Turkey, Canada and Indonesia, a lot of territories.

They needed 8 trainers who would train 19 crews to do this job. None of them would know what and where they were going but only what they were to do. This included the 8 trainers. Aftab produced a video, demonstrating how each task was to be done and provided a fake tree to practice the drilling. He worked with the concept for several days and decided that the risk of detection with so many people was just too much. The least illumination from the moon generally lasted for two consecutive days, and the distance between the golf courses meant that he could get by with two days with just 4 crews heading to the 2 courses in Indonesia and one in the UAE. He ordered one person from each of the 4 crews to be brought to him in Iran.

Later in the evening, Aftab met with his computer experts for an update. As reported, they were now able to hack into the reservation and accounting systems for all Trump owned or operated hotels. They had also hacked into the properties that Trump rented, leased, or sold, except for 4, which, likely, were being handled by the Trump corporate since they were in the New York area. They concluded Trump headquarters must have separate people doing all reservations for those 4 hotels and had not been able to find a computer system to hack. They could also make tee-time reservations for any of the Trump golf courses, and they were still working on accessing the financial data for Trump and his children. They also tapped into several of the Kushner-owned properties and downloaded all the information. Some progress had been made regarding locating the accounts of Benjamin Netanyahu, though they didn't have full access yet.

Aftab said a few words to his team in praise. He told them what they had been able to accomplish was remarkable. Soon, Trump would feel the benefit of the hard work his people had done.

The next morning, Aftab made another decision. That decision was to not wait before making a lot of people who ate at the Trump restaurants sick. His people who were in charge were ready. They knew where to strike, whom the fresh foods were brought from when the delivery was expected. He would tell them in the morning meeting.

Since the operation of installing the acid and stopping up the sewage lines was to be carried out soon, Aftab ordered an 811 call which was a requirement in all of the United States (call before you dig) be made, all areas in the United States had crews who would come to each location and mark where each utility was located underground, this was to prevent damage to the lines when digging. Also, the permits had to be issued for the work to be done. He was sure all this would be done by the next day.

Two of the groups handling the sewage left for New York. Both elected to take a flight directly from Ankara Turkey to New York City. Later in the day, two more teams handling the acid left but through Tehran and Frankfort.

The four teams arrived at the specified time. The United States customs and immigration had illegally put each individual through a rigorous questioning by the US authorities, in spite of the diplomatic immunity each was entitled to. The United States had no information on any of the people in the four groups and wanted more information than just a name or that they were part of the Iranian delegation. All four successfully came through the Kennedy airport immigration. They were well briefed on refusing to answer on anything other than what had been provided to the US immigration services as it was not required. The only questions to answer on their purpose to visit the United States was they are here to represent Iran; Representing Iran was the only requirement for entry. Reluctantly, they were allowed admission by the US authorities. Rasheen Abbasi, the supervisor, was accompanied by Aram Alinejad, the engineer. Earlier, Gulzar Charmchi, the metal expert, and Jamshed Rostami, the Agricultural expert had now arrived and ready to go to work. Rasheen and Aram were already at the UN. When Gulzar and Jamshed arrived, Rasheen introduced them to the other Iranian members of the UN entourage who would assist them with anything they needed. Rasheen, of course, was standing. The Iranian entourage also warned them that the Americans, as they did to all members of the Iranian delegation, would be watching each of them carefully.

Aram, the engineer, wanted to discuss a problem he had worked on while flying. They did not expect much pressure from the sewage pipe leading into the manhole, but the force could well be too much for the thickened gelatin to get set and stop up the pipe from flowing. Aram had roughly designed a .6 meter by .6 meter by 19mm thick piece of plywood to go over the incoming flow until the gelatin got fully set. The plywood was attached to a rope to lower over the incoming pipe. On the back were two pipe flanges with a 60-degree angle. The flanges were of sufficient size to allow two long pieces of lumber to enter and hold the plywood tightly against the outgoing pipe. This would be sufficient enough to hold back and apply pressure until the gelatin sets up which should not be over a few minutes. The local Iranians assured them it would be in the warehouse by morning. They would have to screw on the flanges in the exact spot they wanted. They also recommended four pieces of long lumber and cleats spaced along with the pieces that would fit into the flanges. This would allow the plywood to be held firmly against the pipe opening. The engineer agreed but had them bring 5 pieces since some would be needed to make the cleats. The engineer also wanted a battery-operated SKIL saw.

Gulzar, now in charge of the acid operation, wanted a detailed list of what was stored in the warehouse. He was given the list that showed a backhoe, a trailer, a 5-ton truck, 4 50-gallon drums of acid four coolers filled with dry ice, 4 canisters of carbon dioxide, hot tapping sleeves of several sizes and types, pipe, valves, 20 bags of premixed cement, 3 bags of premixed asphalt, cement mixer, water barrel, finishing tools, shovels, 2 mattocks, battery operated drill with a set of bits, fittings for the pipe, magnetic signs for the truck and equipment, roofers kettles and hot taps for the barrels. A small forklift was also in the warehouse. Gulzar added a sledgehammer and a saber saw with extra blades, in case they encountered roots. The locals stated it would be bought and delivered that night. All were amazed such items could be purchased late at night. The local delegation explained this was New York city and many stores stayed open 24 hours a day 7 days a week.

The four were taken to the hotel for rest. Iran had a delivery van belonging to a local florist that would hide them when they exited the hotel. Inside each person's room was two pairs of blue jeans which had been washed many times so they would look old, white socks three pairs each, American type underwear also three pairs each, western type belts and work boots. None of them had ever worn blue jeans before. Each tried them on and did not particularly like the way they felt but they did look like normal American workers, they also had an assortment of tee shirts with various colors and statements on them. Inside each of their rooms was a leather billfold with two hundred dollars of small bills, fake driver's license, a card from the hotel which gave the address and a credit card. All this was just in case any of them got separated or stopped, they had disguises they would use the next morning when they were ready to leave. The Americans would just have to believe they were still resting.

Chapter Thirteen

At 10 AM, the florist van made its delivery to the hotel where all had rooms, it was a small place where Iran normally put all its visitors. The van parked in the garage near a column that hid the rear door from view and left the back door unlocked. As the driver brought a flower delivery into the hotel, the four slipped into the van. Each was dressed as a typical American tourist with baseball hats and sunglasses. The van was on its way by 10:15, making two other stops before heading to the warehouse. Once it arrived, it did not stop but pulled into a garage and drove to the lower floor. Once the driver knew they were safe and out of view of anyone who may be watching, the four jumped out of the van. Each went a different route to the warehouse, which was less than a block away. Over a period of 30 minutes, each entered the warehouse. A spotter was hidden near the entrance and observed if anyone was watching. All had a throwaway cell phone. The spotter texted everyone that the coast was clear. The Americans had one person watching the front door from across the street of the hotel and another watching the rear. Cameras surveyed each floor and stairwell. The Iranians had taken a video of the hallway and the stairway they would use. They used this facility often and had done this just in case and had used it often. These videos were hard-wired to the respective cameras. They would now only show an empty hallway and empty stairways. Once the team had passed through the security cameras, the feed was disconnected. The Americans would have to verify the correctness at the same time the fake feed was being used in order for them to be aware that the feed they were receiving was not real.

Once inside the warehouse, the four inspected the equipment that would be needed later that evening. Once all had inspected the items needed, they conferred for a short while. Rasheen and Jamshed openly discussed how each item would be used to stop up the sewers once they were satisfied, everything needed was there, they turned the discussion over to Gulzar and Aram. The job they were to do was much more complex so being thorough was critical. They measured the pipe, checked each of the drums and was sure the different types of possible connections were there. Gulzar also checked the battery of the sabre saw and counted the bags of cement, tested the concrete mixer until he to, was satisfied it worked properly. Waiting for them were two vehicles inside the warehouse, parked with a driver sitting behind each steering wheel They were waiting to take them to wherever they needed to go.

After all, had put on shirts showing the logo of who they were supposed to be working for, UG and Manhole Installation and Inspection Services, each had on the correct shirt depending on what task they were to do. They would certainly appear to be legitimate by anyone watching, they also had hardhats with the appropriate logo. Rasheen and Jamshed got into the first van; their job was to stop up the sewers. They were four properties they had decided to hit. Each had been marked by the call before you dig authorities. The list given to the driver included the property in the city at 610 Park Ave, 200 East 69th street, 167 East 61st Street and White Plains at 10 City Plaza.

"Drop Jamshed off when I tell you to", said Rasheen. The driver shook his head up and down.

"Here", said Rasheen. Jamshed exited the vehicle. They were a half block away from 610 Park Ave.

"Drop me off at the end of the block. I will text you when we are ready to be picked up." The driver again shook his head up and down.

The driver began to drive aimlessly around but staying close to the drop off point.

Gulzar and Aram got into the second vehicle giving the driver a list of the addresses they wished to see: 200, 220 and 240 Riverside and 502 Park Avenue. Gulzar wanted to be dropped off near 502 Park Avenue and Aram near the other three. Each was given the cell phone numbers of the others. Since it was so close to a city street, at least judging from the map he had, Gulzar was concerned that the water line at 502 Park Avenue would be too difficult to access.

Rasheen and Jamshed separately surveyed the property at 610 Park Ave and found the sewage manhole with no problem. They also saw where the water, gas, electrical, telephone and internet lines were marked. Jamshed had a small but effective laser distance calculator that looked like and was not much larger than a fountain pen. It had to be pointed at some object, and it would then give the distance on a readout on the side of the pen. On the manhole cover was a slot to insert a tool to lift off the lid. Jamshed shot the lazar down the slot, its red light was easy to see and guide to the hole, it gave him a readout of 3 meters. Jamshed texted Rasheen that he was ready to move on. He then texted the driver to pick them up. The driver picked up Rasheen first, then drove around the block to get Jamshed. When both were in the car, Jamshed excitedly told Rasheen that he was able to measure the depth of the manhole, and it was only 3 meters, easily within what they could handle. The driver drove on toward 200 East 69th Street. They repeated the drop off method. Although a block away, Jamshed was dropped off almost on top of a manhole. He quickly shot the depth which measured 2.5 meters. He then walked toward the actual address, found the nearest manhole. It measured nearly the same at 2.7 meters. Rasheen observed the layout, parking and obstructions they may encounter when filling the manhole. Right now, the traffic was heavy, but he knew that at 4 am it would be light if any at all. 167 East 61st street was nearly identical. Jamshed, measured the depth as 2.3 meters which meant they were going uphill. The last property, White Plains, was 30 or so minutes away. The manhole for the White Plains property was nearly a block away. They both wondered if somehow, they were missing one but could not find anything. The depth was 3 meters. None of the properties looked very difficult. There was or would be enough parking space to set up to get the job done. The worry was, what the line fed. Was it to many buildings or was it a direct line to the Trump property, they would certainly find out tomorrow!

They texted the driver after spending 25 minutes looking over the situation. Rasheen was picked up a half block from the Trump property and Jamshed two blocks away. The driver took them back to the warehouse but stayed, just in case.

Gulzar had a concerned look on his face. He was right. The property at 502 Park Avenue would be the most difficult. The water line was marked in blue; it went a short distance on some grass then crossed a narrow sidewalk then into the street. It would be difficult to get the depth they needed to bury the barrel with the amount of space available. Gulzar decided to add three flat sharp-edged shovels to allow for the ditch to go straight down at a 90-degree angle. He wished he could take an exact measurement but was unable to do so without drawing attention to himself. He texted the driver to get him. The driver picked him up, stopping a half block away from the property. They then drove toward 200 Riverside to meet up with Aram.

When the driver arrived, Aram was just leaving the property at 200 Riverside. Although the addresses were next to each other, it was a good distance from one to the other. Gulzar moved on to the third building, 240 Riverside with no discussion with Aram. The situation with the third building was ideal. The blue line, marking the water, went over grass, with no other utilities in the area. It also had a great spot for setting up the equipment. Aram joined him 30 minutes later. The last building for today was 220 Riverside, it was almost identical to 200 with lots of grass. They did not speak but walked past each other, Aram texted the driver his location. Ten minutes later, Aram was in the van and they drove toward where Gulzar was. They picked him up and drove back to the warehouse. Aram reported that the 502 Park Avenue, the first building would be difficult as the location was tight. It would require the replacement of a sidewalk and involve a difficult dig. The second property had space to get the barrel in with no obstructions and would be all under grass. Gulzar made a mental note to add rakes, a sharp- ended flat shovel and a compaction tool for putting the grass back down firmly.

When all four were back at the warehouse, Gulzar gave them the list of added tools that would be needed, including several tape measures. Rasheen actually raised his hand when Gulzar said tape measure as his team also would need at least two of the 8-meter devices. He then took the SKIL saw and screws and constructed the cleats needed for the long pole types, he also screwed on the flanges to the plywood.

Rasheen took over his supervisory duties and requested everyone to join him, he paced as he talked, including the two drivers plus the other Iranians assigned to New York. "We will have 6 more men join us in approximately 5 hours. The drivers will pick them up at several places. They already have been given the addresses where each is located. We are going to have a long night, and I want each of you to go and get a good sleep on these cots. Food should be delivered any minute. Before you go, I want a pecking order for the property, which one is first, which one's second and so forth. Gulzar, can you and Aram develop the order you will go? Jamshed, lets develop ours quickly."

Food was brought in a few minutes later, they all ate and went to bed except for Rasheen who stayed up to study the pecking order and make some notes before crawling into a cot.

The two drivers set a separate alarm for 4½ hours, got up and left to pick up the others. 45 minutes later they both had returned with the six additional men.

Rasheen had already decided to not tell the six, who were now at the warehouse after being delivered by the drivers, what they were up to except only for the work each had to do. Confidentiality was critical to Iran but, it would assure them no one would be harmed. The work would give them sensitive information that might be used in the future but there was no way to prevent it, they would each always know what they had done.

It was now past midnight, Rasheen sent three of the new men to Gulzar and Aram who then immediately began loading the truck, first the barrels of acid using the forklift followed by the tools and supplies. Within an hour all was loaded and ready to go.

Rasheen and Jamshed took the last three men and put them under their wing and gave them work to do. They had more equipment and supplies than the others so much more had to be loaded. The acid group had larger equipment but was less in number.

Once packed and on the truck, several barrels were filled with water. One barrel for the acid crew and three for the sewage. This took 45 minutes. Gulzar and Rasheen looked over the inventory of tools and equipment with a checklist each had created: all of the equipment was there. Gulzar's truck left first, driven by one of the van drivers. It consisted of a 5-ton cargo-type truck pulling a trailer with a backhoe and a cement mixer. He had decided to first take the three residences at 200 Riverside Boulevard, 220 Riverside Boulevard and 240 Riverside Boulevard. They would be the easiest and would allow the bugs to be worked out before tackling the difficult one.

Twenty minutes later, Rasheen left with his crew. They had two trucks and one trailer. The van driver drove along with one of the three new men. Rasheen had decided to bring the forklift as the kettles were heavy and would require lifting off the truck. Their first address would be 610 Park Ave, they headed that way.

Chapter Fourteen

Gulzar and Aram arrived at 200 Riverside Boulevard. Gulzar marked the spot where they would dig outlining the location with a can of marking paint and his tape measure. Gulzar and Aram reemphasized to all the necessity of wearing gloves fingerprints might prove to be deadly.

"We do not want to leave any fingerprints or anything else that could be traced back to any of us when they figure out what we have done," Gulzar told them.

To accommodate the barrel, they would need to dig a minimum of 762 millimeters (30-inches) deep by 1,016 millimeters (40-inches) wide ditch. He expected the pipe to be 1,200 millimeters (4 feet) deep, which would be perfect to give the barrel 500 millimeters (18 inches) of cover. The marking was going on while the equipment and one barrel were being unloaded using the backhoe. Aram gave the duty of operating the backhoe to the driver. Aram had one laborer place orange warning cones into the street to warn cars to stay away. Two of the cones had yellow blinking lights. Gulzar had one of the laborers dig a straight line around his markings using the sharp edge of the flat shovel. He had him carefully dig under the grass creating sod to put back to disguise what they had just dug up when all was finished. Gulzar worked with the laborer so he understood how the sod could be cut to be reused. The grass had to be cut leaving at least 38 millimeters of dirt underneath (1½ inch) and cut, if possible, as one solid piece. Gulzar emphasized that it had to be a solid piece so that it could not be easily detected by anyone passing by that they had disturbed the area. He hoped to put the dirt back, compact it and then lay the sod on top, rake up the area to make it look undisturbed. They counted on the fact they had proper permits which all law enforcement would have them on a list and no reason to do anything but drive by. Gulzar also knew that early the next morning the building permit would disappear from the site, he would be amazed if any police could remember the exact address, especially if it looked undisturbed.

Gulzar and Aram divided up the supervisory duties. Gulzar concentrated on the backhoe operation, directing it to dig shallow chunks and place the dirt on a tarp. He watched closely as the depth of the ditch moved closer to where he expected to find the waterline. Meanwhile, Aram was working with two of the laborers, first attaching the flange for the air vent then the 2-inch refill connection to the barrel of acid. This was slow work; he also attached a sling to the barrel that would be used to lower it into the hole. He had already installed the hot tap to the barrel.

Gulzar had the one laborer working with him climb down into the hole to probe carefully for the waterline. After 3 minutes, he found it and dug down with a shovel to fully expose it. The line was 6 inches beneath where the backhoe had dug. Gulzar had him completely expose the pipe with the shovel then dig down with post hole diggers until he was beneath it. He climbed down into the ditch, took the shovel and dug on each side until he could feel the bottom of the pipe. The pipe was a 200 millimeters (8-inch) PVC, as expected. Gulzar had Aram throw down one of the hot patch clamps that he undid before wrapping it completely around the pipe. Once it was in place, he instructed the laborer to tighten the clamp around the pipe while he attached the valve and tapping system. The system was ingenious; a drill bit went through the valve operated by a standard hand drill. The operation required two people, one to hold and operate the drill, the other to slowly tighten the tap to balance the pressure as the drill bit entered the pipe. Once the pipe was penetrated, the entire strap had to be tightened, and the tapping system removed. What was left exposed was a valve now connected to the 200 millimeters water line. Gulzar turned on the valve for a moment to make sure that water would spew out—it did. Aram handed him the pipe connection he had prepared; it was connected to the valve. The pipe had a check valve that would not allow water to flow up but only the acid to flow down. The acid would basically be sucked out of the barrel by the flow of water in the main pipe. Gulzar had his laborer fill the hole made around the pipe and then compacted it with a hammer. He made a 'bed' to place the barrel. Aram instructed the backhoe operator to pick up the barrel using the sling and maneuver it over the hole. Gulzar stayed in the ditch and manipulated the barrel over the spot he had prepared. The operator lowered the barrel until it was firmly on hard ground and level. Gulzar connected the barrel to the pipe using the flexible pipe he had just installed. He then connected the airline and the refill line. Aram measured both pipes quickly and had one of the laborers cut the pipe to the exact height. Gulzar turned on the valve allowing the acid to flow, then he turned on the valve connecting the waterline. He could hear the acid being sucked into the mainline. Gulzar crawled out, and the backhoe began to fill the ditch up. The laborers took the tamp and compacted the dirt as it was placed. Luckily, everything was over grass, and no concrete would have to be placed. When the dirt reached the top of the two pipes, now protruding slightly above the replaced ground, the laborer installed a hard-plastic grid on each, then replaced the grass, cutting a neat slot to provide for the new pipe, everything looked undisturbed when it was finished; it had taken an hour and twenty minutes to do all. The crew left and went next door to 220 Riverside Boulevard.

The crew now had experience. Gulzar hoped to improve the timing considerably. Gulzar jumped out of the truck when they pulled up at 220 Riverside Boulevard. He quickly laid out the spot to dig by painting the lines. The laborer, without being asked, took the sharp end shovel and dug the grass so it could be used as replacement sod. This process was slow, but he was getting much faster. He did make a note to have delivered an axe, it would make laying out the sod much easier. Gulzar reminded him several times to maintain the thickness and the size; the end product was what was important. The driver unloaded a barrel of acid and moved the backhoe into the correct position to dig the ditch. Aram and the others prepared and attached the pipe flanges to the barrel. It was difficult to do with gloves on but necessary. The tarp was stretched alongside the backhoe. Gulzar, as before, watched closely as the backhoe dug out the ditch. He was as slow and careful as before. When the ditch reached the level Gulzar believed was close to the pipe, he once again, had the same laborer probe for the pipe. After several attempts, he was unable to find it, finally after digging deeper, he found it nearly 600 millimeters (two feet) further down. Gulzar had the backhoe make two more passes, which took nearly a 300 (millimeters (foot) of soil off the top. The laborer again climbed into the ditch and began probing, he found the pipe approximately 200 millimeters (nine) inches below where the digging had stopped. Gulzar started to have the operator make one more pass but decided instead to dig down by hand. The laborer took the hole digger and dug down as Gulzar dug on top of the pipe with a shovel. The laborer now understood what was to be done and took the hole digger and used it as a shovel to dig under the pipe. Gulzar ran his hand up under, Aram threw him a hot patch-clamp, which he connected. The actual connection was made within minutes as each did what was required without being told. The barrel was lowered, the connection was made once Gulzar verified that the connection was done correctly. The connection to the barrel was made, the pipes were run for the air and refill, and the valves were all turned on.

The sound of the correctly flowing acid satisfied Gulzar. The ditch was refilled, tamped and the grass was replaced. Everything was reloaded and moving toward 240 Riverside Boulevard. Time: 45 minutes. As they drove to the next site, Aram raised his hands in triumph.

It was 5:15 am when they arrived at 240 Riverside Boulevard. Gulzar raised his hand to stop anyone from getting out, "The permit requires that we be out of the way of the traffic flow by 6 am. We cannot afford to be stopped by the authorities. Let's finish the last two by tomorrow." All agreed and they headed back toward the warehouse. They wondered how the other crew was doing.

Rasheen and Jamshed had arrived at 610 Park Avenue at slightly past 4 am. They first reminded everyone to wear gloves.

"Fingerprints could get us killed," Jamshed told them.

Rasheen took charge. He drove the forklift off the trailer and had the kettle unloaded using the forklift. One of the laborers began to fill the kettle using three different hose pipes connected to the water barrels. Jamshed lit the kettle and turned it as high as it would go. The kettle was efficient: it had heating elements on the bottom and sides. The testing of the kettle they had done previously back in Iran confirmed it would bring the water to a boil in 15 minutes. The forklift offloaded the cement mixer which was gas operated. Rasheen checked to be sure that all the safety cones were in place before he took the lid off the manhole. They were all correctly placed. Jamshed measured the correct amount of gelatin and other ingredients after getting a measurement from the bottom of the manhole to 300 millimeters (one foot) above the pipe through which sewage flowed into the manhole. Gulzar had made them a table that would quickly tell them the quantities needed of each depending on the depth of the manhole. Jamshed had only needed to refer to the table to pull together what was needed. He smiled as he did so: Gulzar was a damn genius. The laborers would have to dip the water from the kettle using 3-gallon buckets. Jamshed motioned for them to start the process. He poured the gelatin mixture into the mixer, which was now turning. He constantly warned them that the water was hot and to be careful. The mixer had a handle that could be tilted to let whatever was being mixed pour out.

Rasheen took the plywood contraption and covered up the outgoing pipe as the mixture was being poured into the manhole. Jamshed quickly poured the correct quantity of dry ice into the manhole. The dry ice would cause the gelatin to set very fast and set hard and firm. It started to firm up but much had already flowed out of the manhole down the open drain, Rasheen quickly told one of the laborers to grab the red bottle and spray the carbon dioxide down the manhole onto the gelatin as it hit the bottom. The gelatin turned into solid ice and stopped the outgoing flow. Once the flow was stopped, the mixture did its job, as expected. Rasheen had moved the plywood to stop any incoming flow before they started. He needed both of the pieces of lumber to stop the inward flow. He knew now he would need another set to stop the outgoing. He and one of the laborers held the plywood in place as the next batch was being completed. Seven minutes later, the second batch was poured into the hole. It did not make it above the incoming pipe, dry ice was added, and a third batch was being made. Rasheen held the incoming sewage firm, holding the lumber which held the plywood was difficult, the sewage had pressure once it began to try to back up, every muscle in his body was aching. The third batch was poured, and dry ice added. Rasheen held on for another five minutes then slowly lifted the plywood out of the manhole. It held. Rasheen was thoroughly exhausted. It was 5:30. None of them thought it could be done any faster. They decided it was just too risky to do another and headed back to the warehouse.

Both crews arrived back to the warehouse within 15 minutes of each other. Rasheen was satisfied with what they had accomplished for the day. They gave Aftab the update, who was pleased with the progress. They also, at Aftab's suggestion recruited one more crew to kill the landscaping at the addresses. Aftab believed it would be more difficult once problems were encountered by Donald Trump.

The crew was already in the United States, getting ready to spray the poison that would make the patrons of Trump's restaurant sick. They would spray the fresh fruits and vegetables being delivered to various Trump restaurants in Florida.

Aftab had not told them, as they did not need to know, that the operation in Trump's restaurants was being carried out simultaneously and would be effective probably by the next day. He believed many would be sick as more than 200 guests had eaten a meal there.

After the call to Aram, Rasheen gathered all, including the two drivers and the 6 laborers. He wanted to discuss how they could improve, if possible, before tonight's work started, "I know of two things we need to do. One is, can we install a pipe with a valve to the kettle. It is slow and dangerous to dip out the boiling water and we need another setup with plywood. It is obvious to me that we will need to block the outlet pipe for each until the gelatin sets up."

Gulzar walked over to look at the kettle. "It will be much safer to pump the water out. There are too many heating elements around and at the bottom of the kettle to penetrate it in anyway. We should get a battery-operated pump and buy whatever fittings we need to get the water to the mixer."

"Yes," said Rasheen. "And someone can pick up the materials we need for one more plywood setup."

"We should install the fittings to the acid barrels here. It is difficult to do that properly in the dark," said Aram.

They installed the fittings to the acid barrels at lunch and got some well- needed sleep. They would be ready for the evening. The new plywood, flanges, wood studs, axe and pump were already on their way.

Chapter Fifteen

Iran's deception had reached a new level. They were now using trained actors who practiced their lines in a location safe and secure from American surveillance. The latest was a scenario where the Guatemala government was allowing them to use an abandoned manufacturing facility to make drones with an eight-foot wingspan, capable of carrying 300 kilograms of explosives for up to 500 kilometers. According to the ongoing chatter since the last week, the planners of the drone attacks would be meeting in Guatemala soon.

"General, we have made a lot of progress in constructing our new drones," said actor number 1.

Of course, no General was there.

"The last report I had was that you were searching for a site, as close to the American border as was possible," said actor 2.

"We decided that Guatemala was the safest location. Even though it is 4,000 kilometers to the west coast of the United States, we can fly the drones that distance safely in less than a week or even transport by truck. The Americans are certainly not looking for drones being flown or transported in Mexico. As you know, the Guatemalans hate Trump as much as we do. So, they have been a big help."

"How much explosive can the drones carry?"

"Each up to 300 kilograms. Our engineers chose that weight because the North Koreans assured us, they will have a nuclear device for us soon which would weigh less."

"Also, we can fly to Nicaragua and onto Belize and then to Cuba. If we do so with no explosives on board, Cuba has agreed to rearm when they arrive. From Cuba, we can bring them to the Eastern part of the United States where we can do whatever we wish whenever we want."

"Get me some projected production figures. How soon can you to that?"

"It may take a couple of weeks to give you accurate information. So far, we have produced three, and armed them with conventional explosives. They are in a good hiding place in Texas right now. It was very easy to get them across the border. They can fly at just a few feet off the ground. We flew them just off the water, over Galveston and then into Houston. Most of the refining ability is located near Houston. We will destroy that ability first, as it will do the most damage to the American economy. The next ten or so we produce, we will move them to that general location."

"Are the explosive traceable to us?"

"That is the part of the greatness of this. We bought the materials to make the bombs from the United States. It will be considered an attack from within when we drop the first one. It will keep us safe until the next!"

The CIA operative scheduled to brief the President that day was upset. He, as well as other senior analysts, were aware that this recording had been staged for them to intercept, but the President would not accept this and would react as if this was all true. What would they do? Bomb Guatemala, Mexico, Cuba, Nicaragua and Belize. He also had to report to the President about this 8-foot wingspan drone capable of hauling such weight.

Trump, as expected, went nuts when he was given the briefing!

"I want you to prepare to give this briefing to the senate and house intelligence committee. My own cabinet is convinced this is a setup. You must give them this briefing and convince them this is true!"

"I cannot do that, sir. All our intelligence concludes this was staged for us to overhear. I will have to also tell the congress that!"

Trump's tablet bore his brunt again as he threw it across the floor in rage. "Then I will get my own fucking people to do it! Just get the fuck out of here!"

Trump then called his Deputy National Security Advisor. "Did you get the latest Iranian information on the planned drone attack?

"Yes sir, I did."

"Did you believe it?" "Yes sir, I did."

"Then contact the senate and house intelligence committee. I want you to go tell them that!"

"I will but I must run this by my boss!" "Just keep it between us!"

"Sir, I can't. He has to approve!"

Trump, knowing he would not agree, slammed his fist on the table. "Fuck it, just let them bomb the shit out of us!"

Trump did not stop there. He contacted the Chairman of the Joint Chiefs and ordered him to find the manufacturing plant in Guatemala and destroy it. The General shook his head quietly to himself and ordered special satellite coverage of the area, knowing there was nothing there.

****

Aftab had arranged for five of the Iranian operatives stationed in the United States to contaminate the fruits and vegetables being delivered to restaurants in the area around Miami first and then the others all over the United States. Other than Miami he wanted the poison to be put on the deliveries in New York, Chicago and Los Angeles. His hackers had supplied them with the name and addresses of suppliers and the probable time and dates of delivery. The Trump International Resort in Miami was the first on the list of the suppliers that was scheduled to deliver that very afternoon. Aftab had two of his men, Roshan Moosavi and Shazad Zafar, clothed in the resort's staff uniform and armed with spray bottles hidden in plain sight, all were disguised as cleaning compound, containing the contamination E-coli agent, ready and waiting. It was a simple plan but risky. Like many scheduled deliveries of produce the time period was a several hour window. The two waiting on the delivery had a difficult time hiding while expecting the delivery at any moment, at one point they had to drive away since sitting in the car was drawing attention to them. They pulled the car out of sight of the rear delivery dock but kept the ability to see when the truck entered the area. They did not pull back up to where they could be seen but around the corner. Roshan and Shazad were both United states citizens whose parents had immigrated here well before they were born. The United States mistreatment of Iran made it easy for Iran to recruit them, both had grandparents and other family members who were suffering. Roshan and Shazad having been raised in the area, could easily blend with any of the others who were employed by the hotels. The two got out and mingled with the others until they could safely jump into the truck and spray the produce.

When the delivery truck pulled up, the backdoor was opened. Roshan ask the van driver.

"Can you get fresh broccoli" knowing the season for growing locally had passed.

The driver responded "we can order from California, but we cannot get locally. Do you want me to order?".

"Not yet. We prefer to serve local grown."

As they talked, Shazad jumped onto the back of the truck and sprayed all vegetables and fruits ready to be offloaded. It was over in 45 seconds. The van operator never saw him enter or exit the back of the van.

Both quickly left as the driver began to take the produce inside and headed toward Trump Tower Sunny Isles. The other two Iranians recruited by Aftab were already at the Doral Golf Club, which was also scheduled for delivery today. The Sunny Isles, they hoped, had not received its delivery already. They had the Sunny Isle staff uniform in the car and drove toward the destination. They were lucky as that delivery was also late.

The delivery for the Doral arrived later in the day. The two were ready. The driver opened his back door and walked inside. One took the opportunity, jumped inside and thirty seconds later, he was done. The second Iranian simply watched from outside the truck to be prepared to delay anyone who might be within eyesight of the rear truck entrance.

At Sunny Isles, they were in luck. The truck delivering the fruits and vegetables pulled in at the same time as they. Roshan and Shazad already had on their Sunny Isles dress and quickly blended with the others around. A restaurant supervisor wanted to go over the order before they offloaded because there was a small change he needed to make. As soon as the back door of the truck was opened, Roshan jumped on and did the job, Shazad made sure the back door to the restaurant was fully closed as Roshan jumped onto the truck and sprayed, he now could spray so fast, there was little chance of the supervisor returning before he could finish.

They all wanted to finish Mar-a-Lago, but it was not scheduled for delivery for another two days. Trump Hollywood was on the same schedule as Mar- a-Lago so they would get both together. Roshan and Shazad headed toward Jupiter Florida, which was scheduled for the next day. The other two drove toward Washington DC to the Trump International Washington. It would be an all-night drive; the delivery was scheduled for 2 PM the next day.

The rest of the week and the next four would be busy. Deliveries were scheduled all over the country. There was going to be a lot of people sick in the next few days. Aftab had instructed his computer hackers to get the names, addresses and any other information he could from the hotel registration, or the credit card charges. He also had names and addresses of shyster lawyers in the area who may want to take on these cases against Trump for what would look like food poisoning. They also were able to correlate emergency room treatments with the names. As a convenience, he was preparing the correlated list to be sent to all local newspapers, he felt the people needed to know Trump's restaurants could make you sick if you chose to eat there!

The golf group began work in Scotland. Scotland would be the easiest access and the locals detested Trump's invasion of their area. Also, the courses in Scotland and Ireland had fewer trees but a lot of landscape. They would be much easier to deal with.

The group arrived first in Aberdeen Scotland. There was no security detectable. They scheduled the visit on a moonless night, parked nearly a mile away and walked in through the rear of the course. The course used a type of fertilizer adapter that had to be filled with a liquid. One member of the group cut the line and installed a different one fifteen meters away from the old. The old was left in place. The new one would work much better with the grass killer as it had a greater capacity. It was difficult but a horseshoe type configuration was installed which penetrated the water. It could not be seen as the water had lots of plant life and, thus, was completely hidden. They also replaced the liquid fertilizer used normally by the club with the grass killer. The grass would get a double treatment. Another person had 3-gallon sprayers of plant killer and went across the course spraying all the landscaping. It took three hours. They left and headed to Turnberry roughly 3 hours away. They found a similar landscape and also parked a mile away but this time, unloaded most of the gear much closer. The connections for feeding the fertilizer were the same but the water was clear. They, without hesitation, dug a ditch underneath the line after coming out of the watering pond. The installation of a larger feeder was installed directly on the line, filled and then covered up; the existing feeder was also filled. The members responsible for killing the landscape did not have much of a job. Most of the landscaping was around the hotel and pool area; some on the course but not much. The last course in the area was in Doonbeg Ireland. It was over an 8-hour drive, so it would have to wait until the next night.

The two responsible for spraying the fresh fruits and vegetables with the E coli mixture arrived in Washington DC at 10 the next morning, exhausted but capable. They checked into a hotel near the Trump International Washington Hotel and decided that sleep was important. They each set alarms on their cell phones and collapsed from exhaustion; it was 9:30 AM. The delivery was scheduled for 2 PM. They had the suitable clothing ready; the planners were thorough.

Roshan and Shazad, the two members left in Florida were happy. They even started singing, it would be so nice if Trump himself happened to come down and eat at his fine restaurant after they properly treated the produce! Mar-a-Lago, the prime target, would be handled today. The delivery was scheduled for 10 AM, they would be dressed and waiting. The Hollywood address, to be done after Mar – a -Lago, was scheduled for 4 in the afternoon; it would be a good day. The truck arrived as scheduled, but there was some security in place. It was possible that Trump was visiting, and this was a precaution. The team would have to be careful. Both merged with the other staff and pretended to trim some of the loose edges of the landscape. They grabbed some trimmers when they saw the security. The guards paid no attention to them as they worked their way toward the delivery truck. The guard inspected the contents when the driver opened the back door; Roshan grabbed a clipboard and jumped on the back when the guard exited. The guard never even blinked an eye. Roshan sprayed the vegetables and fruit set to be delivered as fast as he could, signed the sheet on the clipboard and handed it to a passing Mar-a-Lago employee. Shazad continued to pretend to trim the bushes, watching closely for any chance Roshan could be discovered. They both, when finished spraying, walked a long distance away, then turned and headed back toward their car. Both giggled as they drove away. Long ago, they had learned when hiding in plain sight, do what is expected and you will not be noticed. The next stop was Trump Hollywood, which should be a breeze, they thought. It was.

The others had woken and prepared to take care of the Washington Hotel. They had brunch and walked toward the hotel. The loading dock was in the rear; it was now 1:30 PM so 30 minutes until the delivery truck arrived. They walked up the steps to the dock area after slipping on the proper clothing over what they had on. No one paid any attention to them. Ten minutes later, the truck arrived. They simply stood there as if they were the ones designated to unload, there was a risk since the deliveries where normal new faces might draw attention to them. They watched the drivers face as he got out, there was no concern, on his face, so they just stood there. The driver got out of his truck, opened the rear door and went inside as he had done dozens of times before. The two jumped in, sprayed and walked away, pulling off the extra clothing as they did so. The regular hotel staff walked pass them several times but acted as if they were not there, most thought they were above any new people and just ignored them. There was one left in that area: The Trump Riverview golf club. It was scheduled for delivery in two days. They would have time to rest.

The golf group arrived at Doonbeg Ireland and waited until dark before heading to the club. As with the others golf areas, unlike the hotel portions, no security was evident. There was virtually no landscaping, so it would go quick. The pond water, again, was clear, and a ditch needed to be dug. They did not hesitate and began digging as they walked up to the water's edge. In less than an hour, the grass killer was installed. The little landscaping that existed was destroyed, and they headed off. This group would handle the courses in Turkey and the UAE before heading home. Meanwhile, a separate group arrived in Indonesia, and two others were just getting started in the United States.

Chapter Sixteen

By 10 AM the morning after Iran had struck, the Trump organization was in panic. One of their prime properties, 610 Park Avenue, was flooded with sewage. The building housed multi-million-dollar units, some bought for as much as 6 million dollars. Many of these units on the lowest floors were now filled with sewage. On the upper floors, the smell was unbearable. Four lawsuits had already been filed against the Trump Organization, and it had only been two hours since it started. There were many photographers and lawyers, some in rubber boots, walking around inside the lobby. Donald Trump Jr. was in charge, and he quickly blamed the management company. The news media was already aware and had crews on site. The maintenance staff called in a plumbing company that had, thus far, not been able to find the cause. The regular maintenance person got permission to drain directly into the manhole from the outside connection valve from the city. There was an emergency outlet on the outside of the building. This outlet allowed a 6-inch flexible hose to attach to a valve and, when turned on, would drain sewage directly from the building to the outside. When the valve was turned on, sewage began draining directly into the manhole. A different company was called in who also opened the main sewage manhole which now had a line running into it from the building and saw that nothing was draining into it from the regular line. This meant that the stoppage must be in the building or between the building and the manhole. Large sewage 'snakes' were brought in, beginning inside the building. They pushed it down the pipe. It reached its limit and, still, nothing flowed. The company finally took the 'snake' to the end and came back toward the building. They had brought in a type with a cleaning contraption that literally drilled through the stoppage when it was 75 feet or so down the pipe. The sewage began to flow directly into the manhole from the main pipe. The scene was unbelievable. There was a million plus dollar condominium unlivable because of the smell. The owners were beyond upset, blaming Trump for a cheap sewage design that had to be the cause. Experts were on the airways giving opinions regarding what could have caused such a disaster. Trump, on the phone with Donald Jr., ordered him to fire the maintenance supervisor as he had to be the one ultimately at fault. He also ordered him to sue the property managers.

Aftab jumped with joy as he heard the news. Trump was about to have many bad days!

Slightly after midnight, the two responsible for stopping up the sewage and eroding the metal parts were packed and ready to go. Excitement filled the air as they heard of the success from the night before. Tomorrow would not be a good day for Trump. They watched the 'experts' on television and laughed as they discussed their theories about the causes.

Now the schedule called for tackling the White Plains and 200 East 69th Street. Rasheen and Jamshed pulled out first. Traffic was still heavy, so they headed toward White Plains, 30 minutes away, believing it would be less congested. They were right. 10 City Plaza was completely empty. They pulled as near to the manhole cover as they could. Jamshed quickly grabbed one of the laborers and established the safety barriers around them. The driver drove the forklift off the truck after dropping the two loading ramps. The forklift lifted the heating kettle from the rear of the truck, followed by the concrete mixer. Rasheen lit the furnace as two of the laborers filled it from the drums of water. Jamshed took the tool to lift the cover of the manhole, then measured the depth needed to stop the flow; it was 1.7 meters. Rasheen referred to the chart Gulzar had prepared and gave the quantities to the laborer who would do the mixing. The laborer took the correct quantity of gelatin and poured it into the mixer. Rasheen configured the pump to the kettle and watched as the water reached boiling temperature. The pump took less than a minute to prime and begin pumping water into the mixer which already started turning as the water went in. It would take three batches to fill the manhole to the elevation needed. One of the laborers began to add more water to the kettle as the water inside was boiling heavily. Two of the other laborers grabbed each one of the plywood contraptions and held one to the exit and one to the incoming sewage entrance. The third tilted the mixer to pour the contents into the manhole. Rasheen poured the correct quantity of dry ice and Ethylene Glycol into the mixer just before the contents were poured. As soon as the mixer was empty, the process was repeated. The third and last batch was ready 4 minutes later. The laborer was able to remove the outlet plywood as the first batch had hardened. It took 5 minutes for all to get hard, the kettle and mixer was reloaded, the second plywood contraption was removed put on the truck as the forklift was driven back on. The manhole cover was put securely back on. All this was over in 27 minutes, the crew headed toward 200 East 69th Street.

Gulzar and Aram returned to 240 Riverside and went to work. Gulzar laid out where they were to dig as Aram put up the correct safety guards around the work. The driver unloaded the backhoe and one of the acid drums as one laborer dug around and saved all the grass over the digging area. The backhoe moved into place and carefully excavated down to the waterline taking only 150 millimeters (6 inch) cuts for each pass. As he had before but now much more efficient, when he reached a certain depth using the backhoe, Gulzar probed to find the line then directed the operator as the line was uncovered. Gulzar had one of the laborers dig around and beneath the pipe so the hot tap strap could be installed. Once the tap was installed, a laborer created a seat for the drum which was then lowered and connected to the new valve connected to the tap. All the connections were already installed, so all that had to be done was cut the pipe to the proper length and connect using standard PVC connections and glue. The ease and flow at which this was being done amazed Gulzar. These guys had become professionals in just a day. Now, he intended for them to travel around the country and do this to all Trump properties. The crew being used were all US citizens but agents of Iran, they had no travel restrictions and were not on anybody's radar to be watched. The ditch was covered up, tamped properly and the grass was replaced. Time: 32 minutes. They reloaded all the equipment, put back the grass and headed toward 502 Park Avenue.

Rasheen and Jamshed arrived at 200 East 69th Street. The traffic was slow, but vehicles were passing by the address. They again pulled the truck as close as possible to the manhole and put the safety items out, this time further away, and added two blinking warning lights. They wanted to make sure that all vehicles stayed well clear of their work. All was unloaded as before; the kettle was still hot as it was still half-filled with water. The furnace was lit while Rasheen opened then measured the depth of the manhole. This one was deeper and would take 4 mixers to do the job. The flow of sewage which was very little was stopped using the plywood. All were measured and the mixer started 3 minutes later when the water was hot enough for the pump to start. It flowed water into the mixer until full. Rasheen gave it one more minute then added the other ingredients. The batch was emptied into the manhole. As soon as the mixer was upright, more gelatin was added. The mixer was not even turned off as water began to be pumped. The kettle was almost full again with boiling water. As the mixer filled up with the boiling water, Rasheen added the other ingredients which were then poured into the manhole. This process was repeated two more times; they were now very efficient. The equipment was all reloaded as the gelatin set up. The outlet plywood was pulled and the inflow plywood 5 minutes later. The cover was reinstalled. No pedestrian's coming by, including a police cruiser, even slowed down to wonder what they were doing.

Gulzar and Aram arrived at 502 Park Avenue. This would be much more difficult. The traffic had a steady flow, and the drum would be partially underneath a concrete sidewalk. As the equipment was unloaded and the safety items were installed, Gulzar carefully measured the minimum needed for the ditch. They also had added more precautionary blinking lights due to the traffic. No matter how it appeared to him, it seemed like they would have to cut and replace part of the sidewalk. One of the laborers came up with a tape measure and marked the drum at an angle over the pipe. He told Gulzar that he believed they could get it in that way without disturbing the sidewalk.

Gulzar looked at him for a moment, then slapped him on the back. "Son of a bitch, I think you are right. We can do it that way!"

The laborer grinned. The backhoe would be of little use but the procedure for saving the grass and the ditch was started. The backhoe could dig only a small depth before it all turned into handwork. The laborers dug feverishly putting all the dirt on tarps spread out over the sidewalk as Gulzar supervised. When they reached the pipe, Gulzar crawled into the ditch, took the shovel and dug measuring every few inches until he was sure the drum would fit, and the hot patch could be done. Once the hot patch was in place and connected to the main waterline, the backhoe lifted the drum and maneuvered it into place. The connections were made, the ditch covered up, the grass replaced. It took an hour and 55 minutes: handwork was slow.

The two crews met back at the warehouse at 5:20 AM. They were all overjoyed at what they had been able to accomplish but disappointed that they did not have the materials to get more done. They hoped they could get more acid, gelatin dry ice and Ethylene Glycol tomorrow but were unsure.

They tried to contact Aftab but were unable to his cell phone was going straight to voicemail, they assumed it was turned off. Aftab, it seemed, was busy killing Mr. Trump's grass and did not want his phone ringing!

The landscape crew was now on board and were busy going from address to address spraying the landscaping and grass. The crew was made up of three people, one driver and two sprayers. The truck would pull up, the two would get out and immediately begin spraying. They decided any trees would be done on a separate trip.

The next morning was really bad for the Trumps. Hospitals in the Miami area and West Palm Beach had 43 patients admitted overnight, whose common denominator was that they had eaten at a Trump restaurant the night before. Doctors were calling the health department, as they had at least another 25 who may or may not require admittance. The health department moved swiftly and closed all restaurants operated by the Trump organization. To make matters worse, 17 people in the Washington DC area were also admitted. The health department closed the restaurant there as well.

The two who had dealt the blow to the Washington hotel were already at the Trump Riverview golf club, waiting for the delivery. When it came, the procedure was a piece of cake. The driver opened the door and was yelled at by one of the cooks for being 15 minutes late. The two who did the handiwork was on their way within 10 minutes as the driver had left the door open to go inside and be yelled at.

Lawsuits regarding the food now exceeded 75, in just one day. The media estimated that 1,000 people had eaten at these places.

The Trumps, Trump Jr., Eric and Ivanka felt like this was a covert attack on their father and the government should take over to do an investigation. Trump agreed and ordered the secret service to do so. He was quickly informed that they had no jurisdiction and could not. Trump or any member of his family was not under any threat. Trump fired the head of the secret service and called the Attorney General, who also informed him that they could not and if they thought it was a criminal act, the local authorities should be brought in. Trump Jr. called the New York City Police, who said that he could come in and file a complaint. They were not as sympathetic because the Trumps had screwed over so many people that the list of suspects would be never-ending.

Eric contacted the Miami and West Palm Beach police who also had little interest in pursuing what they believed was just bad food served to save money.

The restaurants were Ivanka's responsibility, but she was at a loss as to what could have caused it.

Virtually no new reservations were made that day in any Trump property and nearly all existing customers had checked out. 'Simply a bad day; was not even close to describing what was happening to the Trumps!

Aftab finally contacted Rasheen and Gulzar on their throwaway cell phones. "What's up? How are you doing? I heard good things on the news!"

"We have all gotten rather good at what we are doing. We want to do more, but we need more supplies. Can you get us resupplied?"

"Damn that is really good news. How much do you need?"

"There are at least 10 more properties each of us can hit here in the New York area. We want to do them all and then have the crew who can replace the four of us with people who can move freely. The 240-kilometer limit placed on our people by the United States creates problems when the properties are outside that range. Bring them on now so we can train them. These guys we have are good. It will go well."

"I am sure I can find the people and will see how long it will take to resupply. In the meantime, rest. You deserve it."

The head of the local delegation came to the hotel where all four were staying. He wanted them to come to the UN, fool around in the offices, be seen by the Americans, go to dinner, go to night clubs and enable the Americans to have the information they can report. Being invisible was not good. The Americans needed to know they were still here and working near the UN building. The Americans constantly kept a close watch on the entire Iranian delegation.

All four laughed but nodded their heads in agreement.

Chapter Seventeen

Later the same morning, the Trumps were faced with yet another disaster. Two more properties had sewage overflows, leaving no doubt that they were being attacked. More lawsuits were filed, and those from the previous day's sewage issues piled on. They were convinced someone was putting something into the system from inside the buildings. The first sewage overflow for that day was reported at 10 City Plaza. In White Plains, all were luxury condominiums, and sewage was running out onto the streets. The News media was everywhere; the smell was unbearable. None of the Trumps even bothered to show up. Shortly after the news about the White Plains property, sewage was now overflowing at the Trump property at 200 East 69th Street. News networks were having 'Breaking News' alerts with the discovery of two more properties. It was a nightmare. The upper floors had no problem initially. Customers got up, took their showers, flushed the toilets and did the normal things people do when they first get out of bed. But as all that sewage had nowhere to go, it quickly backed up floor by floor, spurting out of the sinks and bathtubs and then overflowing in on the lower floors. The whole city was getting into the act. White Plains and New York City filed injunctions for Trump to pay fines and clean up the mess his properties had caused. The Trumps were getting no sympathy from anyone, anywhere in the world.

Iran anticipated Trump would be forced to hire some form of cleanup crews to remove any carpet and steam clean all other surfaces. Aftab had recruited and had supervisors on standby to become part of the cleanup crew. The companies who do such work hire lots of temporary workers and have experienced supervision and equipment. Aftab had obtained uniforms of the two largest companies who do this kind of work. Iran had discovered two substances which were originally made for military use that would attach themselves to concrete, tile and other hard nonporous surfaces, also carpet and drapery. Both were clear and had horrible odors after curing which took a few days. Once sprayed on a surface, it would be nearly impossible to remove as the chemical soaked into concrete, tile and even sheetrock, the carpet and drapery would have to be replaced. The only known way of removing the terrible odor was to encapsulate it by painting or spraying over. A clear coating such as varnish which would cover the odor and eliminate the smell. However, this would not be permanent because as the varnish aged and deteriorated, the smell would return. One of the Iranians also had come up with an idea which Aftab approved. He wanted each to have thermos type bottle attached to a holder. The bottles would be filled with fish guts, shrimp pieces and other fish type items. They would put a small amount in any pot, crevice or other opening they found. With the other smells, this would be difficult to locate.

Trump, once the first lawsuit was received, contracted with such a company as anticipated for cleanup. This action, according to the attorneys, would prove they were trying to do the right thing. Aftab's team was ready. They knew from their hack on the computer systems that contracts had been awarded and when they would get started. They did not bother to have Aftab's people get hired by the company, which was the original plan, they just showed up as the work was being completed. The Iranian hired crew, which comprised of three men, came to the site, dressed in the proper company uniform, and unloaded their sprayers; they had two to a person. Each sprayer contained different chemicals. They walked through the building, pretended to inspect the work and sprayed on the surface floors and walls with the chemicals. The spray was more of a mist that covered the surface like a fog. The smell was not immediate. The chemical, once completely cured, which took slightly more than three days depending on the weather, would only then begin to smell. They also had the thermos bottles and looked for anywhere they could place the mixture.

Once they completed on the ground floor where all of the work was taking place, they did not stop but moved to the second floor and began spraying the walls, drapery and carpet. They were very fast and took no more than eight minutes to do a complete floor. They made it all the way to the sixth floor before running out of chemical. They moved back to the ground, eased out of the building, entered their autos and left the area. They did contact the Iranians to have more chemical available for the next. All three were very pleased to damage Trump!

The three stood by until the computer hackers could tell them where to go next. Later that evening, they were given another address and prepared to be there the next afternoon, they had the uniforms required ready, they were supplied with more of the chemical. Several more addresses were given to them later in the evening. They may need more people but would have to wait and see. Trump was trying to negotiate the best deal, which meant the company handling the cleanup in the New York City area would move from place to place but could only handle one a day.

In the other areas, including Florida, separate crews were put to work. A team in Indonesia, India and the Philippines were also created. They would each wait until the cleaning crews were nearly complete before moving in, the crews assumed they were just part of their own workers and paid them no mind.

The locations in Scotland and Ireland had a separate team.

The crews sent to Indonesia had arrived and were prepared to attack the two golf courses which were a great distance apart. They then would plant the acid and stop up the sewage. Aftab had informed them to wait before putting any poison on the foods as the information they were getting from the hacked data was that food sales were near zero everywhere. People were simply afraid to eat at any Trump-operated restaurant.

The course at Lido City. Indonesia was first; it had a large amount of landscaping and palm trees. They needed that training and practice before attacking the Florida courses to include Mar a Lago, the prize Trump property. Even though it would be different people in Florida the Palm trees were similar. Six members of the team went to the golf course. They were going in with a partial moon, which was dangerous, but they had detected no security around the course as had been normal. They had been briefed by the group who had covered Scotland and dropped their gear close to the course but parked a good distance away. Three of the six went straight to the palm trees. The first man drilled six holes around the root with a 12-inch 2-centimeter auger type bit, the next did the same around the tree several feet high but using a 1.25-centimeter inch bit. The third man poured muriatic acid into the holes on the ground and a special poison into the holes drilled directly into the trees. The team continued on to the next tree, becoming more efficient as they proceeded. They had disposable cell phones and one man was assigned as a lookout, he positioned himself so that he was able to see if anyone came onto the property to warn them.

A second team was working on killing the grass. Although they had found that the system used to fertilize was different for each course, the purpose was the same, as it essentially operated the same way. They had also decided that it was more efficient and more likely to work if they simply dug a small trench and attached it to an underground pipe feeding the sprinkler system.

The ones assigned to kill the grass was much faster than the tree and landscape crew, as the trees were slow and tedious to kill. When they finished, they joined the other team. They were assigned the landscape and were given pump type sprayers to spray a bush killer solution on all plants. The group finished at 5:07 AM. Their next target was to install an acid drum connecting it to the water supply. If possible, they would also stop up the sewage flow. This effort would be much more difficult as the hotel was on a septic type system that flowed further and then treated the solid waste. This would be done after dark. They all left and got some much-needed sleep.

They left again slightly past midnight to return to the hotel and Golf Club Indonesians are not known for staying up late and the entire area was empty of any people or vehicles when they arrived at 12:40 AM. The team had never actually done this before but had been trained by Gulzar who had flown over just to train them in both installing the acid and making the solution of gelatin and show them how to use it to stop the sewage flow.

The group had a truck, trailer, backhoe and all the pipe and fittings that may be required. Gulzar had taught them to go ahead and install the air vent pipe and refill to the drums before loading it on the truck. After he had arranged for the water line to be marked, Alzar, the lead man, intended to plant a large tree and wanted to be sure it did not penetrate the pipe. He laid out the spot where the backhoe would dig. It knew the line would not be very deep as freezing was not a consideration in such mild climate. He located the line within minutes then moved the backhoe over a few feet to dig a spot for the drum which would be only slightly higher than the main water pipe. He instructed one of the men to dig under the line sufficient to attach the hot tap strap. The strap was attached, then the valve, which was later connected to the line leading to the drum of acid. The pipes were cut to the correct elevation and covered up. All was just on soil with a straw type covering. They left after 40 minutes to retrieve the tools and supplies required to stop up the sewage. They had to lay the drum on its side to get it hidden and where the acid would flow.

The team needed a roofing kettle, a cement mixer, plywood to stop the sewage flow, gelatin, dry ice and Ethylene Glycol and four fifty-gallon drums of water. The team arrived back at the hotel at 2:30 AM. They had located what they believed was a manhole the day before which was in the rear of the hotel 40 meters away. They decided to use the backhoe to load and unload. The backhoe was unloaded. It picked up the kettle, which was then lit, and water was poured into it. Alzar opened the top to what he hoped was a manhole. It was a type of manhole except modified for this type septic system. The system essentially separated the liquids from the solids and sent the liquids to a field where it was equally dispersed and drawn into the ground. The design was similar in that the raw sewage dropped into the cylinder, roughly one meter in diameter, and then flowed into a separate tank that had a pump and sent it to a treatment facility. When the kettle heated the water to a boil, it was then dipped with a bucket and poured into the mixer, it was dangerous as the water was boiling. They could not locate a pump, the ingredients were added and poured into the cylinder. There was no sewage flow since nobody was up. Alzar decided to reduce the dry ice which was to compensate for the absence of the sewage flow. He believed people would be waking up around 5:30, which should give a good firmness, until around 8 AM, and stop the sewage before the gelatin began to disappear and turn back to a liquid.

By 9 the next morning, the lobby was filled with sewage. The management had no choice but to evacuate the hotel.

The team went to bed and prepared to attack the other property close by the next night. It had no golf course and only housed residences. They installed the acid that night and stopped up an identical sewage system. By 8 AM, they were on their way to Bali.

Bali had a golf course and a hotel with residences. They were concerned that security would be high; it was, but not as high and difficult as it could have been. Guards checked every person entering the hotel or residences. The conjecture by Trump was that somehow a person was getting into the properties and putting something in the sewage system. He had yet to incur any problems from the acid or the grass or landscaping on the golf course. Both would be a major issue for him soon! As such, he had not made any preparations for halting the acid or protecting his grass and landscaping.

The team repeated what they had done in Lido City, Indonesia, installing solutions that would kill the grass and the trees. They also installed the acid and stopped up the sewage. It was a great four days. Aftab had considered ordering them to poison the food in more restaurants but realized no one with any sense would eat at a Trump restaurant.

The team was transferred to India where Trump owned four properties but no golf courses. The properties were in Pune, Mumbai, Kolkata and Delhi. Except for Pune and Mumbai, the properties were a great distance apart. The distances meant it would take at least a week to get them done. The locations were all in large cities. Kolkata was the smallest, a city of five million. The others ranged from Mumbai, twenty million, to Pune, six million. So, the equipment and supplies needed were plentiful in all locations. The large populations also meant obscurity was much easier.

The plan was to start in Mumbai, rent all the equipment and buy the needed supplies. Most of it had already been bought and temporarily stored in a warehouse. The major equipment had already been rented and stored in the same warehouse. The team, which consisted of 8 people, arrived early in the morning after an all-night flight from Indonesia. They obtained two rental cars and scouted out the property in Mumbai and then drove to Pune, which took nearly three hours. For both properties, the sewage and water lines had already been located. The water line was painted blue, and the sewage manholes had a red 'X' on the cover. The team needed rest and, after inspecting the supplies, they rested for 4 hours. Shortly after midnight, they left for the first property.

The traffic was light. They arrived in twenty minutes, created a boundary around the work area for the waterline and a separate one for the sewer. The ability to stop up the sewer lines is a major challenge. Much of India is plagued with difficult to operate treatment centers and the flow of sewage is often hampered by electrical issues. The system at this location flows in two different directions; the first is the water, it flows toward a system that is primarily treated by holding the water in a large lagoon and letting it settle to catch solids which may still be included. It then flows to yet another lagoon where it is sprayed in the air to rid it of most bacteria, finally it goes to a treatment facility which is not much more than a heavy dose of chlorine. The solids flow to a holding pit where they are later pumped to a special dryer where they are bombarded with high heat to remove the bacteria, from there they are trucked and used as a fertilizer. This system means a separation when falling into the manhole and just filling the manhole with gelatin will not do it. Gulzar had figured he must add a high amount of dry ice coupled with shooting carbon dioxide into the manhole to freeze whatever is in process before stopping up the incoming line. The crew had two trucks, one carrying a backhoe and the other the equipment for the acid drum connection and for the sewage. Once offloaded, the backhoe was moved to the second truck and the drums of water, dry ice, gelatin mix, two canisters of carbon dioxide and cement mixer were unloaded, while the waterline was marked for the backhoe to dig. The crew poured dry ice down the manhole and at the same time began to shoot the carbon dioxide as fast as they could. The crew hoped it would freeze solid all that was at the bottom, stopping up both exit lines. The crew also poured cold water as the dry ice was being put down. The backhoe returned and offloaded the drum of acid. The lines had already been installed before the drum was loaded. The operator carefully dug down to the location of the line. As before, one of the men then dug under the line and created a pocket for the drum of acid. The hot tap was installed, and the drum was lowered into the hole. A separate team member connected the hot tap to the drum while another member measured the air connector and the refill line. Forty minutes later, the hole was refilled, cleaned and raked, and acid was flowing into the building.

The sewer team was now moving well. The manhole was not as deep as the one in Indonesia, so the quantity of gelatin was much less, the bottom had frozen solid which gave a base for the gelatin to sit on. Ten minutes after the acid crew completed, the sewage team was finished and ready to leave. It was 1:30 in the morning, the team decided to move on to Pune.

Since there was almost no traffic, the team drove fast and arrived at the Pune location at 3:35 AM. Parking near where they needed to be, was a problem; the team had to offload the backhoe, unload all the needed equipment and supplies then pull away to nearly a block down the street. The second truck pulled up and parked, both teams worked together to block off the area. The backhoe unloaded the cement mixture and other supplies required. Both teams got busy. The water line was quickly located. The team worked hard and fast to install the hot tap, then the acid. The backhoe covered up the hole, the men raked and generally cleaned the area. All was finished in 35 minutes. The sewage team had some problems the sewage was flowing freely, they again had to freeze the bottom to allow for a working base. With the sewage flowing, it took all the strength they could muster to hold the incoming back until the bottom was frozen and the gelatin had set up. It made getting the gelatin in place difficult. The incoming hole had to be held tight with the made-up poles and plywood. One was used by two men to stop the flow. Extra dry ice was used to make the gelatin set faster. At one point, they did not think it could be done, but finally, the gelatin was set and held the flow. It took slightly more than an hour. At 5:15 AM, they loaded the truck and moved the second one back to load the backhoe. They were exhausted and left for Mumbai. Once they arrived, they had to get some sleep. They had 1:30 PM flights to Delhi, a nearly 4-hour flight. It would be another long day.

When they arrived in Delhi, the equipment, supplies and rental cars were already waiting. The water line had been marked as well as the sewer manhole. The problem was security. The properties in both Pune and Mumbai were already flooded with sewage. The Trump organization was now scared. They had thought India was safe. The report received when the crew landed was that security was everywhere, and it may be better to cancel than attempt to damage this particular property. When it was near dark, the India team scouted the property. There indeed was security. A checkpoint existed before the property could be entered. Another checkpoint existed before one could actually go inside. This was obviously upsetting to the people who lived in the buildings. At times, long queues lined up at the entrance. The residents were verbal, threatening the security people hired by the Trump organization.

The India team watched closely as the holes in security became obvious. The security team charged with checking incoming traffic simply asked what their business was without asking for any verification. Second, there was no roving security checking the exterior of the grounds. Checking was being done for the personnel who were going inside. They were checking any and all packages brought in by the tenants with utmost care. This caused some issues as most of the packages contained food and the tenants were not happy about it being handled.

After several hours, the team unloaded the backhoe several hundred meters away from the checkpoint and simply drove around them on a back route.

The backhoe carried the heavy items except for the water. It unloaded the cement mixer, kettle and acid drum then drove back to pick up the water, a few other tools and the supplies needed. The crew boarded the backhoe and drove to the two sites. The backhoe dropped off the sewage crew first and the water. The crew lifted the sewage cover and got to work. The backhoe moved to the waterline and began digging. They had a person monitoring the movement of the security people.

The sewage stops up went very fast. It was a septic type system and relatively shallow, it also had little flow. They filled the mixer, mixed the gelatin, added the dry ice and other ingredients and poured directly into the manhole from the mixer. Twenty minutes, and they were ready to go. The drum installers were also doing well. The line was only a half meter deep. They found the waterline and while the hot tap was being installed, the backhoe dug out a 'seat' for the drum. The drum was lowered into the hole. All were connected, covered up and raked in 28 minutes. The backhoe drove back to the sewer, picked up the mixer, water drum, kettle, remaining supplies and tools and the crew with the drum crew on board. One hour twenty minutes, the entire crew reloaded on the trucks and headed back to the warehouse to park the trucks, a record time!

The crew left early the next morning for Kolkata, nearly 1,500 kilometers away, the last property in India. When they landed, they got the message that the Trumps had sent 'experts' in both security and sewage to the property in Delhi as the sewage overflow was terrible. The next one would be difficult, if even possible, because the property was swarming with security people.

The team checked into their hotel but requested that they be driven to the site to monitor the security situation first. It was terrible; security guards were everywhere. Two checkpoints had been established plus a checkpoint inside the property. There was likely a third which could not be seen from the outside. They also had a roving exterior group who was checking the outside. They had to measure the odds and repercussions of getting caught before proceeding, the good thing was, if they could pull it off with this heavy security, it would mean that Trump could not prevent the damage and it would be a major loss to his management ability.

The group left two people to record the movement of the outside security monitors. They wrote down how often and how long they lingered at each place. Gulzar Charmchi, who had joined the group in India, carefully studied the number of men, their movement and the time needed for a complete scan of the exterior of the property. The security crew consisted of two men in a jeep-type vehicle with no windows who drove very slow around the entire property, never stopping. It appeared that they made frequent radio contact with someone at a predetermined point. Gulzar wanted to verify if the location was the same each time the driver picked up a walkie talkie and reported in. Gulzar obtained a listening device that could overhear conversations of up to 300 meters. He assigned four men to monitor the contacts. The device had a recorder so the conversation could be played back. Gulzar wanted the location, exact time and the conversation to be noted. The four men were stationed at various points around the facility. As the security guard's vehicle drove slowly around, one man from the Iranian team would walk at a distance away, pointing the listening device/recorder at the vehicle. If a conversation was heard, he would write down the exact time and the location. The four men divided the property among themselves and took turns to monitor their conversations. This would allow for 45 minutes' rest for each person as it took roughly an hour to completely make the rounds. The recordings revealed that at roughly the halfway point, the security would report in. The conversation consisted of "Unit two everything is OK" and that was it. Changes of guards occurred every 4 hours. Gulzar now had a plan. The team had darts that could be fired at someone to knock them out instantly; they would be out for one- and one-half hours. Right after the completion of a routine check-in, they would shoot both the driver and the passenger with the darts and take over the vehicle. The men would remain unconscious long enough to get the job done.

The driver called in at the appointed time. The team had four guys very close to the vehicle. Two of them had dart guns and each shot a person at exactly the same time. The vehicle continued to move as the driver slumped over the steering wheel. One of the guys jumped in and took over. He drove it to the spot where it would remain for the next hour and a half. The second guy carefully timed the point where the next check-in would be. He played the recorder at the proper time; he would do this three times while the two were out cold.

Meanwhile, the team moved to the location of the water line and sewer. Gulzar, for a few moments, contemplated abandoning the acid and just doing the sewer, but once he saw what he had to do and how long he had to do the operation, he decided to do both. They had become efficient and did both within an hour and then pulled away from the compound. The one man left behind positioned both the driver and the passenger in the stances they had been before being knocked out. He cranked the vehicle, made the call at the checkpoint and walked away. A few minutes later, both came to, and each was afraid he had dozed off for a moment and said nothing. The driver pushed the gas and continued. The vehicle was an automatic, and in neutral gear. A brick had been placed under the right front wheel to keep it from rolling. The driver when he came out of the sleep induced drugs given to him by the dart, jerked himself awake, realized he was not moving, pulled it into gear and continued as if he had not stopped. The passenger also jerked himself awake as the drugs wore off, he was embarrassed that he may have dozed off and said nothing None of them said a word as the jeep continued its rounds.

Come next morning, Trump's group would be really pissed and concerned. A full security team, inside and out, and still! Sewage overflowed, no matter what they did to prevent them. There was a lot of screaming and accusations going around. Trump's children and management team felt defeated.

Chapter Eighteen

The team boarded planes a few hours later and flew to Manila. The Trump property was in Makati, a suburb of Manila. The entire group was exhausted and went straight to bed. They would visit the property tomorrow. The support team had already rented the necessary equipment, purchased the supplies and other tools and also obtained two vehicles.

The next morning, the team, in two vehicles, visited the property. There was obviously no added security. They were all pleasantly surprised. The team decided that since the property only had the Trump name and another company operated it, Trump and the operators must have thought that it was not at risk. They would be proved wrong!

The water and sewage manhole were marked, both had easy access and were well out of sight from the main road. The Philippine contractors typically established a roped boundary when doing any type of excavation work and added warning lights. They could find no site for a permit to do such work, so they proceeded without one. At midnight, the two trucks pulled up to the spots. The backhoe unloaded the mixer, kettle and water, moved back to the waterline, and unloaded the drum. The markings for the dig were evident, the backhoe began digging and in 9 minutes, they had located the waterline. The crew dug under, installed the hot tap as the backhoe dug alongside for the drum. The connections were made, all was covered up and the acid crew was on its way. The total was twenty-three minutes, a new record. The sewage team had similar good luck, the pipe which spilled the sewage into the manhole was a full meter from the bottom, it had very little sewage flowing into it. They used the plywood to stop what little flow was coming out and began pouring directly from the cement mixer. The mix began to harden almost immediately. Within twenty minutes they were able to remove the plywood, fill the rest of the manhole and began loading the equipment. The backhoe was driven to them the moment it finished with the acid crew. The water was already loaded when they poured the last bit of the mixture into the manhole. The backhoe picked up the mixer, loaded it on the truck then drove itself back onto the other truck. Absolute piece of cake. They went back to the warehouse area and gave the equipment a good cleaning and went to the hotel. The next stop for them would be Istanbul, Turkey. They were now absolute professionals and proud.

Iran now had 8 crews working everywhere Trump's properties were now liabilities, damaging Trump's assets. Five of those were in the United States, and the others moved from place to place all over the world. They had now visited all of Trump's golf courses, except the ones in the United Arab Emirates. Soon, all the grass and landscaping in the others would be dead. The places that had been flooded with sewage would soon be experiencing leaks and the landscaping around those properties would soon die, Trump was having many bad days.

The plan for the United States crews was to move to the Kushner properties and then properties owned by Benjamin Netanyahu in both the United States and Europe. They had been contemplating the wineries owned by Trump. Initially, they had decided to leave them alone. However, after reconsidering, a team was now on the way. They would kill all the vines.

The property in Dubai, United Arab Emirates, was particularly dangerous to attack. Its proximity to Saudi Arabia, who hated Iran, made getting caught especially hazardous. The course had lights on poles, which allowed individuals to play late into the evening, thus avoiding the heat. There were people on the course until around midnight, so one could not even arrive at the property until well past midnight to do what they planned, as maintenance and ground keeping workers would begin their duties only after the golfers left the course. Making matters worse, since the entire area was well lit, most of the maintenance on the course and the exterior was also done at night. The damage they intended to do would be very difficult and also very rewarding. This was the only restaurant left that users were not concerned about getting sick. The Dubai food inspectors were the strictest of any location that Trump operated. Their inspection was always thorough and would close a dining operation in a heartbeat if any sign of carelessness with food was detected. This fact made it even more important that they make the diners sick. The only thing keeping them from tainting the vegetables was that they did not want the security to be worse than it already was.

The plan developed was to steal one of the actual trucks used by the property maintenance crews, dress like them and use two of the golf carts to navigate. It would be a cat and mouse game, staying away from the eyes of the actual working staff and getting the job done. After careful consideration, the team decided to move now as the Trump organization was on high alert all over the world.

The observations had shown a weakness in the manner that the vehicles, including the golf carts, were locked up once the last golfers leave the compound. There was no one watching the carts as the security was concentrated on the hotel and guests. The team obtained the 'uniforms' used by the grounds crew easily as they had located the supplier through the efficient hackers working with them. They simply ordered the correct sizes in the quantity needed. They picked them up, signed for them, had the invoice sent to the hotel and let the Trump organization pay as if they had ordered. They also prepared to taint the vegetables the morning after, as there was a delivery scheduled.

At shortly after eleven PM, the team brought a backhoe to a spot just outside a fairway which was the farthest from the hotel and a clubhouse. The delivery vehicle had a cement mixer, a barrel of acid, a tank filled with water, dry ice, gelatin, a kettle with the other chemicals needed and battery-operated drills along with the three types of poisons needed to kill the grass, landscaping and trees. Most of the ground was covered by palm trees which would make it even more difficult. They offloaded the supplies, covered them with camouflaged tarps including the backhoe. The delivery truck drove half a mile away then parked out of sight. The driver waited a few minutes then walked toward the spot where they had covered up the supplies. Waiting were eight members of the team. With barely any exchange, two guys headed out to deal with the grass. They first needed to steal a golf cart which proved to be an easy task. Most golf courses have a small shack that has all the keys hanging on a peg board with a large round key chain labeled with the golf cart number. They noted that cart number twenty-four was the easiest to drive away as it was in the back and not obstructed by any other carts. They were prepared to 'hot wire' if necessary, then repair the cut wires but they found the key.

Once they had cart number twenty-four operating, they drove to the storage spot and loaded the supplies. They were a team of two men who initially planned on dropping one by the trees while the other worked on killing the grass. However, it was decided that killing the grass was the most important, so both headed toward the water hazard. They had already scouted the area and knew the pump was disguised along the southern border of the artificial lake. They pulled the cart next to the pump and quickly dug a ditch to house the connection device and two-gallon jug of grass killer concentrate. The ground was sand, so the digging was almost effortless. Fifteen minutes later they were done. They could see activity on the course in the form of grass cutters working their way toward them. They moved to the spot where the cutters had already covered. No one was looking, and they were not spotted.

They swiftly figured out the pattern the grass cutters were following and began working on the trees and other landscape. Now, this was the fourth golf course this crew had tackled, two of which had the difficult palm trees. Their confidence was high. One of the teams had two battery-operated drills and two spares just in case. The drill operator efficiently drilled 5 holes along the base of the tree using a 3/4-inch drill bit extending nearly a foot. He then circled the trees, drilling five inches into the tree at a forty- five-degree angle with a ½-inch drill bit. The other team member poured muriatic acid into the holes on the ground then a special poison into the ½ inch holes drilled into the tree.

It took one minute 45 seconds to do the first tree. They would have to do better. The cart was driven to the next tree only forty feet away. The driller had already reached and was done drilling by the time the cart arrived. This was a scary mad race as they had to constantly watch out for the grass cutters and other passersby. It was five in the morning when they finished the last tree. They had yet to spray the other landscaping, but it was too dangerous to continue.

Meanwhile, the other six members of the team were also busy. They had located a flatbed truck the day before, which would do the job. When they arrived, it was unguarded. A search was made, but the keys could not be found. The truck was quickly hotwired and driven to the spot where the backhoe was parked. Next to backhoe was a loading ramp set up against the back of the bed of the truck. The backhoe was driven onto the bed after loading the equipment and supplies onto the truck. They passed by the grass cutters and then the crew trimming the landscape. They waved as they passed, and the crew waved back.

The truck was parked close to the main water supply line. It offloaded the backhoe, lifted the cement mixer and moved it the one hundred fifty feet to the sewage manhole then returned for the heating kettle. The backhoe returned and brought the rest of the supplies needed. It returned to the waterline. One man had marked the spot needed to dig. A watchdog was assigned to be sure no one disturbed the work. He was given an automatic weapon, a pistol with a silencer and a dart gun. His instructions were simple: if at all possible, knock the person out with the dart gun but do not let them see or in any way observe what they were doing. So far, the Trump organization had not been able to figure out how they were stopping up the sewers or how they had been causing all the leaks. Discovery meant that they would have proof that it was espionage.

The watchdog positioned himself behind bushes near the ongoing work. The ditch for the waterline and acid was dug. The team was now professionals and could do so fast. The connection was made, the fifty- gallon drum was installed including the air vents and refill tubes, to include redressing the area. All was done in only 47 minutes—not a record but close to the best time. The watchdog was watching closely one man who was walking around the area, dressed differently than the other workers. The man had a weapon on his side and what looked like a badge on his chest. Even though most of the lights were still on as the grass cutting crew were at work, the lights were being turned off as the crews finished in certain areas. The man had a flashlight, checking behind and around all the bushes. The Iranian watchdog observed him closely, he got down on his belly and began crawling toward where he expected him to come. The security guard walking slowly getting closer to their location. He glanced at the crew installing the acid. They were just finishing but there would be no way to move the backhoe to the sewer crew without the guard being aware. The watchdog decided to strike. He moved to where the guard had just left and carefully worked himself to behind the guard. He matched, step for step, the guard's movement, stepping slightly faster than the guard as he moved. When he was within twenty feet he pulled his silencer pistol into his left hand and the dart gun into his right. He knew if he missed with the dart, he would have to kill the guard. He fired the dart aiming toward his neck. He had hundreds of hours of practice, and his shot was perfect. The guard stood motionless for a moment then collapsed to the ground. The watchdog moved like lightning, first removing the dart then searching for any type of communication device. He found a small handheld device that looked like a small cell phone but only had a button for talking on the side. He put it back in the guards' pocket moved him where he was sitting comfortably, it appeared, on a bench. He literally ran to the crew getting into the truck, told them what he had to do and suggest they hurry! The guard would wake up in 45 minutes then he would wake up all in no time.

The sewer crew was making good progress. The manhole was deeper than expected. So deep they had to locate a hosepipe to add to their water supply. The incoming sewage was not a lot since it was four in the morning. Very few people were up and moving. The complete stoppage was achieved at just the time the backhoe came back to the spot. The crew loaded the mixer using a chain hoist to the backhoe bucket and the tools into the bucket. A few minutes later the truck appeared. The backhoe loaded the kettle, which was still hot and all the other equipment, drove itself with the help of an operator onto the truck. The truck moved swiftly to the spot where it had been originally loaded. The backhoe drove off the truck then onto the original truck after unloading and then loading the equipment and supplies. The truck operator drove it back to the location where it had been stolen, repaired the cut wires and ran back to the others. It was 5:30 in the morning, all but the landscaping had been done.

The next evening, the team offloaded six of their crew at 2 am. Each of them armed with a sprayer left in different directions, avoiding the cutters and trimmers, to spray the landscape. In a few days, there would not be any grass, trees and or landscaping in the course.

The same day, a separate team member had lain hidden near the loading dock of the company that supplied the fruits and vegetables to the Trump property and sprayed them when they were sure that it was designated to be delivered to the Trump restaurant. Nearly all the diners who ate at the Trump property after the food was delivered would be sick by late tonight!

In the United States and Europe, the Iranian teams turned their attention to the Kushner and Benjamin Netanyahu properties. The Kushner properties were primarily concentrated in the East and were mostly rental properties aimed at the lower rental market. The teams went to work. The Netanyahu properties were few but spread out over two continents and several countries. The Iranians decided to do Benjamin Netanyahu last as it may be obvious when they began to damage his property that they were the culprits.

Within a week, several of the properties owned by Kushner had been hit. The impact on Kushner was quick and devastating. The sewage overflows ruined the furniture, carpet and other items in the apartments. Kushner was slow to acknowledge any problem and refused to take responsibility or react to the hundreds of families who were forced out of their homes. They were out on the street with nowhere to go. Kushner's only public comment was to say that they should deal with the insurance companies, that he had bought insurance to cover such a situation, he would however, be sure that had the contact information. The insurance companies were forced by Kushner to hire cleanup crews to deal with the sewage and the smell. The Iranians had people with uniforms for the expected companies who would be hired to do the job. They mingled in undetected and sprayed the substance on the floors and walls just as they had been cleaned and disinfected by the cleaning company. The cleaners primarily used steam along with disinfection to do the cleaning, the substance blended in and was invisible. It would smell terrible in several days and would not be possible to remove through any ordinary cleaning. The Insurance companies stated repeatedly that insurance covered damage to the building and property but not consequential damage to people living in the property. States, cities and counties joined together to assist the renters and also brought legal action against Kushner. The tenants had to find temporary housing and incurred the cost of moving including added cost for meals, laundry and so forth. Trump responded by tweet that the news media and liberal governments were attacking Kushner to get to him and there was no merit to the attacks. as Kushner had no responsibility for such a disaster except to get the damage repaired. The courts agreed with the suits filed and ordered Kushner to provide temporary housing and reimbursement for any losses as the damage was not an act of God or burglary but was because someone was out to get even with Kushner and, thus, preventable. He, of course, appealed.

Chapter Nineteen

The Trump organization, on discovering that most of its buildings were leaking due to the fixtures being corroded, put tremendous efforts into finding out how and why. There were now more than twelve hundred lawsuits filed against them. Trump had filed suits against the manufacturers, which now numbered twelve. The companies had already responded and ask for dismissal since their products were in thousands of properties and no problems had been reported on any others. Only the Trump properties were impacted. It was also obvious that Trump was being targeted, which was not the fault or the responsibility of the manufacturers.

The next morning, all hell broke loose at Trump Tower in New York City.

Don Junior was busy cursing. "Some motherfuckers are going to die! They can't fuck with us and get away with it. Whoever the hell is doing this to us is going to pay dearly!"

"Lots of people hate our dad," said Eric. "Could be the Palestinians, the Mexicans, the Iranians, the fucking democrats, the Kurds and lord knows how many more."

"Well, we have to figure this out and stop it before we are all broke," said Don Jr.

"How much damage have they done?" asked Ivanka.

"Millions. Our cash flow is now near zero. We have had to close or nearly close all our restaurants; people are afraid to eat there. In the hotels, even the ones that have not been hit, vacancies are staggering. The golf clubs are so damaged that we might as well close them down completely."

"How the hell are they doing this to us?" asked Eric.

"We don't know," said Don Jr. "All our experts agree it is being done from the inside. I can't imagine how someone is getting into all our facilities all over the world without our security detecting. We don't have one clue as to how or who is doing this."

"We have to figure this out," said Eric.

"We have placed security people inside and outside our facilities and someone still manages to do the damage, said Don Jr. "Our experts keep insisting it's an inside job, yet our people have searched everyone coming into the building and discovered nothing."

The group read the devastating financial information that was passed out around the table. Receipts had dwindled to the lowest ever; expenses had increased. The cost of the lawsuits was now very high and growing every day. The safety net for lines of credit was fast dwindling.

"We operate under many names. Can we not just file for bankruptcy protection under the primary names being sued?" asked Don Jr.

Ivanka said, "I have been in contact with our lawyers, these lawsuits are unique. They have sued the owner of the building, which is our shell corporation, then the Trump organization as the owner of the shell company and then us as individuals who are responsible for the management of these properties. Our attorneys say the liability we face could be made worse if the primary corporation is released by bankruptcy. The primary claim is that due to our alleged ruthless business and political practices. We should have known that it would lead to retaliation. These ruthless practices, it is alleged, endangered the people staying at our hotels, living in properties we developed and eating in restaurants we own. It may mean that we all must file bankruptcy."

Eric had tears in his eyes. "I just got off the phone with the manager of our Albemarle Estate. They have been hit! The wine manager had tested the vines and they looked 'droopy' as he called it. They have all been poisoned! He has tested the soil. Nothing will grow there for a long time. The sewage has overflowed, and all the guests have checked out. The property for all essential purposes has little if any value. I just asked him to close the hotel and layoff all but a few necessary staff. Why would they do this to such a beautiful place?"

Ivanka rushed and put her arms around him. This property was his baby, and it was a major loss to him. Eric was also an equal owner of the property. This would very badly damage him personally.

"We also, just this morning, learned, that the property we own in Dubai has reported that over a hundred people are sick, all ate in our restaurant the night before. Also, the entire first and second floors were filled with raw sewage. This place is the most secure facility we own. The government is afraid of terrorist attacks and have armed guards everywhere. How the fuck could they do this?" said Don Jr.

"It gets worse," said Ivanka. "I have here a document from the government of Indonesia, received last night. It is an order from their highest court to seize the properties we own. They claim that we refused to clean up the mess created by the sewage overflow, the leaks in the fixtures, or the damage to the grass on the golf courses. I sent this to Dad. The message I got back was, 'he would handle.'"

"Those bastards," said Don Jr. "We looked at what our responsibility should be. It is fucking zero! Our Indonesian partners are managing those properties and they took total responsibility when they signed our contract. The Indonesian government can't just void our contracts, fuck them!"

A clerk walked in and handed a stack of documents in different folders to Ivanka. She leafed quickly through them and said, "Shit."

"What now?" asked Eric.

"These two folders are from the governments of Ireland and Scotland. They have ordered our properties to be closed until the health ministry certifies they are safe for humans to occupy. This folder"—she held it above her head and continued, "is a copy of an order just filed in India declaring the properties uninhabitable and seeking an order to declare them public property to be disposed or handled in whatever manner is in the best interest of the public good. This folder is nearly an identical request from the government of South Korea. It looks like they may have coordinated. Another is a filing by the state of New York and another by New Jersey to take possession of the properties for the public good. I am guessing we will have a similar filing from Florida, Illinois and Washington DC soon."

"Bastards, don't they know it is actually us who are being attacked and all because our father is the President."

Ivanka took over. "Our only hope of solving this is to become sympathetic to our renters, condo owners and operators. We must mobilize and convince the world that we are responsible developers."

"Do you have any idea what that will cost? We have signed contracts with all these people relieving us of any responsibility. I say no fucking way. We need to move against all these people, not step in and accept their responsibility. No way are we going to do that!"

"If we do not," said Ivanka. "We have a high risk of losing all. The risk is too high for us to play tough!"

"I agree with Ivanka," said Eric. "We must at least appear to care about these people."

"You are going to open a Pandora's box!" said Don Jr. "All the fixtures are going to need to be replaced. They then are going to want us to pay for temporary housing, pain and suffering and on and on and on. We should not agree to the first step; it is just fucking stupid."

Ivanka won the argument, and they then called in a procurement person who was ordered to issue contracts to replace the fixtures with the same or better quality and clean up the mess still left by the sewage overflow. This would apply to properties worldwide."

"This is fucking stupid!" Don Jr. threw his pencil on the table and stormed out.

Ivanka also knew they had to have a representative communicate with each of the governors of every state impacted, give them the news that they had contracted with companies to clean up and replace the fixtures and stop the leaks. She also instructed her travel people to book flights for her and Eric to visit each of the countries impacted. She then requested the local embassy to arrange for her or Eric to meet with the appropriate people.

Don Jr. contacted the President who first agreed that it was fucking stupid to give into these people, then pondering it for a few minutes backed off and agreed to support Ivanka and Eric as they had to make an effort. Don Jr. was furious.

Trump's procurement specialist began issuing contracts to do the cleanup again and replace the fixtures. The Iranian hackers were aware of who and when each would be done. They planned the appropriate response! This cleanup was the second as Trump had coordinated an initial group to remove the raw sewage. Iran knew that now the problem was the stuff they had put on the walls and floors of all the properties as they were being cleaned. The horrific smell would be difficult to remove.

****

Through multiple sources, Iran was aware of the Trump organization's failure to even find a hint of who or how all this was being done. While continuing to feed them bullshit on drones, they would also give them a hint of how this was being accomplished, all fictitious of course.

"So how is the drone plan coming?" asked actor 1.

"We are ahead of schedule. Looks like we can begin random strikes inside the United States in two weeks," said actor 2.

"We are hearing rumors that someone is doing a lot of damage to some of Trump's real estate holdings. Do you know any details?" said actor 1.

"The only information I have is that some of the people Trump cheated over the years have come together to get even with him," said actor 2. "We do hear that someone has developed a tiny pill that when wet, will expand to thousands of times its size and stop up a sewage system. After a few hours, it dissipates with no evidence it was ever there. We also hear they are threatening and bribing the cleaning staff to wipe on and or spray a super corrosive concentrate that will cause the fixtures to fail and leak."

"No other information on who's behind this?" asked actor 1.

"No, but we will continue to try and uncover the wonderful people who are doing this to him!" The actor smiled as the words came out of his mouth.

The two actors went on to discuss many other issues which were the normal run of the mill things expected in a meeting. Nothing the United States would have any interest in. Their scripts had been carefully written and practiced before any words were said. This exchange went on every day with different actors. The CIA assumed they were recording real conversations between Iranian officials. But the experts knew that they were being fed bullshit.

Trump was immediately given the transcript. He once more ordered the FBI to investigate. He was informed again that they could not, but he could file a complaint with the New York City police department or any other at the location of the damage but wherever the property was located would have to handle.

He threw the phone across the room, "You forget who the fuck you are working for. You will assign a task force and investigate!" The head of the FBI did not answer. He then called the secret service head and the attorney general, who also confirmed that they could not do anything unless he was being physically threatened.

The FBI, within the hour, sent him a formal reply by letter, telling Trump why they could not and would not assign or create a task force and he must let the local authorities handle. Trump knew that any such complaint with the local law enforcement, would just go into a file and his slandering them, especially the New York City police force, was now definitely a liability. In spite of this, he continued his rampages on their lack of professionalism.

Trump called his three children who were supposedly in charge of the Trump businesses. He had sent them a copy of the recorded conversation with the Iranian even though it was illegal to do so. He wanted to discuss what was recorded.

"Do you see where; the Iranians think it is people I am accused of cheating who are doing all this damage?"

"Yes, we see," added Ivanka who had become the spokesperson.

"Well, I have not cheated anyone! I may have taken advantage of stupidity or arrogance but not cheated! They should blame their own stupidity for any losses, not me!"

"Don't you remember all those contractors and subcontractors we fired because we said the work was shoddy and that was after the inspectors had signed them off as being OK?

"Yes, but we had crappy inspectors who I also fired."

"Well, those contractors threatened to kill us, and most went broke. They are still around somewhere."

"Well, they had incompetent lawyers. That is who they should blame!"

"We made it so expensive that they could not afford to continue the litigation."

"Just business. They should have read their damn contracts before signing."

"We also refused to accept hundreds of thousands of dollars' worth of specialty carpet, drapery and other items even after the architect had approved them. We claimed they were wrong. They all had the Trump logo and were useless elsewhere. We finally paid them ten cents on the dollar and used all of it in the buildings. All of them considered this as cheating and said so!"

"Again, they should have read their contracts. I reserved the right to give final approval before payment."

"Well, we have a lot of people who will never forgive us, and any of them can be behind all of this."

"We should compile a list and start checking them out."

"It will be long and expensive to monitor and check out all these people." "You can't get to the end unless you start. So, get started now."

"Yes sir, but I think we would be served better by reaching out to them. That would at least give us a sense as to how they now feel."

"No fucking way. You will not reopen old wounds!" "Okay, but for the record, I disagree."

The discussion then turned to how to handle the damage to the buildings.

"I thought I had resolved this. I have scheduled a conference with the Indonesian Prime Minister to get their actions undone. I told all of you to file a lawsuit against the different engineers, architect and contractors. Did you not do that? I also said to sue the suppliers and manufacturers of the fixtures!" said Donald Trump.

"We have started the process but for most of these, the statute of limitations has long since expired," said Ivanka.

Eric spoke. "We all agree that we will try to litigate this. We will start it up again as soon as we get off the phone. Have you seen our plan to help those who have been damaged? Junior is in strong disagreement, but he is wrong. If we do not at least appear to be compassionate, we will have those properties confiscated."

"I was told. I do think you are right. Do what you have to before it gets worse. One of you needs to fly to Indonesia and smooth out some feathers. The others, go to Korea and India. This is fucking serious!"

"We already have the tickets," said Ivanka.

The conference ended. Don Jr. was pissed. He flung some papers on the floor and stormed off.

Chapter Twenty

Iran's Supreme Leader, Ali Khamenei, required a personal update on the effort to get even with Trump. It was scheduled for early the next morning. Those invited were Hassan Rouhani, the President of Iran, Aftab Karimithe, Deputy Defense Minister and the head of the task force, and Javon Darzi, the Defense Minister. The meeting started at 8 AM. Hassan Rouhani started the presentation, giving a brief but thorough analysis of what had been accomplished thus far, all 19 of Trump's golf courses are now closed because all grass and landscaping have been destroyed. Every restaurant except the one in Trump tower has been closed by the local health officials, this was worldwide. All his hotels had at least been temporarily closed, due to people being afraid to stay there. The vast majority of his developed condominiums and rental properties were now unlivable. Most of his properties in Indonesia, India, Philippines, Korea and other countries were filing orders to confiscate the properties, none were habitable. Lawsuits have been filed to do the same to the properties in New York and New Jersey. Their prized properties in Virginia and Florida were now near worthless. We understand that the banks are now refusing to honor the lines of credit Trump had prior to this. He is in a huge financial mess! Hassan then turned the meeting over to Aftab Karimithe, Deputy Defense Minister, after he said, "I was a skeptic on this approach and believed this was a waste of time, but I was wrong. Aftab's team has done wonders."

Aftab Karimithe took over and began: "My Supreme Leader, Mister President, and my boss, Javon Darzi, we have been successful thus far because the people assigned to this effort are incredible. Beginning with the group who are not under my control but allow false information to be overheard by the Americans, their effort has put them off guard and looking for answers in all the wrong places. This has kept them from concentrating on what we were actually doing. We also have done much damage to the Kushner family properties. The Benjamin Netanyahu properties are yet to be done but will be soon. There are thousands of lawsuits against Donald

Trump and his family now. We still have much to do. We have, thus far, been unable to do any damage to the Trump family headquarters known as Trump Tower located in New York City. We have just yesterday been able to tap into the bank accounts and personal information of two of the Trump children. I am told that we are very close to uncovering Donald Trump's data as well as one of the other family members. We have been able to hack into Benjamin Netanyahu's personal data. We will do some serious harm to them very soon. One other thing: they have hired a company to repair the damage to properties in Indonesia and India and the United States as they are very close to being confiscated. We installed a backup system on all the buildings we have damaged. It is a simple matter of refilling a large drum of acid beneath the ground. Each has a tube, and this can be done in minutes. We also have been joining the crews doing the cleanup as we have the uniforms they wear. Our people have been spraying a substance over the cleaned surface. When it dries and then cures for a few days, the smell will be horrific and very difficult to cover up or remove. We can refill the acid from a truck with a hose attachment. We will do that the moment the repair work is completed. We must keep the false information flowing. Right now, they are on a wild goose chase believing that people Trump has harmed in the past are responsible. I suggest that we start throwing some real names forward and what he has done to them. This will increase his concern."

"This is all wonderful information. At some point, I will make a speech giving him and the world the knowledge as to how powerful we are. Our enemies who harm us will not go unpunished!" said the Ayatollah.

Aftab's people continued improving the plans to attack Trump Tower. This was only difficult because of security and constant scrutiny. The risk was great. Getting caught meant exposing how they had done all this damage. As much as Aftab wanted this done, he would not take any unnecessary risks. He now had twenty-four-hour surveillance of the locations where the sewage and metalwork would be carried out. All was on camera which broadcasted the recorded information. Aftab had assigned special people to keep watch at every moment to find a weakness that could be used to their advantage. Finally, after three weeks, his people approached Aftab and stated, it could be done.

The weakness uncovered was from 2 AM until 4 AM on Monday mornings. On Sunday nights, the police surveillance decreased and by 2 AM the next morning stopped completely for a two-hour period. There was almost no vehicle and foot traffic. Aftab watched the recording for three consecutive weeks and decided to give it a try. He had the proper permits recorded, brought the now very experienced team to New York, had all the rental equipment and materials delivered. All were stored in a warehouse only twenty minutes from the site. The first team installed the proper barricades around both of the sites which were only 75 feet apart. The second and third teams arrived, one to stop up the sewer and the other to install the acid. The acid would require removing and then reinstalling the sidewalk as the waterline was beneath it. The sewage team expertly dropped the boards which would hold back any sewage entering the manhole and the other preventing the liquid from escaping. They brought two portable concrete mixers with the proper amount of hot water already inside. They had previously opened the manhole and gotten the needed measurements; the water was heated just before they left the warehouse. The gelatin and other chemicals were poured into the concrete mixer then poured into the manhole directly from the mixers. Dry ice was added in the correct quantities to provide for a firm setting until 8 AM. They calculated by that time sufficient people would have used the toilets to cause the pipes to stop up and by the time the backup began to impact inside the building, the gelatin would have dissipated. All this was done in nineteen minutes. The crew removed the barricades around the sewer and was gone.

The second crew had two concrete saws operated by a quiet generator. They each sawed one end of the sidewalk and lifted it away using slings. A backhoe dug down and found the waterline which was nearly six feet beneath the sidewalk. The hot tap was installed along with an air outlet that ran to the side of the sidewalk. Aftab decided to not install the refill as it would be too dangerous and might be discovered. All was installed, dirt was put back in the hole, tamped down with an added final foot of a soil-cement mixture to ensure no settlement occurred. The piece of the sidewalk was lifted and put back in place. A special exact color mixed grout was put into the saw cut which only hid the expansion joints already in the sidewalk. It had taken 41 minutes. The crew loaded everything, removed the barricades and headed home. Aftab was notified of the success and celebrated.

The Trump family members who worked at Trump Tower along with other executives reported to work at 9 AM, as usual. There was a slight odor when they opened the office. It did not occur to them that they had been hit. However, sewage began to fill the lobby and into their offices, and, by 10 AM, the entire building had to be evacuated.

Trump Jr. called his father. "We have been hit. We closed the building. There's sewage everywhere!"

"How the fuck did they do that? You do still have 24-hour security, don't you? And you are still checking everyone who comes into the building, right?"

"Yes, sir. We require everyone including tenants to have a badge. No one can get in without one. I have called a plumbing company and a cleanup crew and also have people reviewing the security cameras. It just makes no sense!"

"Well, this is a slap in the face. Do the news people know?"

"I am sure they do. I have already been handed a legal action by several of the tenants."

Sure enough, moments later, a live television broadcast by several newsgroups was on the sidewalk reporting the event. The broadcaster's line was, "Trump cannot even protect his own building, much less this country!"

Trump Jr. shot them a vulgar finger when they tried to interview him. Several of the tenants and staff did give interviews. All concentrated on the smell and damage. The tenants were furious: "Who is going to pay for this?"

Sewage was flowing into the upper floors before the plumbing people arrived. The stink was horrific. The Trump hotel was evacuated and, later, closed. All the tenants moved out.

Chapter Twenty-One

The news conference began with a brief introduction of each of the representatives of the five countries being represented, India, Indonesia, South Korea, Philippines, and Turkey. The conference was held at the primary government offices in New Delhi, the building was significant in that the cornerstone had been laid by Queen Mary. The site was chosen for its significance to India. Narendra Modi, Prime Minister of India who was the spokesperson for all the countries made the introductions. He began, "This has been a difficult time in India, we have had a major problem with properties which the Trump family owns in India. The fixtures in all the properties are leaking and, even after the initial clean up, there is a terrible smell. The places cannot be used until all this is fixed. A similar problem is also present in Indonesia, Turkey, South Korea and the Philippines. Since the similarities are so great, we decided to jointly look over the possibilities of dealing with this problem together. The President of the United States owns and manages these properties and is, for all purposes, daily involved with India, Indonesian, South Korean, Turkey and the Philippines. He is responsible for everything that happens with these estates. India, as well as the other four countries, strictly prohibit this type of behavior. None of our countries will allow a leader such as myself to own property in another country and profit from this ownership. It creates a conflict with the interest of our country or the interest of the Trump Organization. Donald Trump should have divested himself of all foreign properties the moment he became president. It is sad that he did not.

We have a big problem because so many people are out to get even with Donald Trump and his organization. The Trump family's business interests and methods are reported to have been very cruel over the years. There are many allegations that the Trump organization has ruthlessly dealt with contractors, subcontractors, suppliers, people, they are buying land and other such things. There have been thousands of lawsuits. The tactic claimed to be used by the Trump organization is that the company bringing the lawsuit against them would never win just recover part of the cost because his lawyers would make the litigation so expensive no one could even recover all but a small percentage of their cost. However, it matters little if we believe it or not. We expect that the president of the United States will not take what we must do lightly and possibly take some actions against our decision and attempt retaliation against all out countries. In addition, President Trump has treated very poorly the citizens of various countries which also seek to get even with him and the United States. For instance, Guatemala, Nicaragua and other Central American countries have been harmed greatly by the policies the United States imposed on them when Donald Trump became president. Out of hundreds of thousands of people trying to seek refuge, many have died being confined to overcrowded prisons while waiting to be heard in their quest to enter America but having committed no crime, only asking for a legal hearing required under the laws of the United States to gain admittance into America. The same applies to citizens of Mexico, Cuba, Iran, Syria most of the African nations, Pakistan, Afghanistan, Iraq, the Palestinian people and people like the Kurds, our intelligence reports, who believe that many of their people were killed because of their abandonment by the United States. For these deaths, many blame Donald Trump personally. The significance to us, is that all of these people want to get even with the president of the United States, and it looks like one of the ways in which they are getting even is to damage all his properties. We cannot allow this to happen again to our people or Citizens of India, Indonesia, Philippines, South Korea and Turkey who have also been damaged. Therefore, we have decided that we must confiscate these properties and remove them from the ownership of the Trump organization. This has already been done. Trump or his organization no longer owns or has any interest in properties located in the five countries represented here. We do note that several of the properties located in various parts of the United States, individual states where the Trump organization owns properties are considering the same.

"At the same time, none of us wish to profit from the misfortune of the Trump organization. We desire to fairly compensate them for the property we are confiscating. The value of all these properties has been greatly lowered by the damages done to them. To be completely fair, we have requested the World Court, and they have agreed, to be the final arbitrator of the values. The court will hear evidence from licensed real estate appraisers for each property. The Trump organization may appoint appraisers of their own and question the decisions made by other appraisers. The first monies paid will go to the lien holders of record, the remaining, to the Trump origination. We will be happy to answer questions."

More than 50 reporters raised their hands.

John Thurman, Fox News, asked, "Do you really think President Trump will stand for this? Are you prepared for the retaliation he will impose? He is not one to sit back and let someone get away with this thing you are imposing!"

"We expect that the United States will recognize that we should never have been put in this situation. We cannot allow our citizens to be at risk because of a dispute involving the President or his family. Jointly, we buy more than 200 billion dollars of products from the United States annually. Surely this should not be put at risk by the President doing something foolish."

"So, what do you think he will do?" asked Mary Newer from the New York Times.

"My country has had a discussion with Eric Trump. I think he understands the position we are in. So, I do not think there will be retaliation."

"You must really not know Trump. He will retaliate, and that is just a fact. The question is, what will you do when he does?" said John Thurman.

"If it does occur, we, as a group of many nations, will retaliate with a measured balance. Again, we believe that he is aware that this is a result of his decision to operate in foreign countries while serving as president!"

"Who are the lien holders?" asked Peter Jones from the BBC.

"The properties located in India all have liens filed by Russian banks. Indonesia has stated the same. We have not discussed this with South Korea, the Philippines and Turkey. I have just been given a note stating that Uruguay and the UAE have also confiscated the Trump properties and desire to join us in the legal proceedings. We, of course, will welcome them. I do not know, at this time, who the lien holders are or if any exists on other properties.

Questions continued for another 45 minutes, all different variations of the same angle of retaliation and to what prompted Uruguay and the UAE to join in now.

President Trump watched every news network at the same time, using the multiple televisions he had installed, pacing and screaming out, "Bastards, bastards! They will pay," as he walked. He also had just learned Donald Jr. was on a plane that would land in a couple of hours in New Delhi. His rashness and temper would surely make matters worse. He called Ivanka and Eric on a joint call, "Are you aware that your brother is on his way to India? You have to stop him. I assume you watched the disaster on TV?"

"I did," said Eric, "They are right, you know. This will not stop until we figure out who is behind this."

"Me too," said Ivanka, "Jr. will not listen to either of us. I am sure he will threaten them with all kinds of stuff and expect you to actually do whatever he says to them."

"I am afraid of the same. We have to stop him. One of you check the status of his flight and find out where he is staying. I am going to try and have the Marine security bring him to the embassy. They will record him when he makes his threats, and this will become a large international crisis!"

"We both understand. Had he not fought with us over helping the people impacted, this could have been averted, but he would not allow it." Said Eric.

"Don't forget, we have an equal risk here at home. Both New York and New Jersey are moving in the same direction. Our only hope is to show compassion and help those impacted. Also, we were hit again this morning at one of the places we have already repaired!" said Ivanka.

Eric came back to the phone after motioning for a clerk to find out where Donald Jr. is staying. "He has reservations at the Roseate House. I just left an urgent message for him to call one of us as soon as possible. My guess is, he will not!"

"I am going to call the Secretary of State and have him arrange for security to pick him up at the airport. I also have to remove his diplomatic immunity, for his own good." Donald Trump hung up and ended the call.

Ivanka, immediately then called Eric. "He is going to cause an international incident and make things worst!"

"Yes, he will, if Dad cannot stop him!"

Donald Jr. landed in New Delhi and, as he walked to the baggage claim, he heard his name being paged on the loudspeaker. He also saw text messages to call Eric or Ivanka. "Wimps," he said out loud. "They want me to act like a pussy and agree with them. No fucking way!"

Donald Jr. saw the two US marines at the curb of the airport. Guessing they intended to take him to the embassy where he would be detained, he backed away from the door, went to the backside of the airport where they were dropping off passengers and hailed a taxi. The driver first refused but when Donald Jr. handed him 50 US dollars, he changed his mind. "Take me to a hotel, any hotel. Other than the Roseate House." The driver then drove away. The two marines were still searching for Donald Jr.

Within an hour, the President, Eric and Ivanka were aware that he had deliberately slipped away and was now hiding, planning God knows what.

The President when told Donald Jr. had slipped away, knew it was going to be bad and he would have yet another major problem to deal with, had to call his doctor; he was now gasping for breath. The loss of the properties was a substantial loss but the disclosure that he had large loans borrowed from Russian banks would lose him many of his die-hard supporters. He felt betrayed and just needed to rest right now, all this was just too much.

Donald Jr. found a hotel, paid extra money to the clerk to not register him under his real name. He showed him his identification and reminded him that he was the President of the United States' son and did not want anyone, for security purposes, to know his identity or location. The clerk obliged and registered him under a false name. He immediately went to his room, ordered food and a bottle of scotch. It was now 4 in the afternoon, New Delhi time, too late to do anything that day. He never turned on the news or read his emails or messages.

Donald Trump was frantic. He knew his son was about to do something stupid and he had to stop him. He spoke again to the Secretary of State and told him, "He must be found and brought to the embassy!" The secretary had no choice but to enlist the help of the local police, to whom he indicated that Donald Jr. was in danger!

Eric and Ivanka knew Donald Jr. well and knew what he would do. They jointly went out on a limb and contacted the Prime Minister's office. They could not speak directly to him but spoke with a senior aide. "Our brother is there, in New Delhi. He was given no authority by the company or our father to speak on our behalf. We desire you refuse to see him and contact the American embassy, if necessary. They will put him under arrest. We believe he is a danger to himself and possibly others."

The Indian official assured them that this would be done.

They then called the President to tell him what they had done. They could not get through; his doctor had ordered him to rest and be left alone. They then called Melania and could not get through either. They dared not leave a message.

Donald Trump woke at 5 AM. He was normally a late riser but the medicine the doctor had given him had knocked him out and presumably calmed his nerves. He lay in bed thinking about what had happened the day before. His staff believed the news that he had lied about any business connection to Russia was what had gotten him so upset. He would lie and many would believe that his cover was he did not consider a lienholder as doing business. He would bet that the vast majority of voters did not even know who held the mortgage to their homes. Mortgages are traded often and what does it matter who holds the present mortgage. It is the same money and must be repaid. So, what if a Russian banking group believed his mortgages were a good investment? The real problem was that he had mortgaged this group of properties to well beyond the maximum, as he could do this with this particular Russian bank. His rule always was cash is king: take the cash out as soon as possible then see if you can get some sucker to take over the existing mortgage. The property was mortgaged at its peak valuation, then more was added. At least a 20% premium. If the investment ended up losing money, then it would not be his but someone else's. The appraisals will come back as maybe not even half of what he borrowed since there surely would be a reduction in value because of the damages. This is where he had not only concern but downright fear. These banks are operated by the Russian Mafia. He and his children and grandchildren would be at risk if he could not pay the difference and pay it now. The Russians do not screw around. The secret service, as good as they are, would not be able to protect them from these people. This was a matter of life and death and he could not tell the people who were to protect him why, it would surely be leaked!

He continued to lie in bed, he knew what must be done which was to pay the Russians. There was no other solution. He had a little time until the valuations were known. Even his appraisers would be way short of what was needed. The moment the Russians were aware of the shortfall, the demand for money would come. He must be prepared. Handling it now was the best option. He picked up his secure phone and called Ivanka, "I need you to make an appointment with the Russian bank handling the mortgages on the properties in trouble. Go to Moscow and negotiate a deal where they will take lien interest in other properties if there is a shortfall. Tell them our objective is to ensure that they are protected."

"I doubt they will do that. They have power over us and know it, I suspect they will want more. Maybe even something illegal. We are not dealing with the most honorable people you know. But I certainly will try. Should I take Eric?"

"No, go alone. That will be best."

"I will call now and see if we can schedule a meeting." "Good, keep me informed."

Ivanka had forgotten to tell him about her conversation with the Indian Prime Minister's office regarding Donald Jr.

Chapter Twenty-Two

Donald Jr. woke the next morning, dressed elegantly in not formal wear but an expensive tailored suit and tie. He wanted to appear as 'all business' before he made all hell break loose. This could even be fun, he thought. He took a taxi directly to the Prime Minister's office, went in and demanded to see the Prime Minister. As he was a representative of the United States and the President's son, his work was important. The receptionist had been warned that he would arrive and given strict instructions as to what she should do. She was told to excuse herself to determine if the Prime Minister could see him, go to another room, call the American embassy and inform them he was here. They would send security people over and take him away. She did exactly as she was told and also called a local television station and informed them what was about to take place. Filming, she warned, would have to be secretly done.

She returned to where Jr. was waiting and informed him that the Prime Minister was very busy but would try and break loose as soon as he could. Jr. took her message with no concerns. Then another person entered the room, one the receptionists knew was from the local news station. He also requested to see the Prime Minister. At this point Jr. lost it. He jumped out of his seat and screamed as loud as he could, "You go tell him, I am Donald Trump Jr., the President of the United States' son. My time is more valuable than his. Get me in to see him now. I have things he needs to know!"

"I am sorry sir, but you cannot go until he is free."

"You apparently were not listening when I told you who I am. Get me back there now!"

The newsman was filming every word being said and moved to another side of the room so that he could get every emotion accurately.

"Sir, I cannot. He will see you when he can."

"This delay will cost India dearly. If he keeps me waiting for another ten minutes, I will impose 15% tariffs on Indian products rather than just the 10, I had in mind. Now, get me in there!"

Suddenly the front door burst open. Coming in the door was four United States Marines from the American Embassy. "Mister Trump, you are to come with us now," said the senior Marine, a captain.

"Fuck you. I am not going anywhere with you. I am going to see the Prime Minister and tell him what we are going to do unless he returns our property. Now get out of my way."

The Indian security people entered, turned to Jr. and said, "Mister Trump, you will not be seeing the Prime Minister and we have been instructed to place you under arrest unless you leave with the embassy personnel right now."

"You know you can't arrest me. You can't do shit to me!"

"Mister Trump," the Marine Captain said, "we were told to inform you that your diplomatic credentials have been revoked. They can and will arrest you unless you come with us."

"Who the fuck thinks they have the authority to revoke my diplomatic credentials? My father gave them to me as the President of the United States, and he is the only one who can revoke it!"

"Mister Trump, it was he who ordered the ambassador to revoke your status. I strongly suggest that you come with us."

"Listen, Mister Prime Minister, I know you can hear me. If you do not return our property by the time, I get back home, I will see that tariffs are imposed on all Indian merchandise coming to the United States, and I also will see that our military who is helping you hold Pakistan and China at bay will be removed. You will be risking invasion into your country if you continue this reckless act of stealing!"

The Marine Captain took him by the arm and led him to a vehicle waiting outside. Still cursing, he entered the car. The reporter was filming the entire time.

Within thirty minutes, the entire episode was playing on every news channel in the world!

Donald Jr. was placed on the next plane back to New York. He was still unaware of the news conference the five governments had held earlier, later, adding two more countries. He was still fuming when they escorted him on the plane. No one met him at the airport when he arrived.

Donald Trump was furious. His son came across as a fucking idiot. An idiot who thought he had the power of the presidency and could order other heads of state around. This was bad, really bad. Ivanka was on her way to Moscow. He called Eric to get his input.

"Eric, what the fuck happened? Have you seen the Jr. videos?"

"Yes, I think everybody in the world has now seen them. Ivanka and I tried to call and warn you, but your doctor had put you to sleep. Jr. would not talk to us. He hid from the embassy people, changed the hotel he was to stay in and tried to force the Prime Minister to meet with him. We were hoping maybe you could reach him, but it was not to be."

Ivanka arrived in Moscow and was picked up by the American embassy security and taken directly to her hotel. They obliged her request to be left alone. She contacted the bank the moment she was alone: "When can we meet?'

"Tomorrow morning at ten. We will pick you up. Where are you staying?"
"The Hilton, I will be ready."

The next morning, she was picked up by a limousine, taken to the Bank Otkritie and escorted into a large conference room. There, she was confronted by four older men, each with a folder of financial data in front of them.

"Welcome, Miss Ivanka. Glad you are here."

"It is important that we handle this potential issue before it becomes a problem. As you know, the liens of several of our properties which you hold have been confiscated. Your liens will be paid by the respective nation where the property is located. Our concern is that the country may decide that the values are less than the amount of the lien. We will be powerless to protect you should that be the case. Your liens will be gone for whatever they decide to pay. So, my purpose is to find a way to ensure that should that happen, you incur no loss."

"And what is your proposed method to protect us?"

"Our company has many properties and offer to just transfer your interest to those properties where you have present liens to new ones in the amount of any shortfall should there be one." Answered Ivanka.

"Miss Ivanka, we have many concerns over such an arrangement. These unfortunate problems you are having have greatly reduced the value of any properties you now own. As you know, we are also lien holders on some of those properties. Such an arrangement would only serve to increase the risk we presently have." Said the senior bank official.

"Obviously, we would provide present-day appraisals of any such property. We are going to stop these attacks and very soon."

"You may not be aware, but two of your properties in New York City were hit again last night. Sewage overflows on those properties are all over the news!"

Ivanka turned pale. "I did not know. I am sure it is being handled quickly." For the next hour, the group went over lien amounts and possible scenarios.

"We must be paid any shortfalls and paid quickly. It looks like you may have several weeks to raise any cash needs you may have. Our estimate is that the shortfall may be as high as 500 million US dollars."

Ivanka gasped. "I was thinking possibly several million."

There are several things you may consider. One is the sanctions your government now has in place. Should those disappear, we would certainly add to the existing liens. Second, the property Mar-a-Lago, we would consider purchasing the controlling interest in that property for any shortfall."

"These are things only my father can answer. Let me take them to him, and we will get back to you."

Ivanka was taken back to her hotel. There she called her father, "It is not good news. It is best we talk in person, not over the phone. I will fly directly to Washington. I will let you know my travel plans." She then called Eric and asked, "Have we been hit again?"

"Yes, the property in White Plains and on 6th avenue. Big damn mess again!"

She later found that a flight was available in seven hours. She booked it and informed her father.

Ivanka arrived in Washington at 9 AM the next morning. She took a taxi directly to the White House. She was escorted into the private quarters of the family area where the President joined her.

"OK, tell me what they said?"

"They might as well want a couple pints of your blood. They will do what we requested, which is to take an interest in other properties if you can remove the sanctions the United States has on Russia or as an alternative, they want controlling interest in Mar-a-Lago."

"No way can I or will I do either of those. I thought they would go for the jugular but not this bad. What I want you to do is make contact with some of the major hotel groups and sell the one here in DC, New York and possibly Chicago. That will raise enough cash to cover any shortfalls."

"I will get on it."

Trump walked away. Ivanka collapsed on one of the beds.

Donald Jr. had not surfaced. He had heard on the news that they had been hit again. He still was not aware of the news conference and that he had been filmed making his threats.

President Trump called the head of the FBI as soon as he got back to his office. "I want you to bring over your chief and the most experienced investigator and meet me here as soon as possible." No other explanation was given.

The FBI suspected that it would be about the sabotage of Trump property which they could not get involved in, but they had no choice but to come to the meeting.

Forty-five minutes later, Director Wrag arrived with Jonathan Haver, the Chief of the Investigation Unit. President Trump had never met Inspector Haver and was introduced. "Inspector Haver, as you probably know, I have a problem which the FBI has decided they cannot handle. What I am asking, however, is advice on what we can do. We are getting no help from the local authorities. It appears that I will be forced to hire private investigators to find whoever they are. First, do you know anyone you could recommend?"

Inspector Haver said, "I can send you a list of those I know to be experienced and have the talent and manpower to assist you."

"Second, this has been happening all over the world. Where do you think we should start?"

"That is easy. Start with people who have traveled to the areas near the time of the attack. Also, look at rental cars, trucks and equipment that may have been used. I would think whatever items were used would be required at all locations. It is a lot of work but will most likely pay off."

"Chris, will you allow the FBI to provide us with the manifest for those times and places we have been hit?"

"Yes, I will since this is slowly rising to a level where you may be at risk. We will provide you with whatever data assistance we can."

Trump thanked them then called Donald Jr. "Time to get your head out of the hole and get this problem solved. I have just met with the FBI; they will provide us with data as best they can. I want you to find and hire a private agency to find these people and stop them. An Inspector Haver is sending us a list of ones he thinks qualifies."

"Yes, sir. I will get on that right now, and I could have made that Indian asshole backdown if you would have left me alone!"

"Right! And I suppose you think the same for the Philippines, Indonesia and the other four countries who are doing the same. You must accept they have us by the balls and you only made them squeeze harder."

The news media began broadcasting scenes from all over the world. Iran, Syria, Kurdish country, Mexico, Uruguay, Guatemala, Iraq, Cuba and many other countries were celebrating the problems Donald Trump and the Trump Organization were having. Televisions all over the world were showing the Indian newscast as well as the fiasco involving Donald Jr. There were cheers from the populations of many countries.

A group of reporters hung out outside Donald Jr.'s apartment hoping to get a statement. He peeked out the window but did not go outside. He had now watched the Indian news conference and seen himself on television. Who the fuck filmed that? I saw no cameras, he thought. He now felt like a fool.

Eric had also been very busy. He was handling the latest sewage issue. He now knew what to do and had it down pat. They pumped what was in the lines into a tank on a truck and sent a crew of people inside to clean. Within three hours all was clean and functioning. His attention was turned to finding appraisers in all the cities where properties had been confiscated. He had filmed the cleanup effort and how long it takes to get the entire building back in operation. He wanted the appraisers to know that even though they had not been able to catch them yet, the living areas could be repaired and contained with minimum collateral damage. This was until they caught them! He had not grasped that every time he finished the cleaning process, the property was sprayed with a substance that brought back the smell.

Ivanka slept for three hours, then began making calls to all the top hotel chains. All were interested. She set up meetings over the next several days. She also made contact with appraisal firms in each of the cities they may want to sell. She knew she needed an appraisal number that could be supported and was on the high end.

Chapter Twenty-Three

Ali Khamenei was as happy as any world leader could be. It was now obvious to him that their efforts may, in fact, so cripple the presidency of Donald Trump that he would be forced to resign. A great turn of events. He had been briefed how careless Donald Jr. was. Trump's Jr.'s cell phone conversations were recorded of him trying to hire investigators. He had even spoken of comparing manifest and looking for rental companies. Aftab had picked up this tidbit of information and immediately put his computer expert Rasheen Abbasi into doing what he could to thwart this effort.

Rasheen and his staff hacked into the airline database rather easily. He then simply changed the names of anyone who Iran had actually sent to do the work plus many others in case the changes were detected. It took them less than two hours to get this done. The airline security for old flight data was not very secure.

His crew then went to work on other items which could be uncovered: hotels, credit card charges, auto rental, gas purchases, equipment rental and specialty purchases. The credit card companies' sites were secure and would likely be traceable should they be able to breach the system. This was not possible in the rental companies where they had rented specialty items, they had no online presence and looking at copies of the actual invoices was a manual operation. This worried Rasheen as the charges were paid with credit cards and the charge statement clearly showed what was being paid for. They would keep trying. This was certainly an avenue where discovery could be made. Rasheen sent a memo to Aftab that this was a concern and future rentals should be paid this way with caution. Aftab said he would handle it.

Working off the list provided by Inspector Haver, Donald Jr. interviewed three firms and settled on a Humphrey's Agency with headquarters in Washington DC but with offices in many of the cities where the property had been confiscated. The lead agent, a Maxwell Hamper could not comprehend how the cause had not been detected? There were not that many ways to stop up a sewage line. Fortunately, or unfortunately as the case may be, two of Kushner's properties had been hit just that morning. Maxwell left moments after the contract was signed and a deposit was made. Both properties were less than a hundred miles away. He sent an agent to one property and he went to the other. Once there, the smell was overwhelming. He had to don a protective breathing apparatus to work inside the building. He interviewed the plumbing people as to what they did to unstop the sewage and what they discovered when they arrived. The plumber said the stoppage was definitely between the building and the manhole as the manhole was dry and no sewage was flowing into it. They sent 'snakes' down the pipe with propeller-like bits on the end to grind through whatever had caused the stoppage. When the propeller reached the manhole, the sewage flowed rapidly and drained easily from there. Maxwell could see from looking inside the manhole that it was flowing smoothly. Maxwell sent a camera down the manhole and took hundreds of photos, then sent one down the pipe from inside the building and did the same. He understood that whatever had stopped up the line was now being flushed toward a treatment plant and was gone forever. He needed to examine the situation before it was unstopped. He then made an appointment with a mechanical engineer who specialized in the design of sewage systems.

Kushner had contacted his insurance company who hired a company to clean up the sewage mess. Iran, of course, was standing by to assist in their special way. When the company pulled up at each address, they slipped into the proper uniform at each site.

The mechanical engineer, Michael Letcher, listened as Maxwell described what he had seen at all the other locations. Michael took a plastic water bottle, removed the cap and turned it upside down. He held the end opening so it sealed itself. with the water in the bottle, by putting his finger over the end, he then turned it loose and the water did not flow. Michel then said, "The flow requires air pressure. All you have to do is stop up the outlet until there is no air pressure. In other words, hold it until the pipe fills up. Then it will clog itself up. That is why we design pipes to supply air so the pipe will not naturally fill up. Stop the air and you will stop up the pipe."

"So, someone could plug up the outlet until the pipe fills up, remove the plug and the pipe will stay clogged up?"

"Right."

"Now, how could that be done? And how long would it take?"

"For these types of buildings, probably several hours. They make plugs to do just that."

Maxwell left, called his counterpart visiting the other location, "You find security cameras anywhere within a ten-block area, we need to check them for at least twenty hours before the sewer was stopped up."

"Will do."

Maxwell returned to the area and began slowly canvassing the surrounding area, noting any cameras present.

Maxwell called Donald Jr. and gave him his first reaction and told him what he was doing. Jr. got excited. This made sense. He believed they would have the culprits in hand shortly. He called his father and gave him the news.

The Iranians, since they listened to every word said on Jr's. phone knew instantly about the progress. Aftab acted quickly. He ordered the warehouse location in New York City to be thoroughly cleaned, emptied with no trace, including fingerprints of anyone left. Every piece of equipment was to be disposed of, as well as any inventory of gelatin, dry ice, acid, pumps, mixers. He ordered all that could be disposed of to be poured down a drain. He ordered the trucks and other vehicles to be driven at least 500 miles away in different directions before stopping. The vehicles are to be abandoned at locations unknown. "Leave them legally parked in places that have no security cameras. Remove the tags, any documents, clean them thoroughly and walk away. Find a bus station and come back by bus. Do not tell anyone where you left the vehicle. It will be found and brought in by some local police jurisdiction and sold at a public auction since no one will clam them."

Aftab had also contacted his locations worldwide and gave then the same instructions. He wanted no trace of them ever having been anywhere. Their mission was over! Except, he decided the bedbugs could still be used, it would be the final slap in the face to the Trump organization. He looked over the list of hotels, smiled as he decided that the Trump International Hotel in New York City would be the one to be hit with bedbugs.

After speaking with Donald Jr., President Trump called the FBI director, told him of the progress and requested that they assist in obtaining the video of all security footage. The director first hesitated then realized that a foreign government could be behind this and it was within his authority to do so. Trump felt good. We are about to get those bastards, he thought.

The FBI sent a memo giving the President contact information for the private investigator to coordinate with.

Maxwell sent the location information to the FBI coordinator. The FBI moved swiftly and had agents knocking on doors by late in the afternoon. They had obtained the necessary warrants, if needed, to require the owner to turn over the videos.

The lease on the warehouse property was good for another forty-eight days. Aftab gave no notice, just instructed his people to lock the place up, leave the keys on the floor. Utilities were included with the lease so nothing else was required. Within two hours of being notified, the place was sparkling clean; all equipment and vehicles were gone. Early the next morning, all vehicles had been abandoned. The tags removed and disposed of the vehicles cleaned, and the drivers waited at different bus stations in different towns for buses headed to different locations. Aftab wanted them to head to any large city that was not New York, catch a train to somewhere else then go back on a bus to a different city. He also instructed them to change their clothes each time, keep their head down and wear a hat. They were to buy several hats, to let the security cameras see someone else each time. Iran would coordinate and get them back to their homes, some in the United States and others back to Iran. The same scenario had taken place at all locations Iran had been operating.

By evening, Maxwell and other agents were viewing hundreds of hours of video looking for exactly what, they did not know.

Aftab felt like he needed to brief the President on what had happened and what he had done. He did so in a face-to-face meeting. It was far too sensitive to take any chance of being overheard. The president believed he had done the right thing. He did, however, want Aftab's suggestion on what should be provided as fake information, since this phase was over. Aftab thought for a moment and said, "We suggest that enough direct damage to Trump has been done except we will create a Bedbug infestation at his prime hotel in New York City, other than that, it is time to do indirect. We let him think someone is planning to attack the Russian financiers and make it look like Trump is behind it." The president smiled. "This will make him very nervous; the Russian Mafia is behind the banks and they get paid or they get even! I do like the bedbugs, it will be a great final slap in the face."

Maxwell's people struck pay dirt at 4:30 AM. They spotted a 2-ton truck and a passenger vehicle near both sites; it was the same truck and vehicle. Magnification showed it had a small backhoe, a portable cement mixer, some type of roofing kettle and sacks of supplies on the back of the truck including two fifty-gallon drums at the first site and only one at the second. They could only get a partial license plate number for either vehicle. They also could not be sure about the make and model nor could they tell who the driver or passengers were. It appeared that there were four people involved. One drum observed on the back of the 2-ton truck was gone after the first building was hit and both were gone after the second. Maxwell needed to find those drums. At nine in the morning, Maxwell requested assistance from the FBI. He gave them the size, color and partial license plate of both vehicles. He then updated Jr. who immediately called his father and repeated what he had been told. Aftab got the recording thirty minutes later.

He brought the information to his security people. "What can they learn from this information?" he asked.

"Who and where are the vehicles registered and who purchased the insurance?" said Nash Heydari the chief of security.

"We created a dummy corporation to purchase the vehicles and buy insurance. We paid using a cashier's check. The corporation owners are fictitious. We gave the insurance company a fake identification. The address was a real address in New York but picked randomly. All mail went to a post office box. They were the only ones given that address. The box was rented using fake identification." Said Aftab.

"Sounds to us like there is no way it can be traced to us. What about the application, title and so forth? Are there fingerprints?"

"I hope not. They were instructed what to do."

By noon, the FBI had narrowed it down to ten different addresses. Maxwell set out to visit half, his other agents went to the others. In eight of the addresses, the vehicles were there, but they were not the ones in the video. The other two addresses knew nothing about the vehicles and stated they were not theirs. Maxwell believed them. Now that they knew the complete license plate numbers, they could obtain the insurance data. Both vehicles were insured by the same company and owned by a corporation registered in New York. The officers listed for the company were fake, so were the identification of the buyers of the insurance. They then contacted the postal service and discovered that the same fake identification was used to rent the post office box which was shown as the mailing address. The box had a mailing address but had never been used other than to receive mail from the insurance company. No doubt these were the culprits. They just needed to find the correct address and the vehicles. There also was no doubt that these were professionals who knew what they were doing. Maxwell then set out to obtain the actual documents hoping to find fingerprints. The truck was a black, used 2013 Chevrolet which already had 46,000 miles when bought.

The other vehicle was a Ford Taurus, dark blue 4 doors 2015 bought with 31,000 miles on the odometer.

The FBI put out a nationwide alert for the vehicles. Late the next evening, a 2-ton truck matching the serial number of the missing vehicle was reported as being found at a bowling alley parking lot in Bowling Green, Kentucky. It had no tag which is what led the police to investigate. Maxwell immediately went to Bowling Green and met local FBI agents. The truck was dusted for fingerprints, but none were found except for the tow truck driver who had moved the truck to a holding yard. Maxwell again canvassed the area for security cameras. He obtained the footage but could not make out any features on either of the two men who were in the truck. He did find where two men, similar to the two in the truck, had purchased bus tickets. One to Nashville and the other to Atlanta. He obtained the footage in both cities, saw them get off the bus and then just disappear. He checked trains, airports, rental cars but did not see either of them again. "These are well-trained men we are after," he said softly to himself.

The Ford Taurus was located in Westerville, Ohio in a nearly identical situation. The vehicle was found in the parking lot of Otterbein University. The campus police had ticketed it for having no parking decal then reported it the next day to the local police as it had not moved and had no tag. It was found on the national 'look for' site and reported to the FBI. Again, security footage showed two people were in the vehicle. Local buses were taken to Columbus, Ohio as the videos showed. A person who looked similar to the one in the vehicle boarded a bus to Louisville. The other was not seen. From Louisville no other security footage picked up the person. Maxwell was convinced that all four changed clothing, hats and so forth probably several times.

Maxwell then called Jr., "We need to meet in person. Nothing else can be said over the phone or in your apartment or office. They seem to know what we are going to do as soon as I do."

"OK, where and when?"

"As soon as possible. Where are you now?" "I am in New York at my office."

"Meet me in Philadelphia. Do not talk on your phone. Buy a disposable and call me on it. I am heading by train to Philly. Please do the same."

Jr. went directly to the train station and caught the next one to Philadelphia. He called Maxwell on the train on a throwaway phone that he bought. He told him when he would arrive. Maxwell said, "I will be there. Look for me when you get off the train."

They met. Maxwell was short with him. "Give me your phone!"

Maxwell toyed with it for a few minutes. "It's bugged; every word you have spoken for lord knows how long has been listened to by someone." Jr. hung his head down and avoided looking directly in his eyes. "I don't know. It never entered my mind."

"I am going to give your phone to the FBI. Maybe they can figure out who has been listening in. It would be wise to have all your family's phones checked. These are not run of the mill people. These are highly trained professionals. They have known what we are doing almost as if they were sitting in our conference room. It is no accident that these vehicles were taken far away, cleaned and left for someone to find. Both were driven more than 500 miles away then left abandoned.

"We know that they were mixing some kind of chemicals to temporarily stop up the sewer long enough for the pipes to clog. You said one of the buildings in Indonesia was on a septic system, is that right?"

"Yes."

"OK, give me the details and get me permission. I am going to have someone dig it up and test whatever is down there. Maybe we can figure out what chemicals were used."

Jr. made several calls using his throwaway phone. An hour later, he gave Maxwell the exact address and told him that written permission was on its way.

Iran had heard enough to know that the new detective had figured out Jr's phone was tapped. They would now have to bug the new one again!

Chapter Twenty-Four

Maxwell contacted Donald Jr. late in the afternoon. "I need to meet with all of you and detail what we know and what must be done."

"When?"

"As soon as possible. How about tomorrow morning at whatever location suits you most?"

Thirty minutes later Maxwell received a call. "How about we meet in the morning? Dad would like to be there so let's meet at the White House. He says ten will be perfect for him. The others can be there also."

"I will be there. How will I get in?" "Will let you know in a few."

Ten minutes later. Jr. called back.

"The secret service will pick you up outside the Hay-Adams Hotel at 9:30. I gave them your cell phone number. Dad wants Inspector Haver there as well."

"Good. He will be helpful. I will be there."

Iran had guessed, Donald Jr. would want to use his old number on his new phone. They had already managed to tap into his conversations on his new phone by sending a fake text when opened it downloaded data that allowed for all conversations to be recorded. Using the numbers, he called to arrange the meeting. They also had now been able to tap into Ivanka's and Eric's new phones. The President's number was secure and could not be tapped. Iran was aware of the meeting at the same time as the others.

The next morning, Maxwell was picked up at the entrance to the Hay-Adam hotel, taken to a secure area where he was searched and given a protocol to follow when meeting with the President.

He was escorted into a conference room a few minutes before ten. Donald Jr., Ivanka, Eric and Inspector Haver were already seated. A few minutes later, the President walked in, and, after being introduced to Maxwell, said, "Maxwell give us your breakdown on what you have found."

"Yes sir, but before I do, I would like Ivanka to make a couple of calls," He turned to her, "Ivanka, I worked last night on the leaking faucet problem and may have a solution. Can you call right now and have someone take a water sample at the two new locations and rush them to my office please? Send someone from each location. We need to know this as soon as possible."

"Sure," Ivanka sent a text to an assistant stressing the urgency.

"Sorry sir, for the interruption but this information, I believe, will be important."

"No problem. Now tell us."

"We have been able to figure out how they are stopping up the sewers but do not yet know the precise chemicals used. I hope to know that by morning. Basically, they stopped up the manhole using some form of temporary chemical. It stopped the flow long enough for the main sewer pipe from the building to build up sufficiently to clog up any other sewage from flowing. The chemical used then dissipated and flowed down the sewer system. That is why it was believed that the stoppage was being created from inside the building because the manhole was always clean."

"I don't see how that is possible. Once whatever chemical was used dissipates, I would think the sewage would flow again."

"No, all sewage systems are designed with air vents. Air and gravity are what push the sewage to the manhole. The sewage drops into the manhole and then starts again. This chemical stopped the flow, so the pipe completely filled up with sewage and pushed the air back up the pipe. It clogged up to a point that it would not flow. The design engineer I visited demonstrated this by holding up a bottle of water and removing the cap. Nothing came out until he tilted it, so the air had a way to also escape."

"Damn, I would not have thought that possible! Now, what do we do for the future?"

"The perfect solution is to secure the manhole covers with some type of lock so that they cannot be opened. To do this, you will need approval from the various cities."

"Forget that," said, Ivanka, "New York will never give us approval." "Why not?" said Maxwell, "It is the surest way to protect from this."

"City officials hate us and will not help. We could not even get the police to do anything other than file a report," said Eric.

"Can you not talk to them?" Maxwell asked.

"We can try but I doubt they will even do that; we do not have good relations with them.

"They weren't that bad!" said the President.

"Maybe we can go to plan 'B' which is security cameras. You will have to place them so the manhole covers can be seen at all times. It will require 24/7 monitors, but all your property can be monitored by one person."

"What will it cost?"

"Don't know, but we can find out, but it will be cheap as compared to what this has cost you already."

Eric said, "You know we have had a lot of people get sick eating at our restaurants. Have you looked at that?"

"Not yet. It is on our list. We know some chemicals can be sprayed on food that cause people to get sick. It is relatively easy to spray on food, especially fresh fruits and vegetables. My guess is that is what they have done."

"How could they have gotten access to all these places to do that? Seems impossible. Someone is with the deliveries constantly from the time it is delivered until cooked and served," said, Ivanka.

"The easiest way is to spray it, before it is delivered. They would only need to know who you buy them from and when you get deliveries."

"Now who the hell has been doing this to us?" asked the President.

"Somebody with a lot of resources and sophistication. I doubt an individual would have the ability to do what has been done here. Just the expertise to do this in all the places it has been done is substantial and the technical knowledge needed is great. We have just verified that they had a permit to do work on the two latest buildings. The city is trying to figure out how that was given. It supposedly, is not possible. A permit requires review before it is issued. These permits suddenly appeared as approved! We are likely to find the same for all the places that have been hit."

"What is next?" asked Donald Jr.

"I am hoping to get a chemical analysis of what was used to make this happen. We sent the contents of the Indonesia septic system for analysis. We might get the results back tomorrow. The quantities needed will be substantial. Some of these manholes are ten feet deep. My guess is these are not readily available items. Also, the water samples which Ivanka has arranged to be taken to my office: I suspect they will show a high concentration of acid. The two mysterious 50-gallon drums we have not been able to locate, most likely contain acid. They were plastic drums not metal. I think that when we verify, we should be able to find where they came from and who purchased them."

"Ivanka," said the President, "you see if you can get the different cities to allow us to lock the manholes and if not, retain a security company to install cameras and monitor them. I would think you would also want to do that with Jared's property as it looks like he is being targeted also."

"Will do."

"Maxwell, your folks have done a fantastic job and, I am confident you will find out who these people are. Would you mind keeping Inspector Haver informed?", said the President.

"Not at all."

The meeting broke up; Maxwell was taken back to the Hay-Adam. Ivanka immediately called Jared and gave him a blow-by-blow account of the meeting including getting locks or cameras on the manhole covers. He also told him Maxwell's suspicion that he would find acid in the water samples and identify the chemicals used to stop up the sewers.

Iran, of course, heard every word and gave Aftab a report minutes later.

Maxwell headed toward his office to rush the testing of the water. He was almost positive he would find acid.

Aftab was not unhappy. Someone was now figuring out what they had been doing. He actually thought it would be found out much sooner. He scheduled a meeting with all his people. They must be told. You never know, they may have some ideas about how to use the information.

Maxwell was given the results of the tests as soon as he walked into his office. The test revealed a high concentration of acid. He immediately called both Ivanka and Donald Jr. jointly, "We have the test results. There is most definitely a high concentration of acid in the water. You need to immediately turn off the water before more damage is done. I am sending a team to each address now to figure out how the acid is entering the water!"

"I will have someone do that right this minute," Ivanka said. "What about the other properties?" asked Donald Jr.

"Let us first figure out how then we will go to the other properties and see if the same was done."

"Sounds good."

The teams arrived at the addresses within an hour and a half. Maxwell had sent the water line layout information for each of the buildings on their phones. It did not take long to figure it out. They laid out with blue chalk the line as it would be beneath the ground. For the first address, fifteen feet down the line, the ground had been disturbed and the grass replaced. The agent took a shovel and begin probing what looked like disturbed ground. The agent hit two pipes coming out of the ground. He dug down beside the pipes and sure enough, he hit one of the 50-gallon drums. Maxwell was at the first address by then. He ordered that no one touch anything until it was examined. He sent for some forensic examiners who looked for fingerprints or other evidence. The forensic examiners were excited. They had found fingerprints and likely DNA evidence on the pipe, drum and a contraption drilled into the main water line. Maxwell rushed to relay the information to Inspector Haver with a request to see if the FBI had any information on who these folks were. He then called Donald Jr., "they did this by burying a 50-gallon drum of acid which fed into the water system going into the building. It would feed the acid until empty. We must go to each address as there is also a pipe that will allow them to refill the acid. These must be eliminated. We recovered fingerprints and DNA from the pipe and drum. Inspector Haver is searching for any match he may have right now."

"Son of a bitch, those bastards! I hope we can now find them." "There is a good chance we can identify them."

Iran recorded every word and sent the information to Aftab, the moment it was transcribed.

Aftab wasted no time when he got the information. He already had a contingency plan should any of them be identified. He made contact with the crew that was responsible for the last installation of the acid drums. Two of the men who worked on the crew were US citizens. Aftab wanted them out of the country and back home immediately. "You tell them if they have not been identified, they can return when it is safe. Do not take any traceable mode of transportation back here." He gave them a phone number to call to cover expenses and assist. The other two were professionals and would never have touched anything without gloves but he warned them anyway. Both assured that they had on gloves and it was not them. They also told Aftab that the other two had on gloves the entire time.

Aftab, being an optimist, now believed the fingerprints would be from the salespeople who they purchased the pipe and acid from or the delivery truck which delivered the drums to the New York City warehouse address. Aftab smiled, he now believed this would be a wild goose chase for the Trump people.

Maxwell's teams now went meticulously to every address that had been hit including those in India, Indonesia and other countries. That was one of the big benefits of having offices all over the world. Drums were discovered at most of the addresses, but none were found at Trump Tower. It was assumed none had yet been installed. All were scanned for DNA and fingerprints, none was found.

Aftab began his meeting by updating the crew on what was happening to include the discovery of fingerprints and DNA, "Now that they are aware of how we have been doing this, we likely must close down that part of the operation."

Several of the participants raised their hands, "Maybe for the Trump family buildings but we have ignored Benjamin Netanyahu. He owns an apartment in Manhattan and five other properties: two in Spain, two in France and one in Israel. We should hit all of his properties at the same time.

I doubt he is on the loop of information that Trump now knows. Benjamin Netanyahu needs to be punished!"

Aftab said, "You are right. Can you guys divide his property up and let's see how fast we can get organized to hit him."

"Fortunately," said Rasheen, "the properties in Spain and France are very close together. I think one team for Spain, one for France, and one for Israel would do, and we use who we already have in New York for that one."

The team quickly separated into the groups according to who would handle what and went into separate areas.

Back in the United States, they had raised more than 300,000 bedbugs; they were all gathered and taken to New York City. They were already aware of who did the pest control and what the schedule was for the New York City International Hotel. There was a schedule for the next day. Uniforms were obtained and a man was sent in with a large quantity of bedbugs hidden in a canister. He went to the front desk and got a list of the empty rooms he could treat. He was given temporary keys to the rooms; the keys were electronic and would be good only for the day. He entered to first room which was an elaborate suite, gently raised the cover of the bed and poured bedbugs under the sheets. He knew the bugs would naturally hide themselves until a warm body was nearby. He did the same for three more rooms then left.

Chapter Twenty-Five

Maxwell received the report from Indonesia on the chemical analysis from the septic system. It had some surprising information that made no sense. It found an unusual amount of plain gelatin and a high concentration of carbon dioxide and nothing else out of the ordinary. Maxwell set down with several senior staff members and asked, "What does this mean?" After several minutes, one member noted, "Yes, it does make sense. Carbon dioxide is extremely cold in its solid form. Gelatin is firm but not strong. If it gets really cold and probably freezes, you have a firm solution that will stop up a sewer system for a short period. A short period is all you need before the pipe itself clogs up. This is damn genius. Once the ice melts, the gelatin will just dissipate down the sewer system leaving no trace!"

Maxwell stood up came over and shook his hand. "Damn you are so right."

Maxwell called Donald Jr. to give him the latest. "We have received the information from Indonesia and now know how they did it."

"Great, tell me."

"You won't believe it, but they made a large mixture of gelatin then using dry ice froze it, so it became solid and used it to stop up sewers. The frozen mixture would thaw in a few hours. We tested the concept and it and typically takes four to five hours before thawing. The mixture when thawed just runs down the regular sewer, never to be seen again. The solid would cause the sewage line to run from the building to clog up and stop all flow. Damn brilliant!"

"Son of a bitch, so damn simple but effective!"

"The only way to stop it is to not allow access to the manhole, so security is essential."

"We have awarded a contract to install cameras. The city just laughed, thought it was funny that we would ask for their help in view of all the bad blood between us."

Maxwell then called Inspector Haver and gave him the update. He also added what he did not tell Jr., that many fingerprints and DNA were discovered on the pipe, drums and fittings. They were being extracted and would be sent to him as soon as possible.

Aftab reached decisions on Benjamin Netanyahu's property in his meeting. The decisions he reached was the property in Israel would be left alone; the security was just too great to take the chance. The apartment in Manhattan was problematic. It was located in a large high rise and could not be damaged without also damaging others in the building. "Benjamin Netanyahu would not necessarily know it was him we are after. So, the only way, is to develop a plan so that we can get inside and do the damage just to his apartment. We have assigned someone to download the plans and see how to best do that. The properties in France and Spain should be easy and can be done the same way we have been doing, with some modifications. They are standalone condominiums. However, they may not be on a sewage system that only has those buildings. Several run along the street. It could be, and probably is, these buildings that are connected to the main run going to a manhole. We will see what could be done but we have to go to them to look over. Spain and France both regularly do that and run the main arteries to a manhole. We will have a crew leave in the morning. We have arranged for the equipment to be also there tomorrow morning."

The crew that was assigned to hit the French properties arrived in Marseilles, France. They had a rental car to drive to Saint Tropez. Both properties were located there. The route was a toll road and expected to take 2 hours, however, the traffic was horrible and took slightly more than 3 hours. They found the apartment which had been rented for them, checked in and left to find the warehouse and rental equipment. It took 30 minutes even though it was only a 20-minute walk, Gulzar who was in charge of the French operation assigned everyone to walk to the address of the two properties. The apartments were approximately one block apart on Rue Fontannette and Rue Fontannette Perdu both within walking distance of La Ponche Beach. The property on Rue Fontannette Perdu was the more expensive and elaborate of the two.

Each was a part of several condominiums on a short road overlooking the beach. All were very expensive luxury apartments surrounded by expensive places and from the looks, people with lots of money. Luxury cars were parked all around the places, on street parking and a parking lot was part of the compound.

Each apartment had its own water meter. Gulzar quickly decided that the 50-gallon drum of acid was too much. He contacted Aftab who had his folks recalculate and confirmed. A two-liter quantity was sufficient as it only served one apartment. Gulzar now needed the two-liter bottles and the fittings to make it work.

The sewage was another story. They found the manhole, but it served all the apartments not just those owned by Benjamin Netanyahu. Gulzar gave Aftab the news and wanted a plan to handle the situation. It looked to him like they would need to cut a single pipe and stop it up. Aftab told him they would figure it out and get back to him.

Two hours later, Aftab called and gave the new design to them.

"You are to locate, penetrate but not cut the pipe then use the hot tap concept. The tab will be for a 40 MM hole. On the way is a cement mixture that will be installed like a caulk. The substance is thick and dries almost instantly. It is made to stop a water leak. Put three tubes, if possible. It will stop the sewage flow. Cover it up and leave it alone. For the waterline, dig alongside it, make a hole large enough to allow the 2-liter bottle of acid to be covered up. It must be above the waterline. The water line will be either a 19- or 25-millimeter pipe. You have hot taps for both those sizes. Connect the 2-liter bottle and run an air supply pipe to the surface. Be sure when you cover it back up that the air supply pipe is slightly above the ground. All these supplies will be at the warehouse by late afternoon."

That night, Gulzar and his crew had already confirmed that the correct materials had been delivered. They wisely made the connections to the 2-liter bottles and filled them with acid. Gulzar believed all could be done by hand with no need for the small backhoe. They left the warehouse at 2 AM. There was still traffic but Rue Fontannette and Rue Fontannette Perdu were both off the main streets and almost no traffic was on them. When they reached Rue Fontannette, it was deserted. They first placed the warning barriers which included a readable copy of the permit. The permit was bright orange and could be seen from a distance. It had the permit number in large letters. Gulzar chose Rue Fontannette as the first property because it had the most visibility. Rue Fontannette Perdu could only be seen if you were on the street and in front of the buildings.

The truck, which was a 1.4 metric ton, was a white Renault Tipper type. Magnetic signs were placed on the sides to identify the vehicle as belonging to a utility construction company. Gulzar expected nothing more than a quick glance from anyone passing by.

Gulzar began with two teams digging. He spotted the positions of where the pipes were located very fast as, he had a copy of the drawings showing the placement of all piping. He cautioned both teams to be sure that the proper depth was saved on the sod. Each team had tarps to place the dirt on as they dug. The ground was mostly sand and easy to dig into. It looked like topsoil had been brought in to give the grass something to grasp onto. The team with the sewage pipe reached the pipe in 15 minutes. They carefully dug around and under the pipe, so the hot tap could be made. The strap was pulled under, reconnected and the hole was made using the tap. Once the hole was made, the other pipe was connected, and the cement mixture was pumped into the pipe using a larger than normal caulking gun. The pipe would only accept two tubes. The pipe from the hot tap was disconnected, the valve closed, and the hole recovered, sod replaced, the area raked clean. It looked like no disturbance had been made. The entire work had taken 45 minutes.

The second team had now made the tap, placed the 2-liter bottle and was beginning to fill the hole. They had decided to wait to cut off the air supply pipe after the dirt and sod were replaced. It was just too small an area to take a chance of the pipe getting filled with dirt. The first team had already moved to the second address when the acid installation was complete. They moved onto the second address. Time: one hour ten minutes.

The second installation was easier than the first. The sewer pipe was running along a sidewalk roughly 46 centimeters deep. They cut out the sod, dug down using hole digger, put all the dirt on a tarp, dug under the pipe using a regular shovel, made the tap, installed the pipe and was filling the cement when the second crew started on the waterline. It had become a race and the sewer crew was winning!

The acid crew had a slightly more difficult situation, the water line had a water meter to measure the consumption which was only one meter away from the building. It was running under some landscape bushes. There was no sod just a plastic-type ground cover. They carefully raked up the ground cover and began digging. It was so close to the building that it was difficult. The water line also was slightly deeper than the first. It required a lot of close hand digging, much using very small shovels. Luckily, they had seen no one on the street although, a small crowd was still there on the beach, which was only fifteen meters away. The ones on the beach had paid no attention to them. It had taken an hour and a half to finish the second. It was now 4:30 AM, all were exhausted. They took the truck to the warehouse where they had left the rental car. A second crew would pick up all the equipment the next morning, clean the place thoroughly and get the equipment back to where it belonged. Gulzar contacted Aftab and told him it was done. The crew was to stay in France. They had been provided uniforms of two different companies who likely would be called. They were told to wait and monitor when the cleanup crews arrived and joined them. They also had the substance needed to be sprayed on the walls and floor to leave a bad smell. They waited.

The Spanish teams had reached San Sabastian roughly the same time as their French counterparts reached Marseilles. Aftab had looked at the satellite images of the addresses for the apartments and concluded this crew would encounter roughly the same impediments as the French ones. He modified the material requirements, and the added items were on the way. The Spanish crew had a rental car and drove first to the address before heading to the apartment where they would be staying. The address was on Pageo de la Concha, a beachfront looking over La Concha beach. The team drove by the address several times, both apartments were in the same building. Unfortunately, there were ten other apartments in the same structure. They closely looked at the drawings and now understood there was but one sewage line coming from the building. All apartments connected to the same line. Aram contacted Aftab and gave him the information, "We can definitely cause Benjamin Netanyahu's apartments to flood but not without flooding all others, what do you want me to do?"

Aftab responded, "We have the exact same condition in New York. I do not want to hurt innocent people. In New York, we are installing acid, can you?"

"Yes, we can. There are separate water meters."

"OK then let's just do that. He will know someone is targeting him, that is what is important."

Early the next morning at slightly past 2 AM, the team attached the 2-liter gallon containers of acid to the two apartments. It took only one and a half hours since they had two full crews.

In New York, the same conditions existed. They connected the 2-liter gallon container to the water meter with no issues.

Benjamin Netanyahu was about to have a bad couple of weeks!

Aftab was not satisfied with the amount of damage. He wanted the team to see if they could find a way into the New York apartment, spray it with the substance that would leave a smell which could not be removed and leave. Do the same for the Spanish apartments.

Maxwell had gotten back the results from the fingerprint and DNA analysis. Most were identified as workers at supply houses where the items had been purchased. The fingerprints from Indonesia, India, Turkey, South Korea were still pending. Most is a big word when it comes to fingerprint identification. Two of the prints that came from American Citizens have no connection to any of the supply houses or delivery trucks. The FBI had designated a thorough venting of those two.

The New York crew was now monitoring the apartment owned by Benjamin Netanyahu. The recommendation was rather simple. Sometimes in the next week, fixtures were going to be leaking and workmen would have to come to look at what was happening, then replace the fixtures. The team would simply come in as pest control and do the spraying work. This would be done while the workmen were present. Aftab believed this was 'genius' and approved the plan while the team waited.

Maxwell called Donald Jr. to give him an update. Aftab had the information 45 minutes later.

Chapter Twenty-Six

Donald Trump's poll numbers had reached a record low for a sitting President. Democrats were constantly bombarding the public with excerpts of his claims made during the Russian probe and his claim of an ongoing audit was why he would not allow the release of his financial information, all of which proved to be untrue, the claims stated, "This is just the tip of the iceberg and the senate preventing the examination is now more than dangerous since the entire world now knows there is and was a Russian connection!"

Several of the key Republican senators had made an appointment and were now meeting with the President. "Mr. President," said Senator McConnell, "the impact of this is killing us. We now have three senators who have switched parties. This gives us a margin of only two, and several more are wavering. They do not believe they can be reelected as Republicans. It may be time for you to consider resigning."

"There is no way I'll do that."

"As it stands now, the rest of your term will be so hampered, nothing will be accomplished. I believe that if you do not, our majority will be gone."

"Tell me who they are, and I will talk with them."

"I can but you must be very careful. A threat could push them over." "I know how to be nice!"

****

The crew in New York got word that a contractor was coming to look over the problem with the leaking fixtures for the Benjamin Netanyahu New York property. The leaks had made a mess, soaking all the carpet. Also coming was a cleanup crew and the Iranian group already had their uniforms, as it was the same company Trump had used. They waited and saw when they arrived. As before it was a chaotic group of mostly temporary workers.

They carried equipment to soak up and dry out the carpets, walls and so forth. The crew merged in with the other workers and did what they were trained to do. They subtly walked around the apartment and sprayed the walls, drapery and floors with the chemical. The smell would be suffocating in the next few days.

****

Benjamin Netanyahu accepted that he was also a target like Trump. He contacted Trump to inform him. Both now believed it was likely that Iran was behind this because their common enemies included Palestine and Iran. Netanyahu did not think Palestine could pull this off. Trump agreed and called the FBI to inform them. Later that afternoon, the FBI informed both Maxwell and the president that one of the fingerprints provided by Maxwell's detectives had been confirmed as belonging to a first-generation Iranian. This man's parents had immigrated from Iran 30 years before and was born in the United States. The FBI had, thus far, not been able to locate him. Trump went ballistic when he learned this. He ringed Donald Jr., Ivanka and Eric on a joint call, "The Iranians are behind this," he screamed, "I will get those bastards!"

The FBI cautioned the President on taking a reckless action. The man they were looking for could not possibly know that he was being sought and as far as they knew, he was not in the United States. He was single, had no other family, traveled a lot on his job as a salesman. He would not have needed to tell anyone that he would be gone. FBI had contacted his employer who said that he was on vacation and they did not expect him back until next week. The fingerprint may have been innocent. He could have touched the pipe at the supplier, they just don't know.

Trump's response to the comment was, "Horseshit! The mother fucker slipped and got caught!"

Iran was aware of the latest the moment the President informed his children. Aftab was surprised as he thought they had been more than careful. He knew that the person was now safely in Iran. They would monitor him closely.

President Trump met with three wavering senators. Each had a viewpoint. The only way they would consider staying as Republicans was if Trump either resigned or at least made full disclosure of his finances and completely removed himself from his business interest. Trump reverted to his standard lie about being audited. He just could not release his finances until the audit was complete and said that he was perfectly capable of overseeing his business as long as he had his children running things. The senators responded that then he had no choice but to give up control of the senate or make full disclosure. They would give him a month to turn over control of his business, but the financial information would have to be released now. Their constituents no longer had any trust in him and without the disclosure would throw all three of them out of office. Trump's response was, he would not.

The senators left and informed the majority leader and the minority leader of the outcome. Senator McConnell rushed to the White House but was unable to persuade Trump. His reasoning was, "They will crucify me if this information is released!"

That afternoon, the world was informed that the Republicans no longer held a majority, and a new leader would be elected the next morning. Senator McConnell was out. It was a sad day for the Republicans.

Trump had lost his sanity. He began to issue orders to the military and his cabinet that a coup was likely in process. He wanted the White House surrounding by the military with weapons and the secret service at full force. His cabinet thought he may have become unstable and brought the Vice President into the White House, just in case.

****

The appraisals for the properties that had been confiscated were now in the hands of all parties. The best outcome for Trump, if his appraisals were all used, would be one hundred twenty million dollars short of the loan amounts. The Russian banks would make the demand for the money the moment the numbers were public, which would be just days away. The world court had ordered that all appraisals be turned over by the end of the week. They had not seen the opposing appraisals but knew they were much lower. Ivanka, Eric and Donald Jr. met to decide how best to handle.

"We have to raise one hundred twenty million dollars in cash within the week," said Ivanka.

"And just where is it coming from?" asked Eric.

"How hard did you try to get them to take an interest in other properties?" said Donald Jr.

"Pleaded with them, but they see an opportunity and want blood," answered Ivanka, "The best we can do is give up our interest in Mar-a-Lago or eliminate the sanctions the United States has on Russia."

"With the loss of the control of the senate, that really just leaves the loss of Mar-a-Lago," said Eric.

"I have been working on the sale of two of our hotels, which will raise the money. We are very close to finalizing a deal. It will raise one hundred eighty million," said Ivanka.

"Which hotels?" asked Donald Jr. The one in Washington and Chicago.

"Damn shame," said Eric, "Now can we talk about what we are going to do about the golf courses and the winery?"

"We have reports from three agricultural experts: All basically saying the same thing," said Donald Jr., "We have to either wait a full year or, we can for the greens, till them up and replace with sod. They could be back within six weeks. The fairways can be tilled up and reseeded possibly in 6 months. The plants can be replaced now if they are in at least three-gallon containers. Looks like we can be back in operation in 7 months at best."

"What is the estimate of the cost?" asked Ivanka.

"Three million plus for each course, add another $500,000 for courses with larger trees. We can replace those now. But my guess is they will kill them as soon as we do," said Donald Jr.

"With the cost per day to stay closed, I say we reopen as soon as possible," said Eric. "And as for the wineries, I have an estimate of one and one half million to dig out the old and replace with the new. It will take at least four years to regrow, but we can buy grape juice with the quality close to what we were growing and be back up in a couple of months. I'd recommend that."

"We need to issue contracts now for all of this. Eric, can you take over and get that done?" said Ivanka.

"I will."

****

President Trump convened an emergency meeting of his security council, "I am ordering a task force to begin moving toward Iran. I want us to discuss what we will need." The Secretary of Defense and the Chief and the Chairman of the Joint Chiefs of Staff both bowed their heads thinking this is nuts.

"I have listed two aircraft carriers and the supporting ships, a fighter and bomber squadron along with several of the special forces units of each of the services. I do not anticipate the need for a large ground force. Give me your thoughts on what else may be needed." Continued President Trump.

The Secretary of Defense stood up and was silent for a moment. "Mr. President, this will start a war. We cannot make such a move without diplomatic efforts. Even our closest allies will oppose us. We will have nowhere to land these planes and troops and the carriers will have no land support for supplies, fuel and so forth. This will be an unprecedented disaster and what do you propose to accomplish?"

"These bastards have attacked the United States and we must respond. It is a matter of honor!"

"I am unaware of any such attack," said General Carter. "Where and when was this?"

"Do you not agree that an attack on me is an attack on the United States? Well, they have made attacks on me all over the world!"

"No sir," said the General. "Damage done to your business property is certainly not the same as being done to property owned by the United States of America. And even that, would not necessarily be a cause for war."

"I disagree. An attack on your leader is an attack on America and I get to make that call!"

"Mr. President you cannot send a task force of this size without getting congressional approval, surely you are aware of that," said the Secretary of Defense.

"Under the emergency war powers act, I can and will. This is an attack on the United States in my opinion and my opinion is all that matters! Mr. Secretary, General Carter, you have your orders, I expect them to be carried out. How soon can these be underway."

"Mr. President, we must first have a place that is willing to allow our troops, planes and other things to be accepted. We will begin to try and find such a place. We cannot send troops with no place to land them!" Noted General Carter.

"I will give you two days. If you do not find a place, we will put them all on board our ships!"

The president got up and left. The others sat for a few moments then looked at each other.

The Director of National Intelligence, Richard Grenell, shrugged his shoulders, "So what do we do now?"

"I am going directly to Congress and informing the leaders of the house and senate. I certainly am not going to be put in prison for doing what is clearly illegal," said Secretary Esper. "Meanwhile, I will notify the navy, air force and the army secretaries to begin planning. I also have no choice but to do that."

"I have to do the same," said General Carter.

The Secretary of State made immediate inquiries as to where they may land and house the troops and airplanes needed. Turkey, Saudi Arabia, United Arab Emirates, Iraq and Afghanistan all refused. Only Kuwait would agree to allow some troops in their country because they believed their country may be invaded by one of the other nearby countries, all hated them for aligning with the United States, if America is not present. No country would agree to supply the force with fuel and supplies. This would be a near impossible task if it came to reality. When President Trump was told, he only cursed.

The navy had no choice but to order the USS Carl Vinson and USS Abraham Lincoln to begin preparation for sailing. The air force notified a squadron of B-52s to prepare to relocate; the army did the same with two divisions of rangers.

Ivanka notified her father, Donald Jr. and Eric that the closings for the two hotels were scheduled for Thursday, two days from now. The president divulged to them he was planning an attack on Iran.

Iran listened and Iranian leaders were notified within minutes.

Ivanka received word from their hotel in New York that there were an infestation of bedbugs and those people who stayed in the rooms were furious and likely to sue. She bowed her head then called her Father to give him the news. "Those bastards will pay dearly that I can promise you."

Shortly after, with the help of the Iranians, every major news station was broadcasting the 'new' problem the Trumps had. Bedbugs was a result of poor house cleaning. Reservation cancellations came in by the hundreds shortly after the news was out. Donald Jr. and Eric just shook their heads.

****

The house and senate leaders met to discuss the information just revealed to them by the Secretary of Defense and the Chairman of the Joint Chiefs. Nearly everyone believed that the War Powers Act should be revoked now that it was clear President Trump was abusing the power it gave him. Only Mitch McConnell was against it. They would need a two-thirds majority to revoke it as Trump would not sign it. They were unsure how many votes they could get but knew they had to try.

The senate was now in control of the Democrats, who scheduled a debate on the issue the next day.

Chapter Twenty-Seven

Aftab met with his hackers. He wanted to know if they were ready to launch an attack on any funds Trump or any of his family members and Benjamin Netanyahu may have and also max out the credit cards. He reminded them that all of this has to be done at the same time. "I am expecting a very large check to be deposited into the Trump business account this Thursday. We need to be ready and get those funds the moment it is deposited!"

Rasheen Abbasi, the supervisor of all the hackers said, "We have access to all the bank accounts and credit cards. I have set up computer screens for every account and a person to monitor them. Beginning at 8 AM New York time, we will see every transaction being made in or out of the accounts and the recording of the large checks which we think will be in the range of one hundred eighty million dollars will be the key for us to remove all funds except for a few hundred dollars from each account. This will start with many charges to each of their credit cards until each card is within five hundred dollars of the limits set. We are anxious to get started!"

"Where will the money go?" ask Aftab.

"We have set up accounts all over the world. Those accounts will transfer the money to other accounts. All transfers will be for one thousand US dollars. Many thousands of transactions will be made within minutes. It will not be possible for them to trace where the money has gone or where it is now," said Rasheen. "It will eventually be brought back to us but not for a long while."

At ten o'clock Thursday morning, Ivanka, Donald Jr. and Eric were at the closing of the two hotels. The property required all three to sign. That is what the power of attorney from Donald Trump Sr. required. The closing attorney passed the documents around. Two separate companies were purchasing the properties: one was buying the property in Washington DC and the other the Chicago property. When all had been signed, the attorney entered the transfer data for an electronic transfer of monies from the two accounts to the Trump account. One was for one hundred million thirty thousand and forty-eight cents, the other was eighty million, twenty-two thousand, three hundred dollars and forty cents. A confirmation was received for each transaction which was then printed and given to Ivanka. She had them give her two copies so she could send money to the Russians tomorrow. The Trumps were sad but relieved. They called their father to tell them it was done.

At 10:27 AM, the first deposit hit the Trump business account. It set in motion the transfer of funds in a massive movement. Six minutes later, the second transfer showed up. Money was being withdrawn at a massive speed. Twelve minutes later, the bank balance was $527.83 after the opening balance for the business account, was $6,258,364 before the deposits were made of $100,030,000.48, $80,022,300.40 and $28,645.62. The other teams did the same. Those accounts that had anywhere from $6,000 to $75,000 were down to a $500 range in minutes. The credit cards were the same. All of them had large limits on several cards each. Charges were made, again for $1,000 amounts and transferred. By 11:15 AM New York time, for all practical purposes, the Trumps were broke! They now had no money in the bank, no credit lines and no ability to make credit card charges.

Benjamin Netanyahu's bank accounts and all six of his credit cards were maxed out. He had a total in US dollars of $136,588.67. They left him with $588.67.

Friday was payday for the Trump organization. All payrolls were made via electronic transfer; the transfers were sent out at 4:30 EST automatically. The payroll clerk notified Donald Jr. that all the transfers had been kicked back and were denied for insufficient funds. They had nearly eleven hundred employees. The insufficient fund charges were $70,000 at $35 per transaction.

"They have most definitely fucked up. I will call them."

Donald Jr. called the bank who told him that the company account is now overdrawn because of the charges for insufficient funds with a negative balance of $69,636.00. He called Ivanka and Eric and suggested they all three go to the bank right now. They went and were given a printout of thousands of withdrawals, each for $1,000. The one hundred eighty million was gone.

Their other normal amounts were gone also. Their line of credit no longer existed, and their payrolls have all bounced. They called their dad to give him the news.

A quick and desperate attempt was made to retrieve the funds, but it got them nowhere.

Ivanka checked her personal account and saw that all her funds have been withdrawn as well as her husbands. Donald Jr. and Eric did the same and found that their accounts have also been drained. Tears welled in all their eyes as they realized where they are now. They do not know where or whom to turn to. Donald Jr. screamed, "The Russians will kill us if they are not paid!"

Donald Trump listened, then just laid the phone down on his desk and began to cry, everything he has is now gone, he would lose Mar-A-Lago in the next few days as well. He had never been in such a desperate situation. He had no idea how he would pay his employees. Leaning his head back against his chair, he realized, he did know how, he would have to take it from his campaign account—though he might end up in jail for it—but he would have to borrow it illegally from those accounts. He called Ivanka and told her to arrange for the funds: to go into a separate account to withdraw for the payroll. It was for two million two hundred thousand dollars. Ivanka, knowing it was illegal, told her father that she wanted written permission before she would transfer the money. She was faxed over the authorization from her father, then, after reading it carefully did as she was told. She transferred a total of eight million from the campaign account. She teared up as she did it because she knew when, not if they would be caught, her father would lie and say it was a mistake and he knew nothing about it. She did not know, her father had typed the authorization himself on his secretary's computer, printed it, he signed a blank piece of paper, copied it then cut and pasted it to the printed authorization. He then had one of the secret service agents take it to a place near the white house and fax it to Ivanka. He would deny having any knowledge when they were caught. When the agent brought back the original and proof of transmission, he burned it.

The hackers in Iran believed they may try and set up new accounts and began searching.

****

A heated debate was ongoing on removing the Wartime Powers Act to one that will require Congressional approval any time the military is used. It was clear they had enough votes to pass such a resolution but not the two-thirds required to do so without a Presidential signature. Trump still had enough allies to prevent it. The speakers reiterated the urgency as there was, at this time, two aircraft carriers steaming toward the Persian Gulf, B-52 bomber squadrons were now landing, and the 1st and 75th army ranger battalions were this minute landing in Kuwait, their equipment was being airlifted at a tremendous expense. The counter argument was that the United States was at no real risk since Iran did not have the capability of committing an attack on the United States. The country was not divided on this issue, less than 30% supported such an argument.

Tensions were high in the entire middle east region. Every major country including all the key allies of the United States condemned this action. Israel initially supported it but then joined with the rest of the world. Russia and China stated any attack on Iran would be considered an attack on them. Russia began moving a large force into Syria to counter the actions by the United States.

The Senate passed the resolution by a 60 to 40 margin. The president stated it was a ridiculous bill and he would let it sit on his desk and send it back to Congress with a veto probably on the tenth day, as any longer would make it a law.

No one including the states where the 40 senators represented could comprehend why the bill was not passed 100 to zero. Every major news station rallied for the passing and every major newspaper did the same. Trump stayed adamant. He must retaliate against Iran,

China sent two aircraft carriers sailing toward the Persian Gulf, Russia sent one. The military briefed Trump on the danger but he refused to consider any recall.

The United Nations passed a resolution condemning the United States. Even the US ambassador voted in favor and was immediately fired by Trump.

Trump, in a national speech, reiterated the concept that Iran's attack on him was an attack on the American people. He also stated, "If Iran returns the nearly two hundred million dollars they have stolen from my accounts, I will withdraw the carriers while we discuss the payment for other damages. Iran, you only have a couple of days left to consider stopping this. I would advise you do so now!"

The speech was not well accepted. Most considered he was reacting like a child. The 40 senators had now changed their minds and would vote to resend the power, but they were helpless until the bill was either signed or vetoed. The nation was nervous.

Ali Khamenei requested he be allowed to address the United Nations. Nearly, a hundred percent voted in favor. Trump had appointed a crony to be the temporary ambassador who voted 'no' then attempted to use the United States veto power to block any speech. The UN immediately confirmed it was not within the charter to do so. Trump then demanded the right to address the UN. It was rejected in the same margin with only one positive vote that came from his newly appointed crony.

Ali Khamenei was scheduled to address the United Nations in two days.

Ivanka called her father. She had just received court orders from New York, New Jersey, Virginia that their property was to be confiscated under the same rules that India had imposed except that it would be overseen by a federal judge. She also received confirmation that the countries had agreed to their appraisals numbers which gave them no reason for a hearing. The monies would be paid to the lien holders within the next ten days.

Trump leaned back in his chair. "Those bastards must die," he said only to himself.

Trump then decided he would order an Iranian bombing the moment Ali Khamenei completed his address of the United Nations.

Ali Khamenei arrived in New York with heavy security, the FBI was nervous. They were concerned Trump may have ordered his assassination.

Attorney General Barr rendered his own resignation. He believed coming shortly would be a claim of mental incapacity of the President and he would have to rule on the claim. It would be a no-win situation for him no matter which way he ruled.

Two days later, Ali Khamenei stepped on the podium at the United Nations. He was greeted by a large standing ovation from the member nations. Trumped watched and screamed "bastards" as they clapped.

"Everyone here knows why I am here. Iran has suffered greatly under this man who is now president of the United States, it appears to us he is mentally unstable. We worked with all nations to achieve an agreement for the world to ease the crippling sanctions which we had been under for many years. We had begun a nuclear program that was primarily to be used for peaceful purposes. The world negotiated with us for Iran to stop all developments of nuclear productions in exchange for the sanctions to disappear, and we would get back the money that is ours and had been frozen many years ago. Iran lived up to every word of the agreement, allowing inspectors into our country, cameras to record our every move in all of our nuclear facilities and most of our military facilities. This current United States president decided the agreement reached by most of the world was not enough. He wanted much more than what had been agreed upon and breached the agreement. His desire was to renegotiate another agreement which he then could breach again. He has caused great damage to our country as we were not prepared for such unprecedented behavior.

"His reasoning is our support of the Palestine people who are being treated like a conquered country by Israel. They can do this because the United States supplies them with weapons to be used against the Palestinians and we choose to try and even the field by supplying Palestine with defensive weapons. Israel considers what we are doing as a 'terrorist' act and what they are doing as defending themselves. The United States believes their supply of weapons to harm the Palestine people is justified, but we consider it as terrorism. We have been open for many years to come to a solution but have been blocked by the United States and Israel. The solution must include the rights of Palestine as a people, which is not much to ask. This man then slapped the face of the Palestinians by relocating the Israel American embassy onto property which the Palestinians deem as theirs! In addition, then allowed and even encouraged Israel to build settlements on land that is not theirs. Remember, Iran is being punished for standing up to such injustices.

"Iran decided that such behavior and damage to our country could not go unanswered. Our leadership first decided the American and Israelite people must suffer as we have been made to do. However, it was pointed out that we really have no issues with the American or Israelites. They, as a people, have done us no harm. It is two people who have led the charge to damage us, and it is they against whom we must seek retribution. Donald Trump and Benjamin Netanyahu, the two men who collaborated to damage us.

"Yes, Iran has worked hard to seek and damage the assets of those two men as well as their families, as they have done to Iranian families, it is just, yes we declared war on two men. We did damage the properties of these two, but we harmed no one! We also confiscated the money that they rightfully owe us for the damage done to many Iranians."

"Donald Trump now threatens us with war if we do not reimburse him for the damage. Iran says multiply that by 1000 and you will come much closer to what he and Benjamin Netanyahu owe the Iranian people."

"Now let me get to the facts that America faces if they allow this man to continue. It was thought when Iran signed this agreement that we had no nuclear weapons. We agreed to turn over any that we may have developed which was none. Iran did have and still does have weapons which it acquired from other countries that the United States and Israel were unaware of. For verification, I have just now provided photos of those bombs via email to each of you. You may pass them on to your weapons experts to verify."

Iran emailed photos of two of the bombs taken with a copy of a daily newspaper, dated two months ago."

There were immediate gasps by the people in the audience, many grabbed their cellphones as they received the emails. The news media covering the speech went berserk.

Ali Khamenei paused for a few moments as the audience settled down. He continued.

"We have planted those weapons in the United States and Israel. We also have planted a number of traditional weapons which we can detonate to demonstrate that we have such abilities".

The crowd again gasped as this information sunk in. The Israeli and the United States contingent were on the phones.

"I can only assure you this, if America or Israel drops any bombs on Iran or sends any of those soldiers, they have massed on our borders into our territory then millions will die. I can also assure you that nothing will happen if Iran is left alone!

"America and Israel have suffered because of the actions of two men: one, a madman and the other, misguided. Removing them will go a long way toward bringing peace to all our countries.

"I thank you for listening to me."

Ali Khamenei stepped from the podium to a stand-up applause of nearly all the members of the United Nations.

Donald Trump picked up the emergency phone in his office which connected directly to the Chairman of the Joint Chiefs, "Iran just admitted to attacking us. I want you to release the B-52s on Tehran right now!"

General Carter who had also listened to the speech contacted the secretary of defense, "Sir, I have just been ordered by the President to bomb Tehran. I will not issue that order. If you wish to fire me then you may do so."

"No, do not. I have already contacted the Vice President and the other member of the cabinet. We all agree that a 25th amendment action is justifiable. We will enact it in the next thirty minutes. The President, of course, will disagree and it will be thrown to Congress. I have also contacted the leadership in Congress who will also convene in the next hour to independently vote to enact the 25th amendment. He must be removed from office right now and those weapons moved away."

The cabinet arrived at the White House twenty minutes later and convened in their standard meeting room. Donald Trump was furious as he had not called a cabinet meeting. When all were seated, the Vice President stood and turned to Trump, "We all agree you must be at least temporarily removed from office. The purpose of this meeting is to vote on enacting the 25th amendment. He then turned to the cabinet and requested hands raised who was in favor."

Donald Trump jumped up, "None of you are eligible to vote as I have just decided to fire all of you! So, get the fuck out of here. You no longer are on my cabinet!"

The Vice President pounded the table, "Raise your hands if the answer is yes!"

All raised their hands.

"Like I said, you have all been fired. The only one I can't fire is the Vice President which makes the vote a tie. You all lose! Goodbye. Get the fuck away from me," He then called the secret service to order them removed.

The secret service came in. They were unsure as to what they could or should do.

The vice president stood, "I am now acting President. This man," he pointed to Trump, "is mentally incapacitated and it is obvious that he is. The Congress will affirm my appointment in the next hour. Please take this man to a hospital where he can be cared for."

The secret service men stood silent for a moment then took Donald Trump by the arm, "Come Mr. President, you do not look well," They forcefully took him to the White House doctor. He cursed and fought them every step of the way/ When they reached the white house doctor's office, he gave him a shot which would put him to sleep, he gave it as the guards held him down. One of the guards did call Melania who did not come down.

One hour later, the Congress voted with a 100% majority to, at least temporarily, remove Trump from office.

Vice president Pence, now President Pence, immediately ordered the two carriers to return home as well as the ground and air force planes. China, Russia and the other countries did the same.

Ivanka, Donald Jr. and Eric discussed plans with an attorney for their personal bankruptcy. The now thousands of lawsuits and near-worthless property the Trump Corporation held was not worth enough to even fight to keep.

Epilogue

Donald Trump was kept in confinement and sedated until the bill passed by the senate which terminated the emergency war act became law. The congress also passed sweeping legislation eliminating the power of the president to enact sanctions without the express approval of the senate. Acting President Spence signed into law the legislation to be effective immediately.

As to Iran, Acting President Spence issued executive orders eliminating those signed by President Trump taking the United states out of the Iranian agreement and also, the Paris climate accord. The entire country celebrated as well as the rest of the world. Also, congress enacted, and Acting President Spence signed into law revisions to the Inspector General act. Inspector generals can now only be removed with approval the senate.

When Donald Trump was released by his Doctors, he immediately sent a letter to the Speaker of the house and the senate majority leader that he was well and able to resume his duties as president. Both the senate and the house reacted within minutes of receiving the letter and by a near 100% margin voted to remove permanently the President until such time as the congress was assured of his ability to continue as president. That assurance could only be obtained by an inquiry before the senate. His attorneys filed for an immediate hearing before the supreme court but was denied within hours of being filed. As he only had six months left on his term, he decided his best option was to accept his fate and leave the white house. His approval rating was below 5% and had no chance of reelection. Melania refused to go with him opting instead to return to her native country with her son. The Russian bank had taken over Mar-a Lago but had agreed for Donald Trump to keep and maintain his residence.

Iran and acting President Spence agreed to high level meetings in France. There, they debated the nuclear and conventional bombs Iran had planted in the United States. Iran's position was clear, the United States could not be trusted to live up to any agreement. Any terms negotiated could be broken and breached by any future US president. Iran would agree to divulge the location of the conventional bombs and would at some point in the future dismantle the nuclear devices if Israel will work toward recognizing Palestine has a right for self-governance.

Eventually an agreement was reached but Iran held fast that its nuclear devices would remain until the United States and Israel proved themselves to be trustworthy.

Trump's children would be able to survive, each had investment accounts that were not touched.

It is only hoped the world has learned its lesson.

www.ingramcontent.com/pod-product-compliance
Lightning Source LLC
Chambersburg PA
CBHW041052310726
48978CB00011BA/530